To [illegible]

Hope y[illegible] ...ith
of where human[illegible]
all its potential and failings as
we enter the 21st century

The Covenant At Stedman Woods

The Covenant At Stedman Woods

by

Steve Scott, Sr.

Stay Blessed!
Steve Scott Sr
2001

ISBN NUMBER: 1-58721-253-6

1stBooks rev. 4/18/00

ABOUT THE BOOK

Dr. Richard Stedman, young highly regarded Theoretical Physicist from U.S.C., Berkeley, has been in a state of deep depression for nearly a month. His spirit is exhausted. His constant companions are debilitating migraine headaches, accompanied by frightful dreams, with shadowy figures beckoning him into the unknown.

For months, Dr. Stedman has carried the burden of possessing an awesome scientific secret. A secret so startling, it has the potential for paving the way for a New Scientific and Social Age. He has made the astounding discovery of the ages. What Dr. Stedman has discovered is "TOE," the Theory of Everything in the Universe. He has successfully integrated all of the known forces of matter, including Einstein's General Theory of Relativity, into one simple, elegant formula that would fit on the front of a T-shirt, as predicted by the great physicists of the twentieth century. He has nearly completed writing his findings for publication in the prestigious journal <u>Science</u> when his father dies unexpectedly, at the family farm in Greencastle, Indiana. He is now the sole heir to the 700-acre farm, and Executor for the family estate, publishing his discovery must be delayed.

By happenstance, [perhaps] he is drawn into a tight cable of dreamers. Dr. Jessica Harrington, beautiful, young, gifted microbiologist, is very close to discovering a vaccine for the AIDS virus. Dr. Stanley Davis, a black Sociologist and childhood friend of Dr. Stedman, sees himself as a visionary for the New Age of Aquarius. He has nearly completed a lengthy manuscript addressing the relevancy of Science, Religion, Technology, and the woeful state of the nation's inner-city schools. He seeks reforms through national debates, as we enter the new millennium. It is his dream that his book will become a national best seller. And there is Reverend Donovan, whose faith is being sorely buffeted by the winds of social change and scientific discoveries threatening the old paradigms of theology.

Dr. Stedman will not have long to wait to become embroiled in the debate.

One evening, while walking through a wooded meadow of the Stedman farm, Dr. Stedman has a mind bending alien encounter. One that attacks the boundaries of human imagination and sense of reality. He is forced to make Faustian choices directly affecting the course of the new millennium. Will mankind cast its lot with the scientific and technological knowledge potential of Dr. Stedman's new discovery? The secret known only to the Gods. Or will mankind continue to stumble into the next century carrying with it the old baggage of social, religious, and educational decay. Only Dr. Stedman, out of some six billion people on earth knows the outcome.

INTRODUCTION

To be perfectly honest with you, the germ of the idea for this book began as I was preparing for retirement. I had timidly purchased a home computer to join that mystical breed of men and women who, through the years, bombarded me with their computer wizardry. Even my six year-old grandchild, Mackenzie Gayle Scott, was dazzling me with her mastery of her personal computer. What was a grandfather to do? The answer came in a flash of inspiration. I decided to use my fledgling computer skills to complete two long delayed personal projects. One was to write my autobiography, <u>A Walk Through Time</u>, for my two children, Steve Jr. and Wendy Gayle Scott. That I have done. The second project, you are holding in your hand. A novel for the New Millennium for my three very young grandchildren, Mackenzie Gayle, Cennie Lyric, and Ruby Sage Scott, all showing burgeoning signs of making a ripple in this tiny part of our universe.

For sometime it has been my belief that our great thinkers, the movers and shakers, the scientists, the theologians and educators were not providing mankind, especially the young, with a grand vision of our potential as we enter the 21st century. I feel on a visceral level that we have failed the next generation by not conducting, in the 1990's, all-inclusive seminars, plenary sessions, and national TV debates that address what directions we should be taking as we enter the new millennium. One might rightly ask, "where were the national debates in the 90's about the future of our legal system; "the Four Horsemen of the Apocalypse"; the environment; global warming; improving our decaying cities; the morals decline of our youth; racial hatred and civility toward one another; the startling advances in science and their effect upon our daily lives; unchanging, dogmatic religious doctrines that ignore advances in physics and cosmology; and the sorry state of our educational systems? Where is the dialogue of our great philosophers that might show us the potential for order in our lives? Where is the debate about a New Age of reason whereby the nation makes a commitment to a more rational, more meaningful society? Where were the debates about the ethics of making "designer babies" and the appropriateness of having the capabilities of offering human genetic enhancements? We're entering a period when breakthroughs in biology, technology, and cosmology are out pacing the culture's capacity to deal with the ethics and potential social impacts of such discoveries. These are real questions and issues facing us in the near term as we peer down the road of the early 21st century. The reader may wish to add his own list of missed opportunities.

I am humble enough to admit that I am not a great thinker or a mover and shaker, but I do profess to being a life long learner. And on deeper reflection, I regret the fact that as a nation, we seem content to stagger mindlessly into the next century, slaves to TV charlatans, irrational politicians ripe with malice and torment. And then there are the quick confessions of fallen entertainment and sports figures who write books, and present their naked souls on TV talk shows, presenting themselves as reformed role models to our young people. I am also fed up with "In your face" media moguls who produce television programming attacking every person that makes a mistake. And then there are the newspaper journalists who believe that all people of responsibility are hiding some dirty secret that is their duty to uncover. It is also a very curious fact that when they themselves make mistakes, they are never held accountable. I guess it has always been easier to rile against those in authority, and others, when you are bereft of responsibility. Could it be that is the reason, we as individuals, are so troubled and ready to explode with violent acts? Could it also be that we have grown so desperate, lonely and unable to find satisfaction with our own lives that we seek out others to rid us of our own quite desperate, unfulfilled lives? Could it be that our failure to face the issues detailed above are the underlying causes of why we are constantly seeking the Primrose Path-one that leads us to a merry life of indulgence and sensual pleasures of life. Are we becoming like Odysseus, that fabulous person who ate lotus fruit, which induced languor and forgetfulness of home?

As I looked over the landscape of existing print, electronic media, major talk shows and ordinary discussions over coffee klatches, I could find no meaningful dialogue related to such issues. I decided to conduct my own sophistry.

See Selected Readings at the end of the book for reference material used in the formulation of certain ideas expressed throughout the book.

x

ACKNOWLEDGMENTS

My thanks to my wife Marilyn, who along with infinite patience and grand class, endured many hours of my absence of personal attention, as my computer became my surrogate wife. I must also offer my debt of gratitude to Furness Holloway who edited the manuscript and endured much patience and hand wrenching as she guided the book with expert care through its many polymorphic developments. The Views expressed in this book are mine alone and she should remain blameless for them. Likewise, any errors in grammar and content must fall upon me and my stubbornness to accept her learned advice. Also, see the Selected Readings at the end of the book for reference material used in the formulation of certain ideas expressed throughout the book, and in particular the dialogue chapter.

Bon Voyage into the new millennium.

Steve Scott Sr.

DEDICATION

The Millennium is at hand. For many souls, it will be a time of fear and Foreboding. For others, it will usher in a time of unfolding promise. This book is For those who dare to go Boldly into the 21st Century . . . The Age of Aquarius.

TABLE OF CONTENTS

Chapter 8

Chapter 9

Chapter 10

Chapter 11

Chapter 12

Chapter 13

Chapter 14

AUTHORS NOTE

The much hoped for discovery of the Grand Unified Theory [GUT] is based on the prediction and views held by many physicists of the existence of magnetic monopoles. The monopoles have exotic, if not mystical properties, mainly their mass. Ordinary, elementary particles weigh scarcely anything at all. Billions and billions of them would weigh only as much as a speck of dust. However, one GUT monopole would weigh as much as that speck. They should be observable and move in space very slowly and have existed at the time of the Big Bang. Some scientist thought they could be found deep in the earth, in mines, in the moon rocks. Monopoles were sought in the giant particle accelerators; yet, none have been discovered.

It should be noted however, that James Maxwell, the Scottish physicist who merged electricity and magnetism in the 1860's, produced mathematical equations that permit the existence of monopoles. Unfortunately, his original equations were not quite symmetric. They produced broken symmetry. Nature and physicists have long abhorred broken symmetry because it lacks elegance. Magnetic monopoles would produce the needed elegant symmetry. They were never found. But, perhaps one was found. In 1982, just before two o'clock in the afternoon of St. Valentine's Day, an astonishing thing happened. Blas Cabrera a physicist at Stanford University, almost, or perhaps did, experimentally, find one using a superconductivity experimental apparatus.

Despite intense, worldwide experimentation by many physicists, they could not duplicate Cabrera's finding on that Valentines Day when the needle on the graph monitoring system signaled the illusive monopole. It was ironic but the exotic potential of the original experiment had precisely the value predicted by James Maxwell. Cabrera worked tirelessly to improve his original apparatus, but in 1990, he and his fellow researchers abandoned their efforts. He announced that his original "monopole discovery" should be withdrawn. But should that invalidate his original finding? It just might be that one day soon, some young researcher, peering into Einstein's theory of relativity, Maxwell's equations, or examining background radiation from the stars, may vindicate Cabreras' almost magical moment on St. Valentine's Day, in decades past.

One should also be reminded of the fact that down through the ages, many of the great discoveries made by our most renowned scientists have come in a sudden flash of awe inspiring insight. A Pure Thought Transmission, if you will. For example, Archimedes had an instant perception as he was getting into his bathtub. Suddenly, out of nowhere, and without forethought, it dawned on him that a volume of displacement is independent of the shape of the object. It was such a flight of insight that he cried out "Eureka." That simple word "Eureka" has bounded down through the ages. It signifies a sudden blinding flash of enlightenment and insight. But, where and from what source do such enlightenment and insights come? The following story might be an example of just how such divine and mystical events, of sudden insight and discovery, could happen.

CHAPTER 1

Day One
Morning
Summer 2000
Berkeley Hills, Calif.

Dr. Richard Stedman, renowned physicist, was barely moving through time. He did not know it yet, but he was about to embark on an Odyssey that would change his life and that of the world, forever!

Dr. Stedman, having just showered, was preparing to shave. He wiped the shower steam from the mirror, and then stared at his reflection with deep melancholia. His entire body began to shudder. But it was more than that. He looked terrible, despite the fact it was 5:00 a.m. But it was more than that. He should have felt exhilarated. He could scarcely recognize the face staring back at him. His curly dark, wet hair was matted to his head and face. His eyes, deep within dark sockets gave him the appearance of the undead he had seen in horror movies in his youth. Richard was in trouble and he knew it. The migraine headaches were returning, and to make matters worse, so were those damnable recurring dreams. He knew how to control the headaches, but what darkened his spirit the most were . . . the fitful dreams! They came almost every night now, always bathed in eerie blue lights, shadows, and clouds. It was as if he were watching lightning flashing through an approaching storm, he would find himself in a thickly wooded area, driven there by compulsion and a strange glowing light. The nightmares made him grateful for the reality of the morning.

Richard sucked in deep breaths of air, in vain attempts to clear his mind of such thoughts. He was not an early riser. He was fond of telling his associates who chided him about his aversion to early morning, "There is no world outside until after 8 a.m. Down through the ages, Man has always cursed the

1

darkness." He cursed the fact that he had to catch an early morning flight to Indianapolis, Indiana, rent a car, and drive the thirty miles to Greencastle by early afternoon. Once he arrived there, he would be meeting with a minister, hand wrestling with a lawyer, funeral director, and heaven only knew whom else before the day was done. Dr. Morris Stedman, his father, had died unexpectedly of a massive stroke just two days ago. Richard, as the sole heir and Executor to the family 700-acre farm, had much tidying up of personal affairs to complete in short order. He had given himself thirty days to complete the necessary details. His manuscript submission for publication would have to be put on hold for the interim.

"That's why my migraines are back. At least my father doesn't have to suffer from his painful heart condition any longer." His death had come swiftly after his massive stroke. Richard regretted the fact that the full effects of his grief at his fathers passing had not seeped deeply into his being. For the moment, he would rid himself from remorse. "I'll think more about him on the long plane flight. But, not now. I've got to get dressed. My plane leaves in two hours"

As he hurriedly began to shave, he tried desperately not to look to closely at himself in the mirror. But, he couldn't help it. The image that stared back at him looked like bread dough rising in a baking pan, colorless and lumpy. He groaned and licked his lips, as he continued to stare at his reflection. He saw gray threads in his hair that he had not noticed before. "How can that be? I'm only thirty-seven years old." But he knew why? For two years he had worked night and day on his new theory of how to make a marriage of gravity to the other two forces of nature, the electroweak interaction, the electrostrong nuclear force, which holds protons and neutrons together in the atomic nucleus. No one, including Albert Einstein had been able to do it. He knew that Einstein had spent the last thirty years of his life in the effort, but never succeeded. But he, Richard Stedman had. He now possessed the greatest secret man has ever known. Proof of the Grand Unified Theory. [GUT] He had not told a soul in the scientific community. Only his graduate student assistant, Eisa knew that he was close to some awesome secret. He knew that carrying this lonely secret contributed to his migraines. "But what about the dreams?" He said aloud. "What do they mean?" He nicked his chin below his lip and swore lightly under his breath. "Now, I really look a mess. Well there is nothing I can do about it. I've got to move faster. I can't miss the plane. I've got to meet with the damned lawyers today, as soon as I reach Greencastle."

Richard finished his shave and took one last look at his naked body in the full mirror attached to the bathroom door. Despite his disdain for athletics he had an athletes body. He was tall, six foot two with broad shoulders, small waistline and well-proportioned buttocks, thighs and legs. It was his sunken eyes and swollen face that bothered him. It was the lack of sleep and the dreams that were always the same. He had an answer for both. He reached into the medical chest and quickly retrieved a packet of Benadryl antihistamine tablets. He swallowed two of them. They would reduce the facial swelling and make him just drowsy enough to sleep on the plane. Suddenly the front door bell began to chime. Stedman knew it would be Eisa Chang, his young Chinese graduate assistant. She had promised to give him a ride to the airport in San Francisco. "Damn, I am really running late. The travel time to the airport will take at least forty-five minutes under ideal conditions and if the check in lines are long, and they always are, we may just barely make it in time. Why is it that the human race seems to love long lines and impossible waiting delays? Stedman bounded down the stairs clad only in his red and white checkered briefs, ignoring the blue silk robe hanging on the bathroom door. "Surely Eisa has seen a man in his shorts before," he growled. He opened the door and quickly made his way back up the stairs, hurling a lackluster, "Good morning Eisa. Make yourself at home. I'll be just a few minutes."

3

"Good morning Professor. It looks like a wonderful day for flying. Plenty of sunshine. I could see the Bay Bridge on my way up the hillside. We're going to have to hurry if we're going to make your flight. You know how unpredictable the traffic can be in the Bay area. Where is your travel luggage? I'll put them in the car trunk while you finish dressing."

"Ah, Yes. Go ahead. That's very kind of you. The bags are right next to the kitchen door. I'll be down in a minute."

He began to dress quickly, thinking how uncommonly, bright, soft-spoken, and well-mannered Eisa was. She had been very instrumental in compiling the data and doing the difficult mathematics associated with the radio astronomical data from the black hole discovered coming from the center of the galaxy known as M87.

Richard's breakthrough came when, in a flash of brilliant insight, he decided to look to the heavens for a solution to GUT and not the particle accelerator. Richard knew that the biggest accelerators in existence and those dreamed of could never achieve the tremendous energy levels necessary to observe the monopole. The best and most widely held theories of GUT would remain forever untestable and proved by the standard method of observation and experimentation. However with the aid of his astrophysicists friend, Dr. Claudia Peters, at the Lick Observatory, she was able to provide him data from the Hubble Telescope on a peculiar galaxy known as M87. This system was known to be shooting out material at the incredible speed of light. The source of this violent activity at the center of M87 is a black hole, the ultimate energy producer. The energy it produced was the equivalent of billions and billions of watts of energy. In one second the energy produced is equivalent to all the energy potential put together of all the known galaxies. Obviously more than enough energy to produce the much sought after monopole particle. It remained a matter of utilizing the Hubble telescope in conjunction with the Vela Satellites that were arrayed secretly in orbit in the 1960's to determine the presence of Russian launched

4

satellite weapons that could attack the earth from space. The Vela satellites utilized Radio telescopy, just what Richard needed to detect the monopole. It was an ingenious method that had escaped the best scientists of the day. He felt extremely fortunate that the idea for this methodology came to him in one of those Damnable dreams that were his constant companions since childhood. He would make sure Eisa, along with Claudia, would be predominately mentioned in his "GUT" paper in the Science publication, <u>Nature.</u>

He continued to dress, choosing casual, light brown trousers, white polo shirt and a light summer weight, dark blue blazer with shiny gold buttons. He started to reach for his buff colored tennis shoes for ease of travel, but thought better of it, choosing instead a pair of dark brown oxfords.

As Richard reached for his briefcase, he could not help but pause to reflect for a brief moment upon what it contained. What awesome power he would soon deliver to mankind as the 21st Century dawned. The impossible! The unthinkable was now at hand . . . boundless energy supplies, time travel, going to other star systems, other dimensions instantly were now in the grasps of mankind. Nor could Richard resist at that moment thinking how modern man was paralleling the caveman as he and his family peered outside the campfires of his cave, terrified while lighting flashed across the darkening sky, booming thunder claps reverberating everywhere, as they wondered what the gods, goddesses, or demons were up to.

Day one - Morning
Hotel room of
Dr. Jessica Harrington

Dr. Jessica Harrington was a defined beauty- a vision of dreams unarticulated by most men. As a teenager, she had modeled for several leading women's magazines. Her long, fluffy, brunette hair, cradled an exquisite mango colored complexion. Her eyes were large, almost bovine like. Her aerobic honed body rested on a five-foot nine and a half inch frame that moved with the grace of a cheetah moving stealthily through the high grass of the Serengeti Plain.

Despite these commanding physical attributes, she did not have a current man in her life. In reality, many eligible suitors shied away from her, not so much because of her beauty as because of her clear insightful intelligence. "Nothing new about that." She often confided to her female friends that young men would feign approaching her, saying, "You can live your life like a movie queen." She would have none of that. Her mission in life became clear to her long before she entered high school. Her destiny seemed to arrive in a flash, a dream. Jessica knew that she would dedicate her life to curing the sick and conquering the diseases that plagued them.

She was an excellent student in high school and in college. Jessica had attended Cambridge, and then moved on to Oxford, England, as a Rhodes Scholar, earning a Doctorate in microbiology. She had returned to the United States where she did post doctoral work in immunology, at Indiana University, Bloomington. But she would have no time to think of her past. Her future bore down on her with immense pressure, as she was very close to producing a vaccine against the HIV AIDS virus.

Fortunately, on this particular day, the pressure gave way to a great sense of controlled excitement as she prepared to leave U.S.C., Berkeley. She had been at Berkeley for nearly a week,

6

attending a worldwide conference on the progress being made in destroying the AIDS virus. She also felt a tinge of pride at being selected one of the presenters at the seminar. She had given a general overview of her theory and her experimental research that had the potential of effecting a vaccine against the dreaded disease. Although she had received many daunting questions from her peers, she was able to hold her own, even receiving polite applause at the conclusion of her session.

Nevertheless, she had little time this early morning to bask in her triumph. She had a plane to catch to Indianapolis, but first she had to get to the San Francisco Airport, fighting the peak, early morning traffic crossing the Bay Bridge. She had to get a move on. She had two hours to get there, return the rental car and move through the maze of harried passengers at check-in. She was not looking forward to that part of her travel.

Jessica had already showered, and was selecting her travel apparel. Her first impulse was to travel very comfortably in gray slacks, a black turtle neck sweater, and matching jacket. "No! I won't wear slacks today. I want to feel feminine." She said, as she continued to rummage through her garment bag. "I'll travel in something more daring. Perhaps I will be lucky enough to be seated next to some dashing young man for the plane ride east." She chuckled at the thought, knowing that fate had not been kind to her in the past. She finally decided to wear a red business suit; the one with a very short, pleated skirt that clung to her well shaped body. It also revealed her long, tawny legs.

She selected a white, high-necked blouse to wear under the blazer jacket. After dressing, she quickly packed her other garments. Then she rang for a hotel bellman, checked out of the Holiday Inn Hotel, retrieved her new Taurus rental car, and sped through the heavy traffic snaking its way toward the Oakland Bay Bridge.

7

Jessica could never fathom how the commuters could endure the daily agonies of such a drive. She longed for the simplicity and ease of the staid Midwest- for the amenities of the small college town of Greencastle, where reflection and study came easy. These and other reveries of her past made the elapsed time to the San Francisco Airport seem very short indeed. As a matter of fact, after dropping off the rental car and checking in with the ticket agent, glancing at her watch, she discovered that she had nearly half an hour before her flight departed. Rather than open her briefcase and review some of her research models of cells and how they mutate once infected by the AIDS virus, she decided to await her flight time by people watching. As she looked at passengers come and go, she couldn't help wondering, who were these travelers? What were their final destinations? How many would one day be infected with AIDS, or did they already have it, and were unknowingly spreading it to others? It was a chilling thought which gratefully disappeared quickly.

Suddenly, out of the corner of her eye, she saw a tall, handsome, scholarly looking young man approach the ticket agent, a young Asian female. She noticed that the ticket agent smiled at him broadly, revealing white teeth that literally flashed with brilliance. The young man acknowledged her smile with a confident air. Jessica noticed he was wearing tight fitting, light brown trousers, white polo shirt and a dark blue blazer, his apparel revealing an obvious, athletic build. His dark brown oxford shoes were scuffed, denoting he had done considerable walking. Perhaps he was a young professor on the Berkeley Campus and walked a great deal to and from classes.

The young man turned with his boarding pass in hand and glanced across the passenger waiting area, searching for a vacant seat. Slowly he moved in her direction. His eyes suddenly met her gaze. They lingered and he smiled at her with a gentle ease. Jessica could only blush. A reaction which she was sure did not go unnoticed by the young man. She audibly sucked in a deep breath, regretting that there was no empty seat next to or near

8

her. Her dark eyes followed him. He glanced over his shoulder at Jessica and moved off to an empty corner of the waiting room area and stood, leaning against a wall, near the point where passengers would egress to the waiting plane. Jessica thought how lucky, and perhaps wonderful it would be, if fate would make him her seatmate for the long trip to Indianapolis. The ticket agent broke her fantasy by announcing the boarding procedure and seating sequence.

"We are now ready to begin boarding passengers for flight number 486 to Indianapolis. All passengers holding seats 16 and higher may begin boarding. Those passengers needing special assistance and passengers with young children may also board at this time." Jessica's seat number was 18c and therefore among the first to board. She would have one more opportunity to pass close to her new fantasy. As she did so, she felt an explosion of warmth trickling through her body. Their eyes met and remained locked for a brief moment in a ghostly magnetism. She then moved quickly up the ramp to the waiting plane.

Despite his ravaged physical state, Richard never tired of the breathtaking beauty surrounding his home, high atop Grizzle Peak, in the Berkeley Hills. By day he could look out of his huge picture window and drink in the majesty of the gently sloping hills. Each hill was dotted with lovely, contemporary homes that perched precariously against the top and sides of the foothills. And, when the morning fog burns itself out from the heat of the morning sun, he could enjoy the view of cities, Oakland to San Francisco far below. And off in the distance, but clearly visible was the most distinctive landmark of the Bay area, the Golden Gate Bridge. At night he would be thunder struck by the thousands of twinkling, yellow and amber lights of the two cities, as they blurred into one vast kaleidoscope of power and seduction. His mind lingered on those thoughts because he knew that it would be at least a month before he would return home.

His melancholia was broken by two distinct, physical sensations. One, being tossed about by the Volvo's struggles to remain on the winding road, as Eisa negotiated the narrow, hairpin turns descending into the city of Oakland. The other visceral sensation was the euphoria he felt knowing that nestled in his briefcase was the mathematical proof of the formula for the Grand Unified Theory, the most sought after physical solution to nature's secret in the history of Science. Even though Einstein could not solve the riddle, Richard often quoted one of Einstein's more popular sayings, "The only incomprehensible thing about the universe is that it is comprehensible." The thought comforted him as he pulled his briefcase closer to him, as though fearing it might fly through his opened window.

Eisa remained mostly silent during the entire descent into Berkeley, obviously aware that her mentor wanted this time for reflection. She also was painfully aware that he was monitoring very closely her driving technique for negotiating the precarious curves in the road that had no guardrails.

As they crossed the Bay Bridge connecting Oakland to San Francisco, Dr. Stedman broke their silence by giving Eisa final instructions. "Eisa, I want you to go over all the equations you have been working on so laboriously. Especially, the daunting Lorenz Transformation and those defining N Space."

Eisa looked at him quizzically. She had reviewed them dozens of times over the past two months. She couldn't be more confident in her solutions to the mathematical equations. She called upon her rich vocabulary for a response, but could only manage a mundane, "Yes sir, Dr. Stedman. Is there anything else?"

"Yes, I want you to make absolutely sure you discuss your work with no one. And I do mean no one. You do, of course understand that Dr. Abel and his staff at MIT have been working diligently on the same problem. I have reason to believe they are heading down a blind alley. But, we can't be sure."

"Of course Dr. Stedman. I will do just as you say. And one thing more. I want to convey to you again how sorry I am about the passing of your father. You'll recall that I met him once, several years ago when he stopped by your office en route to a business trip to San Francisco. From all accounts he was a brilliant and good man, like yourself. Please call me once you arrive in Greencastle, or at anytime you think I can be of any help to you on a personal basis." Richard was deeply moved by her thoughtfulness.

"That is very kind and thoughtful of you Eisa. I will do that!"

He continued to look out of the side window, noticing as he did that they were passing Three Com Stadium. He stifled a laugh as he recalled it was first called Candle Stick Park. Where in the world do they get such names, he mused. Richard liked the latter much better. They continued in silence down Highway 101 South, toward the airport.

The check- in routine went smoothly enough, a fact that Richard found to be a rarity for this busy International Airport. There was one curiosity, however. For some strange but welcomed circumstance, he had become unusually drawn to a beautiful lady in a striking red dress. Their eyes had met and they exchanged telepathic waves. There was a promise of something that lay dormant for now.

The early morning sun bathed the airport tarmac in golden rain as Dr. Stedman stared out his window seat. His attention was focused on the men and women as they scurried around the plane. Some driving tractors trailing baggage and luggage carts.

Others were loading the plane with food trays from trucks proudly displaying the name of the caterer. Men with long hoses leading from a fuel truck pumped hundreds of gallons of fuel into the belly of the plane. Richard was happy he had chosen a window seat for his long flight. Being able to look out the window gave him an opportunity to read landforms from on high once the plane reached altitude. It also gave him some relief from the claustrophobic closeness of the tight seating arrangements on board. Richard grunted a phantom "hello" when the male passenger settled awkwardly into the middle seat next to him. He did notice that the man was short, thickset, and sported a grayish beard perched stately on his chin. The depth of his eyes seemed forever hidden from the observer. Richard knew immediately that he would not be talking to the stranger.

The beehive of activity suddenly settled down and the aircraft begin to pull back from the gate. The female flight attendant's voice droned into the familiar take off routine. The only thing she said that registered into his consciousness was, the information about "using the seat cushion for a floatation device." That meant the airplane would be utilizing the east west runway and the aircraft would be flying for a couple of minutes out over the Pacific Ocean. Never a pleasant thought for a person like himself who was not fond of flying.

Nevertheless, he settled back in his seat with a sigh of resignation. The rumble of the engines grew to a deafening pitch as the plane screamed and lurched down the runway, and then vaulted into the air, groaning as it strained for an altitude. Those sounds would be the last he would hear for some time. Sleep came quickly and deeply . . . along with the pitiless and familiar dreams!

CHAPTER 2

Departure for Indy
Aboard USAir Flight 247

Jessica settled comfortably into her passenger seat, if one could use the word when referring to seating on any passenger aircraft. She preferred the window seat, as it gave the feeling of space and roominess as she looked out the window. In addition she loved interpreting the landforms and geological structures from the vantage point of thousands of feet in the air. It was as if she were reading a book. Jessica never ceased to be awe struck as she thought of the millions of years it took to forge the hills, mountains and streams on planet earth.

No sooner had she made herself comfortable, than an odd looking man struggled over the passenger on the aisle seat and plunged into the middle seat next to her. Jessica's worst premonitions were coming true fast. Fate was not going to deliver the handsome, smiling college professor to her on this day. She would be sitting next to a walking, breathing, magpie for the next four hours. Perspiring slightly from his dash to catch the plane, and struggling to board the full flight, he nudged her arm lightly and muttered, in a Texas drawl, Howdy young lady? I hate full flights, don't you? It wouldn't surprise me if it were over-booked. They do it all the time, you know! I see you are glancing around at the ground crew outside the window like you're nervous, or something! I betcha, you got a lot on your mind haven't you? Are you some kinda doctor?"

Jessica could not believe her ears. Now it became abundantly clear to her that she would be doomed to sit next to this creep, for the next four hours, just when she desperately wanted to be alone with her thoughts about her work.

She looked closely at the stranger. He was wearing a dark blue designer sweater, summer weight, over a white polo shirt and cinnamon colored trousers. Jessica judged his age to be about 45 years. His graying hair and wide, salt and pepper mustache masked to some degree, his well-chiseled face. However, she did notice that he had a one-inch scar next to his right eye, high on his cheekbone. "Probably from some bar room fight." She thought. He was tall, over six feet. His eyes, a piercing ice blue, were shaded by thick, eyelashes. His nose was large and hawk- like. He had a ruddy complexion, as if he had spent a great deal of time out of doors in the sun. Like the pictures she had seen years ago of the Marlboro man. Although his demeanor was lepreconish, he gave the impression that he had seen too much over the years of life's troubles.

"You look like a professor ma'am. Yep, you're a professor all right!"

Jessica hesitated before answering but felt she had no choice but to reply. However she did scan the passengers in the immediate vicinity, fearing the stranger was talking too loud. She was right. Several passengers were staring at her.

"Yes, I'm a professor of sorts," she said in a husky, deep throated voice, despite the fact she tried speaking softly. "I'm a scientist."

The stranger was right on another count as well. Before she could continue, their conversation was interrupted by one of the stewardesses over the intercom. Her voice sounded much too cheerful.

"Our flight is oversold. We are looking for two volunteers to relinquish their tickets. We're offering two tickets each to any destination in the continental United States where US AIR flies. We're also including one hundred dollars each and we'll try to get you on one of our next flights east." Two young people, apparently college kids, leapt from their seats, yelling as one. "We'll take it."

The plane was delayed for another ten minutes while the transfer of passengers took place. The stranger appeared unimpressed by his several correct guesses. He only smiled and looked straight ahead, as the jet engines roared to life and taxied to the main runway for takeoff. The plane moved forward on its roll down the runway. Suddenly and with great straining, it leapt in to the sky. After gaining about 2,000 feet of altitude out over the Pacific Ocean, the plane made a wide circling arch and came back over land, seeking more precious altitude. Finally, crossing over the Sierra mountain range at 5,000 feet, the stewardess made the usual plea to "keep your seat belts fastened when not moving about the cabin." "As soon as the captain reaches our cruising altitude of 35,000, we will be coming around with beverages and our complimentary breakfast."

This was also the signal for the stranger to begin his conversation again.

"Young Lady, did you say you were, a scientist? I guess I'm like most people," the stranger said. "I find it hard to follow what science is doing today. Back in my hometown of Lubbock, Texas, a small sheep ranch outside of Lubbock to be exact, we don't have much use for all the grand, mysterious discoveries being made today. Our lives are quite simple, you know. We depend on ourselves and each other, not technology, to rule our lives. You know, we spend a lot of time alone, under the sun and the stars. It gives a man a sense of freedom and control of knowing he is master of his own fate. Each person has his own world and space, hidden from all other eyes with power and magic. You don't find that kind of feeling of personal security and control in the big cities. We ranchers have a lot of time to meditate, to be centered in ourselves for a while. Out on the prairie and farm fields, the ability to meditate makes everything one does have a kind of real significance. You're part of the rhythm of life. It's like everything in the universe is really simple, connected, understandable, like breathing in and breathing out, you know. Maybe that's why breathing exercises are recommended by doctors for city folks who are all stressed out. But . . . I am talking too much. I'm accused of that all the time. I think people are so . . . interesting. What kind of scientist did you say you were?"

Although Jessica was only half listening to the stranger, for some reason she did find him rather interesting and attractive too, in a rugged, masculine kind of way. She was convinced he was a great, skillful master of the droll, sarcastic put down, and that is probably what he is up to. Certainly most of the people she came in contact with on a daily basis did not easily expose their inner thoughts and feelings so easily. Especially the researchers she had just met at the science seminar. She decided to play the little probing game a little longer. If she became too bored, she could always feign busy work by taking technical papers out of her briefcase and beginning to read.

"I didn't indicate what scientific specialty I'm involved in." She demurred. Nevertheless, Jessica felt compelled to appease him. She continued in a matter of fact speaking voice, hoping to smother her bewilderment of where this line of conversation was going.

"Yes! It would be fair to say, that I am a research scientist. A microbiologist. It is a big word, but it really means those people in this particular field study the structures, functions of organisms, living things that exist on a very tiny scale. Mainly we observe these creatures through an electron microscope. It magnifies them to thousands of times their actual size."

The stranger blinked, but smiled another capricious smile and hurried on.

"Well dear lady, all my life I've felt close to nature and have observed her majesty first hand. On my Dad's ranch I observed cows giving birth. I witnessed other animals repeating the life cycle of birth and death on the prairies of the Texas Panhandle. I have felt close to the meaning of nature and my own connection with plants, rocks, water ponds, earth, and sky. You know, it gets awfully dark on the ranch at night. One could observe the heavens vault, pregnant with shimmering stars, stretching vast and infinite. You feel a oneness with them.

"It is surprising what you can see and feel on deep starry nights on my ranch. I didn't look through, what do you call it? . . An electron microscope? No one needed to teach me in schools, and universities about life's" great questions. You know, Truth . . God . . . Man's true existence! Life after death. Human urges of love, hate, meanness in individuals. No! I don't need a microscope to contemplate them. Perhaps it is best that in this century many such questions have been considered meaningless. Maybe in the next one coming it will be different. I think they have been neglected along with other mystical rituals.

"There are too many issues that affect our daily lives and those of the world, which our best brains are not addressing. Issues we could solve early in the next century, if we just turned our minds to them. Questions like, "Are we looking too much into the nature of things, advancing technology, instead of understanding basic human needs, and how to get along with one another? Why are cities dying along with the hearts and souls of the people in them? Why isn't religion relevant to a great many young people today?

The stranger was becoming exorcized with his passion. Passengers nearby began to turn in his direction. Jessica put a finger to her lips, urging less audible passion in his conversation. The stranger took the cue, but continued his line of thought unabated.

"In a complicated world, scientists should be bringing to bear their great brain power on such weighty questions as, "Why are cities dying along with the hearts and souls of the people in them? Why isn't religion relevant to a great many people today? Can science and religion coexist, given the miracle advances being made by science in the fields of space, astronomy, and

17

medicine? Where is the cure for AIDS, after billions and billions of dollars have been spent on research for a cure? A simple rancher like me should not have to be raising these enigmas. And one last thought, Why aren't scholars and scientists thinking of these things? But I don't want to be too hard on you as a scientist. You are probably a very good one at that, but I hope we plain people will be asking you more and more of these questions as we begin the next millennium."

"This is idiotic," thought. Jessica. "Who is this man? Why is he asking me these questions? Don't they drink beer in bars in Texas and spend their non-working hours seeking pleasures of the body, and not the soul? I've been working too hard in Academia. Maybe I should spend more time in the future talking to other people besides mainstream scholars and scientists. Do people like him really think about ideas such as those he is speaking of? What does he want from me? What would he think if I told him that several of my associates at DePauw discuss such issues in monthly dialogue sessions? What would he think if he knew I was one of the select persons heading a team at the Center for Disease Control in Atlanta? Would he care if he knew we might be as close as months away from a vaccine against Aids? He would probably like the fact that we call it M99. The M signified the coming of the millennium and the "99" for the year of breakthrough discovery technique to produce the vaccine."

The stranger did not have to know that she was unable, at this point, to develop her ideas fully about the patient's vulnerability to anti toxins of M99 and that a few more serious anomalies remained. But she was confident that her team could manage it in the near future.

" What if I told this cynical stranger that just yesterday, I delivered a paper stating the same thing at a Berkeley symposium? And what if he knew that several DePauw

University colleagues and I meet once a quarter to discuss such mainstream issues as he has been talking about.

"No, I won't tell him that between working on my Masters and my Ph.D. degrees, I had to come to grips with the same childlike questioning of my own beliefs, my own sense of purpose, nature's purpose. Curiously enough, I still don't know the guiding meaning to such questions. But I came to realize I could make a contribution to mankind. So I put such weighty questions on hold. I pursued microbiology to vitalize my life."

Jessica decided to give the stranger just a few more minutes of her time and then to either sleep or reflect on her next strategy for dealing with the damnable Aids Virus. She didn't know it, but the plane was now passing over the Rocky Mountains. Time was no longer the master, and the trip was taking a lot less time than she had thought. Jessica surprised herself by answering the stranger's questions. She knew how to play his game.

"In a way I find your viewpoints very interesting. Most of the time, I believe as you do that all the answers we spend a lifetime seeking have been hiding just below the surface, within us. The secret is that regardless of what is known or unknown, one's fate resonates within ourselves."

She noticed the stranger was now looking at her with new and youthful eyes, as if he had been reading her mind all the while. She began to analyze her situation, to think. "He certainly seems to know a great deal more about science and the world than would appear from what he is telling me. A rancher in Texas would normally not spend his time thinking of things of the higher order. She wanted to, no, she was compelled to know more about him. She gently eased into a lighter, less threatening topic.

"Ranching must be busy, hard, and time-consuming work. How do you find the time to work on the ranch and read so much? You must really enjoy reading?"

"As a matter of fact I do," said the stranger. "I was never able to go to the university. Oh, I wanted to, but I was needed on the ranch. I have two older brothers and sisters. They graduated from the University of Texas. But when it came my time to go, there was no more money left. My parents felt bad about that too because I was an honor student in high school. My dad needed me to help him manage the ranch. My parents and I always considered that after a couple of years, we could save enough money for me to go to college. But it never worked out. So I tried to educate myself, I read countless books in my spare time and on many different subjects. I guess I have been reading about philosophy, religion and eastern mystics, since I was a small boy."

The stewardess reached their row with a snack cart and began to take beverage orders.

"I'll have a 7-UP, "said the older gentleman in the isle seat.

"I'll have one of them small bottles of Hennessey whisky, with coke," the stranger barked, looking directly at Jessica, as if seeking her approval.

Jessica thought to herself, "I hope it will act as a sedative for him," but she knew better. Alcohol is a stimulation in the initial stages of drinking.

"May I have a bloody Mary mix, with a twist of lime, please," Jessica asked? She knew she certainly did not need an alcoholic stimulus that would match the heightened state of the stranger. It would be far more comforting in her current situation if she settled for a non-alcoholic drink. She turned her gaze once

20

again toward the view outside the airplane window and permitted her mind to wander.

The plane must now be over the vast expanse of flat lands, which means they were beyond the majestic Rocky Mountains and entering the plains states of Iowa and Missouri. The city of St. Louis stretched somewhere out there in the not too distant horizon. The trip is taking far less time than any trip from the West Coast that I could remember. Could it be that the stranger and his ramblings were far more interesting than I have imagined, or care to admit. He was making the trip seem like condensing times arrow. The stranger talked on.

"I hope I'm not bothering you too much. If I am, please tell me."

Jessica cringed and gave him a plastic smile.

"No! No! You're not bothering me. I was just . . . "

The stranger didn't permit her to continue. He leapt at the opening.

"I would like to share something very personal with you that happened a long time ago. It's about the Lubbock Lights."

Jessica groaned silently. "The Lubbock Lights" did you say?"

"When I was a boy, about nine years old, my Uncle Starky would often take me out onto the prairie lands surrounding our ranch. We would fish and hunt rabbits. He was smart too. He also knew about the constellations in the sky and would point them out to me with great excitement. Later I was delighted when I could discover the different ones without his aid. I would amaze my friends when I pointed them out to them on dark starry nights under the Texas sky. I was familiar with Pleiades, Virgo, Taurus, Orion, Ursula Major and Ursula Minor. Then there were the stars, Vega and Regulus. I liked to gaze at the

21

Southern Cross the best. Many nights my Uncle Starky would sometimes build a campfire to take the chill out of the night air and to keep wild critters at bay.

"One night, in 1956, I think it was, we were looking at the Three Sisters constellation. You can find it just off to the right of Orion's Belt. Then Uncle Starky began telling me a story."

The stranger lowered his voice and his demeanor took on all of the trappings of an old prospector telling tall tales around a dying campfire. He prefaced the story by saying it was true.

"Do you know son," Uncle Starky began, "I don't think I have ever told you about the time Unidentified Flying Objects, UFO's they called them, flew over Lubbock."

When the stranger mentioned the word, UFO, slight, gnawing shivers climbed the length of Jessica's spine. It was like a shadow had crossed the sun on a chilly but sunny afternoon. She didn't understand why. Luckily the stranger didn't notice, as he continued in a dreamy voice.

"No sir, Uncle Starky," I said. "You never did!"

"Well there were 12 of them. Yes sir! I think there were twelve. They appeared over the city in late afternoon, just before dark. Huge objects they were. And, they flew in a tight V formation. The whole town saw em. The young Carter boy even took movie pictures of them. One of them broke formation and flew off in the direction of your Dads' ranch. We never saw it return.

"There were pictures in all the local and surrounding newspapers. They showed disc looking objects in a large, V formation. The whole time of the sighting was about twelve minutes so we all had a good look at them. They were silvery in color and oblong. Some of them seemed to be pulsating, in

22

different colors of reds, greens, and yellows. Occasionally, one or two of them would break formation in a flash, only to return again, just as fast as they left . . . Instantaneously! The whole formation was moving too fast to be airplanes or birds or anything else we knew about that could fly. The local newspaper and the wire services all across the country carried the story. Our little unknown town became instantly famous.

"Of course scientists debunked the whole thing, calling them flights of birds. Even the United States Air Force came to interview the young Carter boy who had taken pictures of the sighting. The Air Force men, in black uniforms, took the original negatives of the photos for examination, for authenticity they said. A funny thing though. They never returned the negatives. However, copies were sold to one of them major television networks. For five hundred dollars I think, which was an awful lot of money for the time. For several years, the "Lubbock Lights," as they came to be known, appeared on documentaries about UFO's. You never hear about them anymore. But Uncle Starky said that they were real, all right.

"The frightening thing about the story is that Uncle Starky said he felt he was kidnapped by one of them UFO's for about an hour. It seems he was chasing down some stray cattle on horseback, when it happened. He used to tell my Dad about it on occasions when he would come to dinner. He said two little men, in silvery suits, did it. They had large heads and eyes like insects. They hypnotized him and took him aboard their small craft for examination. He has had strange dreams and nightmares ever since. I still have em, too, and have often wondered whether or not the same thing happened to me. My folks used to tell me that about the time the "Lubbock Lights" incident happened, that I came up missing for nearly two hours. All I could remember was that I was alone late evening. I was returning from hunting rabbits with my dads' rifle. I was on horseback. At the time, I had a pinto horse named "Ole Nokomis." Named after one of them famous Indian warriors. Suddenly, without warning, "Ole

Nokomis" started getting' kinda skittish. It was at this point that I knew something was wrong. When I looked off to the west, I noticed a brilliant light, hovering over the ground, about a quarter of a mile off in the distance. Being a curious child, I took off at a slow trot toward the light. When I got about two hundred yards from the light, I noticed it was a metallic object, and glowing with lights of all kinds of colors. "Ole Nokomis" gave a shuddering whinny, shook his head violently, and would go no further. I didn't either; cause a bright blue light zapped straight at me. That was the last thing I saw!"

"When my folks found me, they said I was staggering, aimlessly and lost. "Ole Nokomis was trailing behind me in the same condition. My parents were scared to death for me. I couldn't tell them much more than I have told you. They didn't believe me, of course. All I know is ever since then, I seem to know a lot about a lot of things I didn't know before. Science, astronomy and technology. And, I have premonitions too.

"Do you know young lady, surveys have shown that more than 20 million Americans say they have seen UFO's?" Jessica shivered again! "That our astronauts have reported seeing em in Space and that they were there, observing from a hillside, when they walked on the moon. Even our bomber and fighter pilots in World War II observed them as they darted around their aircraft. They called them "Foo' Fighters then, because they appeared and disappeared instantaneously. What do you think about that?"

Jessica noticed that during the entire time the stranger was talking about UFO's, he scarcely looked at her. He was glancing out the window, as if searching the skies for the alien visitors. Jessica could not rationally explain why the term UFO had such a profound effect upon her. She had not seen or heard the word for years. She took a last sip from her Virgin Mary, and shifted the conversation to more familiar topics.

"As a scientist, she finally said, "I'm sure there are many scientific explanations for what people see. I'm fairly certain many UFO observers are convinced they have witnessed a truly unexplainable and frightening event. But, it is probably due to arcane, long suppressed dreams.

"I'm also sure that there are many things we scientists do not understand. Some things exist in nature that we will never be able to adequately explain. We are just now discovering things that a decade or two ago we had no clue as to their meaning or existence. For instance, in my field of research, less than a decade ago the AIDS virus was unknown to us. Now it is one of the world's great mysteries. We are frantically working now to stop its deadly march through mankind. It has probably been lying dominant for hundreds or thousands of years in our bodies. Now it was surfaced again. I don't want to frighten you, but it is now believed that nearly 30 million people on earth have been infected with the HIV virus. Sometimes I feel convinced that viruses have a human like intelligence. They mutate into other forms when our drug treatment becomes too powerful for them. Then we have to fight them all over again with new weapons and techniques."

She looked at him for a reaction, but received none. He finished the last of his drink and placed the empty glass and bottle on the tray table in front of him. He smiled at Jessica as he said, in a reassuring voice, " We'll find a cure and vaccine . . . and soon. I don't think fighting AIDS with powerful drugs is the final answer. Oh, for the time being, drugs are our best intermediate hope for many desperate souls now dying from the disease. We have to develop a vaccine to cure AIDS. You, dear lady, just might be the person to come up with it too. All it takes is new ways of thinking and imagining possibilities for solving the problem."

Jessica found it difficult to keep her incredulous thoughts about this man from coming to the surface. How could he be so sure of himself? From the way he talked he seemed to have some special kind of knowledge or premonition. He said he had that power. He couldn't possibly know that it was the exact approach she and her colleagues were taking, and that they were getting close to working out a formula for a vaccine. In the next few months she would be performing experimental trials with monkeys. All she knew for sure was that he was more than just a stranger and rancher from Texas.

"I hope you are right," Jessica said. "I hope you are right, for the sake of all mankind." He just offered her a calming smile that would tame a ravaged soul. But it was the captain who offered her the most welcomed respite.

"Ladies and gentlemen, we are now passing over St. Louis. We will begin our descent into Indianapolis in about 10 minutes. We are expecting to land at Indianapolis International Airport in about 28 minutes. The weather in "Indy" is 72 degrees, with some light rain showers in the area. I don't expect much turbulence ahead, but I will continue to keep the seat belt sign on. We'll be back with another update on time and weather for our arrival, in about 20 minutes."

Somewhere over the awesomely flat topography of the Midwest plain states, Richard awakened from his deep sleep. He was scarcely aware of his surroundings. He was reminded of the way small infants awaken. First, they open their eyes wide, as if in slow motion. Almost like a tourist seeing a big city for the first time. Then they howl for attention. Perhaps, he would have done so as well. But he felt strangely refreshed. And grateful that his numbing migraine headache was gone.

Richard confirmed in his mind that he was well into the flight as he looked out of the window. Between scattered cirrus clouds, he could see flat, verdant green landforms. The flight was obviously well beyond the lofty, Rocky Mountains. Perhaps they were nearing St. Louis. That was a welcomed prospect. He would soon be in Indianapolis. He mentally began to review his strategy once he reached Indianapolis.

First, he would call his farm estate. He knew his dad's longtime friend, Mr. Jeremy Jarvis, would be there looking after things. Mr. Jarvis and his father were nearly inseparable through the years. They seemed to have gotten even closer since his mother passed away four years ago, leaving his dad all alone on the large farm. His dad had hired Mr. Jarvis as the caretaker of the farm and had so advise Richard of his action before he died.

Richard had known old man Jarvis since he was a child. He always got along well with him, mainly because Mr. Jarvis would take a great deal of time with him when he would come over for evenings of chess and Sunday dinners. Invariably he would hustle Richard off to the pond for an hour of fishing and conversation. In many ways, the quality time he had spent with Mr. Jarvis was more quality time than he had with his dad.

Richard remembered Mr. Jarvis as a great storyteller. He knew everyone in the city of Greencastle and the surrounding area. He was now a retired schoolteacher, having taught math and science at Greencastle High School for more than forty years. Richard was pleased he was staying at his Dad's place. He had pledged to do so as long as Richard needed him to. Next on Richard's "To do list" for this day was to rent a car at the Indianapolis airport for his drive to Greencastle. He would commit to leasing it for one week at a time; since he was unsure of the total time commitment he would give to this trip. He would go immediately to the mortuary to complete the funeral arrangements for his father's burial. Since his family was small, with few living relatives, he would opt for a quick burial, within two or three days, if he could arrange it.

He would try to meet with lawyer Ernest Flownery. Since he was a friend of the family, he would entrust him to handle his fathers' insurance and the sale of the family farm. He had absolutely no intent of nor interest in moving from California to live out his life on the farm. He would give himself until the end of the month to complete the sale arrangements. He could use the time to great advantage. The solitude of the farm would provide the perfect atmosphere to continue working on the write-up of the "Gut" Theory. Richard smiled deep within at this last thought and excused himself from his seatmates and made his way cautiously to the lavatory at the rear of the plane. He needed to wash his face and perform other ablutions, so there would be no delay in his dash to Greencastle upon landing. Of course he took his brief case with.

On his return to his seat, Richard stole a glance ahead to look for the lady in the red suit, but it was to no avail. There were too many people on board for instant recognition, and he was in a hurry. There was no time for flirtation. Nevertheless, he took solace in the fact that the Captain's voice broke through the general silence hanging over the passengers. "Ladies and Gentlemen, this is your captain speaking again from the flight deck. We will be making our descent into Indianapolis in just a few moments. We expect to be on time for our arrival at the gate. The weather in Indianapolis area is cloudy, but the rain has moved out of the area. The remainder of the day in Indianapolis should produce a nice display of sunshine with the temperature expected to reach 84 degrees. On behalf of the entire crew, we want to thank you for flying USAir with us today. We hope to see you again soon on another US AIR flight. Hope you have a good day in Indy. We'll be on the ground in just a few minutes."

Richard now felt pangs of hunger, and regretted the fact that he had missed the beverages and snacks. It would be a couple of hours before he could get something to eat. He didn't plan to make any stops for fast food along the way to Greencastle. He wanted to get his itinerary out of the way first. He clutched the briefcase tighter as he settled back into his seat. The next few days were going to be hectic. And for some reason, unexplainable, he felt they would hold troubling surprises.

"We'll be landing shortly", said the stranger. It has been a pleasure talking with you. Don't worry! Something tells me you were born for greatness. I can feel it. You don't know it but you will be recognized as a great and brilliant scientist one day. Perhaps a Nobel Prize is in your future. And it won't be long either!

"You know another thing? We've been talking all this time and I don't even know your name. " The stranger began to chuckle aloud but continued before Jessica could answer.

"I mean . . . I have been talking for a long time. You've been a great listener and seat companion. I know you will save the world from the next AIDS pandemic with your research project?"

Jessica gave him a full smile in reaction to his last comment. The stranger took it as a genuine sign of affection toward him.

"I appreciate your confidence in me and my work. Sometimes, just when you think you are making real progress in the battle against a virus like AIDS, you run into a blind alley.

"The virus will become impervious to our new drug treatments by mutating. Then you're pretty much back where you started. That's the big challenge my research team is working on. It's that point in which the media will make a premature announcement about the little progress we are making and the worlds hope for a cure rises, only to be dashed in short order. Even the patients that seem to be making real progress are fearful that their low blood counts will rise again. They watch their afflicted friends who are in advanced stages of the disease as they look with envy, through hopeless and yes in many cases, envy at the second chance for life others are getting. A cure must

29

do much more than clear HIV from the blood stream. It must rid it from other places that it has been lurking until the time is ripe for its activation and survival."She thought about the wonderful work done by Dr. David Ho, who just a few years earlier, who had made great strides in arresting the virus in patients who had never contacted a full-blown case of the disease. The drug cocktails he used at the time perhaps still can be made to work in patients in the later stages of the viral attack. But even so there is still the question of high costs. They are now certainly much too expensive, unfortunately, to do much good for the tens of millions in this country and in the developing nations who are already infected, or soon will be.

" I do appreciate your confidence. My name, by the way is Jessica. Jessica Harrington. I'm a research fellow at DePauw University. I've been attending an AIDS virus symposium in Berkeley. I must admit that I wanted only to be alone with my thoughts on this flight. But, you've made the long flight pass very quickly. I think I have learned a few things from you as well. Especially, how to be humble again. Too many people in my field and in the other sciences are so busy with their own struggles that they have forgotten just how important, and knowledgeable, others outside academia can be. It's nice to know that everyone is not a "couch potato," depending upon Russ Limbaugh, and other soothsayers, for instant knowledge."

She laughed at the analogy she had quickly come up with. So did the stranger,

"OK'" She said coquettishly. "Now you know my name, what is yours? You told me what you do, but not what your name is."

"Normally, I don't give my name. I prefer to really get to know someone first. You are an exception. I think I have come to know you very well. It's Clay, Clay Haskins."

30

"Well, Mr.Clay Haskins, we may have a lot more on common that you think. I too am a bit enigmatic. I had strange nightmares where I seemed to be walking alone at night, near my home and see strange beings invading my private space and few are invited in. When you were telling me about the UFO Lubbock Lights, they seemed strangely familiar to me. Sometimes I wonder why I to see white lights and strange, shapeless forms. They beckon to me. I try to get close to the figures and the light to touch them, but the apparitions remain just beyond my reach. However, through the mist of the dreams, I get the feeling they are trying to be reassuring and somehow assist me in my work."

Jessica was interrupted by the stewardess, whose voice again came over the intercom, giving final instructions for landing. "We'll be landing at Indianapolis International Airport in just a few minutes. Please return your tray tables and seat backs to their normal positions for our landing. Keep your seat belts fastened until the aircraft comes to a complete stop at the gateway. We appreciate your flying with us today, and we hope the next time you have travel plans, you will include US AIR."

Clay smiled again, without looking at Jessica. At the same time he extended his hand toward her. With a great deal of hesitancy, her hand moved toward his. The touch was ghostly at first, but as his handshake became gently firmer, Jessica felt a certain bonding with him. It was comforting, and discomforting at the same time.

"I wish you well, Clay, wherever your journey may take you. I have this feeling I will long remember our conversation."

Before Clay could answer, the plane shuddered as the wheels touched down on the runway. Once at the gateway, the rush of passengers making last second adjustments before deplaning prevented any further conversation. Jessica had a difficult time collecting her thoughts as Clay joined the other passengers in their mad dash toward the exit door.

31

Jessica decided it was time to join the rush. She didn't want to wait in a long line to retrieve her luggage and pick up her rent-a-car. She caught a finale glimpse of Clay Haskins as he strode with infinite confidence down the concourse walkway, his shoulder bag bouncing lightly against his muscular form. It was only fitting that his black western hat tilted slightly toward the back of his head, like the renegade he seemed to be. Jessica looked at her watch. It was 1: 46, Indianapolis time. "Where did the time go?" It was like missing time! The thought of the words "missing time" gave her a chill. But, Why?

"I've never been so happy to end a flight in my entire life", Jessica thought, as she exited the Indianapolis International Airport complex. She now entered the entrance ramp to interstate I-70, heading for Greencastle, Indiana. "It's only a short, pleasant drive to home now. I can clear my mind of everything that has happened so far today. I'm not sure whether it has been good or bad, but at least I'm here, and alive. I'll just permit my mind to run its course. A stream of unconscious thoughts is fine with me." She decided however, that her thoughts would be restricted from locking in on her research project and, above all, on Clay Haskins. She had enough of both for a while, although she readily could admit that the world could use more people like Clay. Lots more, she thought as her mind raced on. "The world needs more discussions about what national and global issues should be debated and addressed now, before the new millennium arrives. Regrettably, the government doesn't appear willing to or capable of holding a national debate on what compelling issues we should be addressing. Research budgets are being gutted just at the point in time when disease, famine, natural disaster, global warming, science and technology are rampant. We're developing new ideas faster than we can cope with any of them.

"I'm scheduled to host the next monthly in- gathering of the informal discussion group. My God! I almost forgot it was my turn to act as host. How did that come up so quickly? When is it? Soon, I know. I've got to look at my calendar as soon as I get to my apartment."

Just then, Jessica became aware, through her rearview mirror of a green Honda Accord approaching fast, much too fast. The car swerved quickly into the passing lane. As the car moved along side, Jessica tried to get a look at the dammed fool who was speeding and driving recklessly. The driver looked straight ahead, as if he were in deep cosmic thought. He now cut sharply back into Jessica's lane, causing her to break abruptly to miss his car. Jessica swore out loud. "Lousy driver! I thought only Californians reigned supreme in the lousy driver category." Although she couldn't explain it, the brief glimpse Jessica had of the driver, tugged at the back of her mind. She thought she had seen that person before, and recently.

"Oh well, she thought." It's really not worth my time thinking about it. The Lord knows I have enough other demands on my iced brain not to give the matter further thought. She permitted her mind to expand in other directions.

"Lets see, Jessica, she asked herself, if you are the host for the next group meeting, what will you serve for dinner? Spaghetti! That's it! A spaghetti dinner! Along with a nice, crisp spinach salad, garlic bread, and some of my famous raisin bread pudding with crème sauce. That should be a big hit with the men. It will surely top the stiff, tasteless lasagna Dr. Stanley Davis served at the last meeting." "Since the host must come up with the topic for the evening's discussion, I've got to develop some categories. As I recall, Stanley after the last meeting, said he would assist me. He probably forgot. Since our last meeting was a lively discussion about modern religion, what if we carried that discussion further with a general umbrella topic of "science, religion, and philosophy: Where to in the 21st Century?"

"Jessica, you little devil you. What a great idea! I can see it all now. Dr. Davis and Rev. Donovan, tangling with each other like two fraternity brothers showing off their dialectic skills at a late night beer and bull session. Then there would be lawyer Ernie Flownery talking away like an Iowa insurance man, knowing a little bit about a lot of things and nothing much about anything of value."

She smiled at this thought. Jessica knew he was not a bad person, and his ebullient personality guaranteed that an evening in his presence never made for dull moment.

"Lets see Jessica, the unspoken rules of the meetings stipulate that each regular member could invite one additional person to dinner. It just so happened that the last few meetings, only one or two guests were in attendance, I would hope there will be several guests for my meeting. If so, they will probably be boring," She thought.

"I might as well prepare for several guests. Frankly, I find additional guests very stimulating; they keep the rest of us on our toes and prevents the meetings from becoming stagnant."

Jessica was now entering the city of Greencastle. It shocked her to some degree that she had driven from Indianapolis, without being aware of the passing miles, having negotiated turns and arriving at her destination . . . Safe! It was as if the car had been on automatic pilot.

Going to Greencastle

After the plane touched down and taxied to the gateway, the passengers began their usual jostling of each other as they moved forward to the exit. Richard remained seated and looked up ahead for a glimpse of the " Lady in Red." It was in vain. She was gone. Vanished! When his eyes methodically searched the maze of fellow travelers making their way through the airport concourse, he detected no sign of her. "Oh, well" he thought,

"Such a pity. It is too much to expect fortune to smile upon me twice in one day."

Richard went straight to the Hertz rental car booth located on the main concourse at

Indianapolis International Airport. He could not help noticing the young, attractive female attendant standing attentively behind the counter. She had long, shoulder length blond hair, that teased the sides of her slightly sun tanned face. Her large wide, almond shaped eyes danced above her sculptured nose and full red lips. She greeted him warmly. It was just what he needed after the long plane trip from the coast. Another time and place he might have lingered longer to chat, and perhaps more. But, Richard needed to be in Greencastle in a hurry.

After completing the paper work for his rental car and retrieving his luggage from the baggage carousel, he hastened to an assigned 1999 Honda Accord and drove directly to I-70 West, only a quarter mile from the airport. It was drizzling rain. Despite the wet and perhaps slippery conditions of the Interstate, Richard decided to put the Accord cruise control on 70 miles per hour. He knew the road well, having driven it many times before on trips to and from his home in Greencastle to Indianapolis to visit his girlfriend Amy Stillwell. He smiled at his ability to snare the name and thoughts of her at a time like this. His smile quickly vanished however, as he pulled his brief case, containing the half-written write-up of "GUT" sitting on the front seat, a little closer. For the first time in many hours he began to relax as he drove on toward Greencastle, unconscious of the passing miles.

CHAPTER 3

Ma Mayes Restaurant

Dr. Stanley Davis, successful black author and professor of sociology at DePauw University, had just finished his last two-hour lecture of the day and was now en route to a noon luncheon appointment. Dr. Davis was medium brown skinned, with a large round face and eyes that danced with excitement when he talked. His large, but perfectly aligned teeth, flashed brightly as a comet in the night skies when he smiled. Stanley's voice was not authoritative, but one felt compelled to listen to his every word because he spoke with such sincerity. He moved with a youthful, athletic grace, despite the flecks of gray that were now sprinkled throughout well kempt hair.

Today, Stanley felt a great sense of anticipation at the thought he would be meeting with his old friend from Indianapolis, Rayford Moses. Rayford was a black community activist. He was also a journalist, story- teller, drug addict, and a religious zealot. He was definitely unique, supremely passionate about those social issues that he cared most about. Stanley was eager to hear the opinions of Moses regarding his solutions to several, mainstream issues effecting Black Americans entering the 21st Century: especially, the problems of educating our black youth. Stanley was convinced that immediate radical changes and new approaches were called for if we, as a race and as a nation, are to rescue black children from a downward spiral into the abyss of ignorance and despair. He understood that the next decade of the new millennium would be pivotal for saving black children who are falling woefully behind in preparing for the job demands of the future. Stanley wanted to ensure that mainstream black thought would be included in his book. He was confident that Moses would be adroit and forthright in his opinions. It was Stanley's idea to hold the meeting off campus, where Moses might feel more comfortable. It seemed only fitting that their meeting would take place in the community's only black owned "soul food" restaurant. It had some faithful following of blacks, but also had many white, faithful patrons as well.

The area of the city where most of the black population lived consisted of some twenty-five families. Most were homeowners who had lived there all their lives. The homes were in reasonably good repair and the yards and streets were neat and clean. Many of the homeowners were in their advanced years. Their children had long since moved away from Greencastle to Indianapolis, in search of a better quality of life. But enough remained to work at the University, or at the plant and in the food service industries. Saliva begun to flow to the corner of his mouth as he gleefully thought of the soul food restaurant. It was located in a small red and white building that had seen better days. Yet, it only seemed to add to ones dining pleasure.

It was not well lighted, and perhaps it was just as well. One got the feeling the somber lighting hid many things one was not anxious to see. The dining area featured booths and tables. The flooring was covered with white tiles, which were clean, but well worn. Nevertheless, "Ma Mays" was a clean, well-run restaurant, which seated about 30 patrons. It featured a large steam table filled with the standards, fried chicken, barbecue ribs, meat loaf, Kosher franks, deep-fried perch and catfish. The side dishes were also those familiar for decades to black kitchens in private homes for decades. Tantalizing, aromas instantly enticed the patron upon entry to the restaurant. At various times, depending on the day of the week, one would dine on black eyed peas, with ham hocks, kidney beans, cabbage, macaroni and cheese, stewed tomatoes, fried corn and green beans, highly seasoned with onions and bacon. " Mayes homemade cornbread and apple cobbler was the people's choice. Especially the apple cobbler, which featured a layer of thick, sweet, syrupy topping, on top of a thick golden brown crust. All of the foods were high- caloric intake, but most of her customers would not deny themselves a weekly, or biweekly visit. The customers loved it anyway, and they loved "Ma Mayes"

38

When Stanley entered the restaurant, he found Rayford Moses waiting. They embraced warmly. Stanley couldn't decide, after looking at Rayford, whether he was glad to see him, or just happy Stanley was on time so he could begin tasting "Ma Mayes" food. "Ma Mayes" was an absolute delight to witness in action behind the serving line.

A heavyset woman in her mid sixties, Ma had unbridled energy: moreover her laugh and perpetual smile were infectious. With hands on hips, she would bark out instruction to her serving staff. She would hurl a steady, playful banter of chatter toward her customers challenging them to taste certain foods. "Now you be sure to try some of my meat loaf today, Honey! Ya hear! It's extra good." Or, "I put some of dem really meaty ham hocks in my greens today." When she spotted Stanley in the line, she shouted. "Dr. Davis, you be sure and try my liver and onions. Dey taste jist like you like em, Honey."

Stanley was embarrassed, but only mildly, as other patrons turned to see what food choices he would make. Of course, Stanley decided to have "Mama's famous liver and onions." What other choice did he have? He decided it wouldn't hurt for one day to forego his usual soup and salad lunch. He would go for the gusto! He ordered side dishes of, greens, pinto beans and mashed potatoes. He would decide later whether or not to have one of her famous desserts. Rayford opted for fried chicken, green beans, and macaroni and cheese. He didn't hesitate to put a slice of apple cobbler on his tray, either.

Stanley paid the modest bill of fourteen dollars and sixty-eight cents. They gathered their trays and made their way toward the last window booth that looked out over Elm Street. After they strategically placed their food in front of them, Rayford was first to speak.

"Ok, Brother Stanley," he said. "You asked me to think about how to tackle the massive travails of Black Brothers in America, and meet you here for lunch to discuss them. Well I did, and I'm here. But, ya know Brother. I ain't sure I can tell you much you don't already know. What with your formal training. And big time degrees, and such. I guess there is some hope for us Black folks Brother, when you Black professor types, take the time to discuss such weighty matters with a plain ole Brother like me. Take that book you are working on. Most social scientists I've read about, would be taking surveys, interpreting all kinds of fancy data to fit their theories, then writing a book. I'm happy to see Brother; you didn't take the easy way out.

"Apprenticeship programs that teach youth real jobs needed by business and industry. Especially, for the better service jobs in the outlying areas of our major cities. Even inner city service jobs can be vital to a young adult entering into the workplace. I would grant that McDonald couldn't be the employer of last resort. But, they can teach youth positive work ethic qualities necessary to add personal value and growth potentials that are transferable to the skilled job jacket. Values like dependability, how to take direction, and probably just as importantly as anything, teamwork.

"We need to empower young people, at the earliest age, with the skills necessary to become self sufficient. That is why learning computer skills are so important. Seeing, touching, manipulating ones environment is far out of the reach for too many of our poor youngsters. But it is now possible for them to do so through the technology advances of the computer. Without their leaving the classroom, CD ROM technologies can place students in real time and places they would never be able to visit or interact with. With teacher guidance, young students can edit their homework and correct spelling and poor grammar habits. And where it becomes really powerful is the ability of the computer to assist young students in staying on task longer, because learning can be made fun and the student is actually in control. We should take the best of what technology has to offer and integrate it into the "tool chest" teachers already have at their disposal. It would appear to me that we are only scratching the surface of the benefits technology can bring to the classroom. The real success will be adaptability not the accessibility."

Rayford stopped talking and attacked the greens and macaroni, which were starting to cool. The pause in his rapid fire, sometimes highly excitable voice, gave Stanley a chance to ask Rayford a question or two. He wiped his mouth with the small white napkin, took a drink of his iced tea, and began slowly, deliberately, and with a professor's insightful delivery.

"You know Rayford, I have no real quarrel with anything you have said thus far. And you are definitely right about many of your points, which I will try to expand upon in my book. But I'm curious though about the fact that you didn't say much about educational needs of young blacks and their potential for success in the coming millennium. Many of the schools they attend were designed at the turn of the 20th century and are ill equipped to prepare youngsters for a knowledge-based 21st. Century economy."

Rayford held up one finger, signaling another brief pause was needed. He used the moment to attack, with relish, the remaining food that had gone untouched for several minutes. Several sips of iced tea left him feeling cool and refreshed for another assault on the dismal state of educating inner-city youth. Choosing his words with the precision of a surgeon's scalpel, he began addressing the question posed by Stanley.

"You are right. I haven't used the word black children very much. I suppose it is by design, because all poor children, black or white, are handicapped with the same set of negative circumstances. One might say that education is the ticket out of poverty and out of the imprisonment of the ghetto. Period! It appears throwing money at the problem of the deficiencies in education won't help much. A new national view and understanding of what is actually taking place in the work force, the work place, and in our schools needs much more attention than it is getting. New approaches, leading to a new mind set stemming from that review is what needs to be crafted in our schools. Perhaps the "Head Start" program is a lonely exception to this view. Nevertheless, I still have the feeling that a good education, starting in kindergarten, is the key. It is tragic that many people seem too distracted in endless, and mindless debate from that one essential. Change! We keep going back to the travail of the past, and I'm afraid the world is changing so fast that we don't have the luxury to do that. By the time the debate ends, our kids will have fallen further and further behind. Simply put, education is the first resort and the last, for the national solution to the problems of freedom, poverty, and racism. However, everyone seems to be hung up on the "blame Game." Could it be that no one is stepping up to the plate and saying what really needs to be said because they are afraid of attacking "sacred cows?' Why is it that we are afraid to say that, it's time to expect more from, and for, our children? No excuses accepted! Low expectations yield low results and of course our kids suffer. Kids starting school not knowing about elementary computers, not knowing numbers to fifty, or primary colors, never catch up. Their future is predictable. They will fail! They will be the troublemakers in our schools and in our streets. They will be the Hardees' clerks who can't count, unable to read a bus schedule, or fill out an employment application."

Stanley was getting caught up in the sincere excitement put forth by Rayford. He wanted to continue in this vein to test other ideas he was incorporation into his book. He continued to bait Rayford by asking simple questions: "Is business to blame? Could it be that our major corporations and businesses in general are partly responsible for the rotten state of our education system?"

Rayford willfully accepted the bait. " We only need to look around at the downsizing of our major business corporations, wherein thousands are laid off at a stroke. The reality is that we've been sold a bill of goods. We've been had! Even those

42

employees with college degrees are finding no safe heaven in the workplace. There was little concern raised when the poor blacks and high school dropouts lost their jobs. But now the hue and cry is coming from the ranks of those with college degrees. Only those employees with a willingness to learn adaptable and transferable skills and willing to be lifetime learners will succeed in the next century. This adaptability attitude is not learned suddenly or over night. It must be instilled in our children at the earliest age, by our schools."

Rayford continued to take the bait. He, too, was probing for agreement with his own ideas and agenda for social change. He now became exorcized. He hoped the other patrons in the restaurant were secretly eavesdropping on their conversations.

"And another point my dear friend Stanley, I don't hear any debate on television or radio talk shows, school boards, the political arena, that lays down a strategy to help our kids learn . . . NOW! So they can begin the next century with hope that one day soon, they will be productive members of our society. No child wakes up in the morning wanting to fail at school. It's what they see around them and what happens within the school walls that contribute to their failure. Much of the problems facing education come from words, not deeds, words of derision, scorn, skepticism, cynicism, disbelief, even hatred toward our kids."

Stanley interrupted Rayford. He had grown weary with attempts to shift the blame to different segments of society. He moved closer to Rayford. His hands tightened, clutching his coffee cup. So tight that the veins ballooned in his hands and neck as he continued.

"All I hear is blame and finger pointing. Parents blame the teacher. The teacher blames the parent. The teacher's union blames the school board. The school board blames the Superintendent, and the Superintendent blames the State Legislatures. The State Legislators blame Congress. Of course

Congress blames the President of the United States, Where does the blame lie and when will it end? What are the solutions that should be in place now to help our young kids?"

Rayford began to feel the rage displayed by Stanley. His nostrils began to flare as he was caught up in the impassioned pleas of Stanley. He blurted out his strong agreement with him. "Sometimes, I think I would like to take mankind by the throat until it turns blue, then turn it's face toward a brighter future that is just waiting out there for us, if we have the courage to find the right path. There comes a point when we can no longer beat our children with the carcass of our ancestors, nor, can we afford to permit people who should know better to talk the issue to death. What's the old saying? " Paralysis by analysis?"

Stanley could not permit Rayford's last remark to escape the moment and accepted it for what it was intended to be comic-relief. He began to laugh a genuine belly laugh but quickly reverted to his professional posture and pressed the dialogue forward. After all, they were trampling on his profession . . . education.

"No other segment of our society is under such probing and scrutiny. Federal and state interveners, local municipalities, consumer groups, ideologues and just plain idiots, on a daily basis poke, probe, litigate, and look into every nook and cranny of the education system. After all is said and done, nothing is done and they start all over again. Where is the truth . . . Now?"

The sumptuous meal and the depth of their conversation seemed to have lulled them into a new found sense of oneness and passion for the subject. This sense became evident when Rayford spoke his final thoughts. His words came like pure beams of light from a darkened sky. "The answer to the education issue, in my view, is fairly straightforward. We should be taking our queues from American businessmen. Many businesses would not survive for thirty days if they were run like a school system. In business, you either fix a train when it is off the track, or go out of business. It's called survival. American business has made fundamental changes over the last decade in how they operate. Most so radical and far reaching that they are scarcely the same companies, structurally, that they were in our fathers' day. The most basic change is in the workforce. Workers are expected to learn new skills, requiring greater knowledge than ever before. They are expected to be "lifetime learners, as well. They are also expected to work in a teamwork type setting. No longer do they scratch and claw at each other to get ahead. They are required to make progress . . . together! I don't see this happening in our schools.

"I guess you are right, " said Stanley. "The work place is certainly different today. The change was borne out of necessity and competition, both at home and abroad. So, change had to come and fast. Those companies that couldn't or wouldn't change were doomed. There is no question that our educational system is at the same crossroad."

Rayford was quick in his rejoinder, as he presented Stanley another with another envelope from his pocket. Its content and intent were clear and unmistakable at first glance.

"One of the most ridiculous aspects of the crisis in education is that no one seems to be pressing home the fact that the world has changed and is changing faster than we can keep up. Even those of us who have a good education are feeling woefully inadequate to the demands of the work place. The old ways of doing things just won't do any longer. They belong on the scrap heap. Technological skills and information processing are what will be the drivers and demanded of the workers of tomorrow. Business, which can gather and process information accurately and fast will be the winners of tomorrow. Employers who can supply the intelligence to drive this process will be most in demand for their services. Computers, phone systems world money managers, people who understand how a dollar works in

45

the world economy will also be the survivors, as we enter the 21st century."

Stanley was quick to agree with Rayford but he but went much further. "The educational system is no different from these business systems you talked about. It is my firm belief that all students can be successful and learn if the right atmosphere for learning is provided. As you mentioned earlier, no student starts out wanting to fail in school or life. Albeit, children learn at different speed limits. Other limiting factors, such as innate abilities, home and social impediments eventually take their toll. But most students can learn skills necessary to be productive and maintain self worth. Every school in the "New Age" should factor this into their educational model. It's idiotic to think most kids are going to go off to college. Our school systems don't seem to think so though. Our big focus should be on grades K-9 These students should be focusing on improving basic skills of the majority that don't go to college or universities. But, there is no reason such children cannot succeed. My definition of success is how they lead satisfactory lives after high school graduation. That means solving life's fundamental problems for living a decent life. Like raising families, possessing marketable skills and growing personally, on a continuous basis."

At that point, Rayford reached into his vest pocket and brought out two envelopes. The first was titled <u>GOALS FOR EDUCATIONAL CHANGE</u>. He meticulously opened the envelope and handed its contents to Stanley. The twinkle in his eyes and the sly grin spoke of an inner pride at what he had produced for the meeting. The gesture caught Stanley totally by surprise, but he began to read the typewritten contents with great curiosity, and anticipation. <u>Goals for Educational Change</u>:

1. Every Student, on a yearly basis, from K-9 would be required to take computer courses.
2. Every student, on a yearly basis, K-9 would be introduced, on an elementary level, and as a requirement

in the middle school, to take math courses in algebra, geometry, and calculus would be part of that requirement in the middle grades

3. Every student K-9, on a yearly basis would be required to take a foreign language

4. Every student, on a yearly basis, K-9 would be required to learn how to manage money, including how it flows through the economy.

5. Students, K-9 on a yearly basis, must be introduced to and demonstrate a familiarity with the values and virtues of a civilized society and how they translate into how we should get along with each other.

6. Every student, K-9, on a yearly basis, must be familiar with the major races and their cultures. They must demonstrate appreciation of the contributions each race has made to humanity they have made to humanity.

7. Every student, K-9, on a yearly basis must demonstrate a familiarity with how to communicate effectively. Speech classes would be mandatory.

8. Every student, K-9 on a yearly basis, will be exposed to the physiological and psychological tools necessary to manage aberrant behavior, with the primary focus on how to control anger.

9. Every student K-9, will be encouraged to play a musical instrument of his or her choosing. Rental fees for the instruments will be provided for those who are unable to afford them.

10. All courses such as Art, Gym, Ebonics, woodshop are to be abolished. If parents want their children to learn such

subject matters, they are to ensure that teaching, elsewhere.

11. Philosophy, Ethics, and virtue will be introduced to all students in some manner of course work in middle school. K-9.

12. Every student, K-9 must demonstrate how to prepare meals, sew, iron and wash clothes.

Stanley was astonished as he read the contents of the paper and quickly scanned the list again. He gulped his rapidly cooling coffee. He ordered more. He had asked Rayford to be creative in his thinking, but he had no idea he would be That Creative. Stanley could only suck in his breath, as Rayford handed him the second envelope, titled,

GOALS FOR TEACHER ACCOUNTABILITY

1. All educators, superintendents, principals, and teachers must be held accountable for their performance in the classroom. These accountability measures will be the standards and goals established by the parents, teachers, principal and the superintendent. State, and local politicians will have no say in formulating such standards.

2. Successful teachers accepted into the new system will be given the designation of "Master Educator."

3. A school social worker will be on site at each school.

4. Only the best-accredited teachers will be hired and their salaries will be 20 percent higher in inner city schools than surrounding counties and township schools.

5. Each individual school will have in place a there own individual teacher recognition program.

6. A dollar bonus system will be in place for all Master Educators and support employees when the school reaches specified goals that include, but not limited to:
   A. Attendance
   B. Social behavior incidences in the classroom
   C. SAT score improvements in:
      1. Math
      2. Reading comprehension
      3. History-U.S. and global

7. Educators not performing to expectations and measurements that gauge such performance will be given one year, after skills training, to demonstrate improvement.

8. The measurement standards at the time of a yearly review would be as follows:
   A. Did students, teachers, and administrators meet acceptable standards as prescribed in formal guidelines and hand booklets?
   B. On an ongoing basis skills will be required to ensure the programs in place are meeting the students' needs.

9. Performance reviews of master teachers would be mandatory on a quarterly basis by the principal. The next layer of supervision would have performance reviews by administrators. Superintendents will have performance reviews on a quarterly basis by an accountability committee of the school board.

10. At each level of performance review master teacher and administrators failing to meet acceptable standards after an opportunity to improve in the course of one year, will be dismissed or transferred to a different assignment that has no direct bearing on teaching students. Every effort would be expended to move the non-performers into the acceptable standard's performance level. All master teacher and administrators who fail to accept remedial skills training

would be denied a contract for the coming year. Their only option would be to make another career choice.

There are too many cases where teacher training is a national shame. Too many are not trained or qualified to teach the subjects they are teaching. Too many don't even have a minor in math. Additionally not enough states require their new teachers to know how to operate a computer. The school system would recognize that the new accountability should carry with them certain rewards. It should be noted that these change recommendations toward more accountability standards are no different from those already adopted by most other professions, including most businesses that have adapted to meet changing domestic and foreign challenges. Although the Accountability measures are high, so is the reality of the cruel fate of our children face when they fail to learn under our current educational system.

One must remember that CEO's are dismissed. Airline pilots are called upon to maintain a certain proficiency scale. Insurance managers are held accountable for their performance. Bankers, food service mangers, employees all across the business spectrum are held to certain standards of job proficiency. The standards are not to punish people, but to make them better performers. The Army is doing it. The Air Force is doing it. Even the government is doing it, for heavens sake! Education is not doing it. It is my thesis that people, in general, do not come to work every day to do a poor job. In too many cases it is the system that does not allow them to perform up to expectations.

The bottom line is that too many of our children are already lost or face a bleak and dismal future. Many can be saved, if immediate, and drastic actions are taken. While there is no "Silver Bullet" to improve schools that don't work, a model school system could be put in place, tomorrow, in any local system, that could be the model for many schools elsewhere.

Rayford ignored the slackened jaw of Stanley, and continued headlong into his final sermon on education.

"So, you see Stanley, it's not so hard to effect change after all. His grin widened. I believe a school system built something like the one I am proposing should be debated in homes, on talk shows, and in the national media. But the debate should not be long. One year only. What do we have to lose? Americans of all colors and creeds have shown an abundance of creativity during this century. But great ideas don't belong to just the elite or the giants from the best universities. We live in a vast arena where creativity and ideas are natural to all of us. Most of us are not born innovators or visionaries. I suppose it is a fact that most people even resist change and innovation. But we are talking about a New Vision. I would like to see the nation establish an environment where all people have the freedom to be creative in their thinking. But, regrettably, I don't see that. I see only endless debate. And usually between people who have no stake in or could not care less about our children's future. They care only about ivory tower debate."

Stanley could almost read Rayford's thoughts and was quick to grasp what it would take to reestablish a new priority paradigm shift in approaches to improving our schools. "You're right Rayford. I am impressed. I find favor with many of your ideas for the new, ideal inner city school. You've given me a great deal to think about as I sharpen the focus of my book. I think I can proceed without fearing that I might be too radical for the general public." He laughed a sinister laugh. "Again, as in the past, when I have called upon you to give me some "grass roots" thinking, you have not failed me. I knew you wouldn't and, as I promised you over the phone, you will be recognized in my book as a significant contributor. Ma Mays doesn't know it yet, but she will get a brief mention as well. I think her sumptuous food stimulated your brain. " As the two of them rose from the table and walked to the parking lot, Stanley offered up a final affectionate hug to his friend. As Rayford walked away, he yelled over his shoulder,

"Yeah, Stanley, don't forget to spell my name right in your new book. I have a feeling it will be a best seller." His laughter could be heard throughout the parking lot.

CHAPTER 4

Arrival in Greencastle

Richard was happy to make the turn off the Interstate as he neared Greencastle. He recalled the Interstate was seven miles south of the city, and as he exited at 231, the early afternoon sun bathed the near empty two-lane highway. He thought about what road travel was like before the advent of the interstate systems. Certainly they made for easy travel but those travelers miss a great deal of the beauty that lies just beyond. He had long contended that some of the country's most breathtaking sights could be appreciated only by exiting these super highways. He couldn't recall the author but he remembered reading a book titled Zen on a Motorcycle. It was about a man who took to the back roads of America on his motorcycle, witnessing sights and sounds undreamed of by the average American. It turned out to be a best-selling book, probably a testimony that people still longed for the romantic adventure and the simple pleasures to be found in rural America.

Richard, like so many people born in the Midwest, had left his small hometown to make his way in the much larger world. He still considered that tiny dot on the map called home as the center of the universe. He began to reflect more on his city of Greencastle.

Located 40 miles west of Indianapolis in Putnam County, Greencastle is a small town with a population of slightly more than 10,000 inhabitants. Like most small Indiana towns the city had grown only by a couple of thousand people in many decades. Greencastle was more fortunate than many small Indiana towns. It was the home of DePauw University. The Methodist Church in Indiana selected Greencastle to be the site of its new college. Indiana Asbury began as both a college prep school and a four-year residential college. Indiana Asbury

College changed its name to DePauw University in 1884, and has grown but slowly, ever since.

Richard recalled from his visits to the University that it was a friendly place- Midwestern in its best sense of openness, informality, and lack of pretense. The lives of the students seemed casual, but active and fun. The University is couched in low relief on 175 - acres of land. Bowman Park is surrounded by lovely, old, but sturdy buildings. Scattered among the older buildings are modern fraternity houses. One such structure is the Kappa Alpha Theta sorority house, the oldest sorority in the nation. It is one of two national sororities founded at DePauw. Fortune magazine from time to time has ranked DePauw as one of the nation's foremost producers of corporate chief executive officers.

Richard thought about the quality of life that has not been lost there. He found it in the ready smiles of the city's residents, the local business people and the college students, all eager to share their pride in a city that retains its down to earth Hoosier hospitality. He was tired but somehow happy to be away from the Bay area and its hustle and bustle, particularly Berkeley, where people dash around like a lunch crowd in Uptown Manhattan. He knew instantly that he was, at heart more Hoosier than West Coast.

Outside Thompson Mortuary

Thanks to the 3-hour time differential, Richard was grateful it was only 1:45 in the afternoon, local time. Richard had entered the city in what seemed like only minutes from the time he left the airport. He drove slowly but directly down the main street, South Jackson, where he pulled into the parking lot of Thompson Mortuary, largest and most modern of the three mortuaries in the city. Unprepared mentally to go directly into the mortuary to see his father's remains. He noticed a park bench at the far end of the driveway. It was nestled, in picturesque fashion under a large, aging sycamore tree that stood as a silent sentinel overlooking a large flowerbed with a dazzling water fountain in its center. Richard decided to rest himself on the park bench for a time and mentally gather himself for the difficult moments that lay just ahead.

Richard leaned against the back rest of the park bench, taking notice of a pair of monarch butterflies doing an in air dance as they flitted from one gorgeous flower to the next, seeking their sweet nectar. He began deep breathing exercises to relax his mind, body, and spirit. All were leaning over the edge of his endurance, knowing what he must do in the next few minutes. He would have to look upon the death mask of his father, whom he had not see in over a year-the father whom he had virtually ignored for an even longer period. He could hide behind the denial that his work had him bottled up. But he knew in his heart that it would be just that, denial. He decides to let his subconscious drift to whatever level it might choose. Random thoughts soon began to fluctuate in an out of his conscious reality.

.....Death! Immortality! What are these mysteries that even scientists cannot explain, even as the 20th Century comes to a close? Immortality is what the greatest Kings of ancient Egypt sought in vain...

.....They had looked in the wrong places. With their pyramids they tried to bargain with God for eternal life. Their sarcophagus filled with awesome treasure and untold wealth came to no avail. Only grave robbers and archeologists reaped their heavenly rewards here on earth...

..... The ancient Kings had no way of knowing that centuries later, a man would walk the earth and offer eternal life to anyone who would believe in him-for Nothing!.....Earthly troubles and sufferings of course are, after all, quite small and won't last very long. Yet, this short time of woe will result in God's highest blessings upon us Forever and Ever! ..... And didn't this rare person say...But I am telling you this strange and wonderful secret..... We shall not all die, but when we do, we shall all be given new bodies! It will all happen in a moment, in the twinkling of an eye, when the last trumpet sis blown. For there will be a trumpet blast from the sky and all Christians who have died will suddenly become alive, with new bodies that will never, die..... For our earthly bodies, the ones we have now that can die..... must be transformed into heavenly bodies that cannot perish, but will live forever...

Richard could see these words in bold red letters and he knew them to be from 1 Corinthians' 15:1-55. And there was more!

.....This is what God has prepared for us and, as a guarantee, he has given us his Holy Spirit. Faith maintains this principle, and we must believe it. Neither the soul nor the human body suffers complete annihilation..... At the resurrection, the substance of our bodies, however disintegrated, will be reunited....

Richard saw more words in red letters.

..... St. Augustine Doctriana Christiana "21'19." ..... Everything we are and everything we have touched, sands on the beaches, grapes on the vine, chairs, or beds, is made of atoms that once were adrift among the stars.....
Richard now knew that his father was adrift among the stars.

Richard felt a slight jolt. Perfumes, colors and sounds brought him back to awareness. He now felt a sudden peace within himself and he could now face the reality of his father's death.

He became aware of the fact that tears had been streaming down his cheeks, unwiped, while he had been in the trance. He wiped them away gingerly. He could now see pigeons flying randomly nearby, but eventually finding their way to a church steeple across the street from the funeral home parking lot. He also became aware of the fact that much time had passed while he sat on the park bench. Too much time; it was now late afternoon. "I must have fallen asleep", he thought.

A small cloud drifted across the afternoon sun, as Richard walked briskly toward the mortician's funeral parlor entrance.

Inside Thompson Mortuary

"I'm so sorry to meet you again under such tragic circumstances," said Mr. Leon Thompson, the owner of the mortuary. "Your father was a friend to a great many people in this city; I was privileged to call him a friend as well. We were even members of the VFW together. He was a good man."

"Thanks very much for your kind thoughts," Richard said, hating awkward moments like this.

" I've been keeping up with your career through your father. He was very proud of you and the work you're doing at Berkeley. Everyone around these parts is. We always knew you were a very bright young man. I know you are very tired from your long plane trip and you would like to get on with the arrangements."

Mr. Thompson led Richard into the back room where bodies were prepared for the viewing parlor. Mr. Thompson made a motion toward the far corner. Richards's knees began to buckle slightly and he sank down in front of the casket. Leon Thompson walked away, head bowed, leaving Richard alone with his father and his maker.

As he knelt next to the table where his father's body lay covered with a white canvas blanket his mind flashed back to the previous day when he had first spoken with Mr. Thompson who was the first to notify him that his father had passed away suddenly and unexpectedly. The part of the conversation that bothered him the most came to him again, in fragments... "It's difficult for me to ask Richard but the hospital wants to perform an autopsy to determine the exact cause of death. It's up to you of course, as the only surviving sibling, to make the decision."

"No! Mr. Thompson, there will be no autopsy. Some things are sacred and further violations of my father's body would be just that, a violation of something sacred . . . to me!" I want you to pick up my father's body from the hospital morgue and bring it to your funeral parlor. I want the funeral to be held in the early afternoon, two days after my arrival. He is to be buried next to my mother. I want the pastor of his church to officiate at the services, and they are to be brief . . . No longer than 30 minutes. I will talk to Pastor Donovan myself when I arrive. I want a closed casket, which you are authorized to select. I trust your judgment and spare no expense in your selection... "I want you to know that I made my peace with my father when he was alive and I am grateful for that. I'm satisfied to hold my memories of him as those I have held dear in the distant past for my mother."

Richard emerged from the back area-viewing parlor after some thirty minutes time. He appeared to be much more calm and relaxed. He asked Mr. Thompson if there was anything else he needed. "No, Dr. Stedman, it seems you have covered everything. I'll be happy to take care of everything. Will you be spending the rest of your time at the family farm? I hear your father's best friend, Mr. Jeremy Jarvis, has been staying there for the past few months, trying to keep your father comfortable during his illness. Do you need transportation while you are here? I'll be happy to lend you one of our company cars."

"No thanks Mr. Thompson, I have leased a car for the next thirty days. It's very kind of you however. You might do me one last favor. I don't have time to see lawyer Ernest Flounery right now, but can you give me directions to his office? It will save me some time tomorrow.

"Oh sure, it's not far from here. Nothing is far from here, as small as this town is." Mr. Thompson was sorry he said that. It was certainly no time to be making jokes. Richard did not smile. "His office is just off the east side of the downtown courthouse square. It's in the Heflin Building, second floor."

"Thank you very much Mr. Thompson. You have been more that helpful. You came with very high recommendations and you certainly have not disappointed me. I'll call you again some time tomorrow. I hope you can release someone to come by the farm to pick up Dad's burial clothes."

"Sure Dr. Stedman, just call me whenever things are ready."

Outside the mortuary once again, Richard noticed the sun was in its final downward spiral to meet the horizon, as Richard walked out into the fresh air. He hated the smell and atmosphere of the mortuary. But, the thought that the same beautiful sunsets that can be seen hanging precariously over the Pacific Ocean, from his home atop the Berkeley Hills, are the same ones he could now see hanging in the late afternoon skies over Indiana - that thought was good for his soul.

Richard felt relieved and pleased as he drove out of the mortuary parking lot. He had been able to handle the difficult decision making process and had chosen options of dignity and brevity, because he knew that would be what his father would have wanted. He had also spent much longer than he had anticipated, chatting with Mr. Thompson about the people in the city he and his Dad had known through the years. Richard glanced at his watch. It was exactly six o'clock Indiana time. Darkness would not settle in completely until about 8:45 p.m. this time of year. He had plenty of time to get something to eat and make the 25 minutes drive to the farm. To some degree he regretted the fact that he had slept through the meal on the airplane. The thought soon passed. The tasteless, complementary meal on the plane was not what he had in mind. He wanted a real steak dinner with all of the trimmings, and a glass of Cabernet Sauvignon wine to wash down the meal.

He also knew from the past that his options were limited for a decent steak in the small town of Greencastle. Certainly there would be nothing available like the haute cuisine in California. Suddenly, he remembered the Old Hickory Golf Club, located 2 miles North of Greencastle on highway 231. Old Hickory, an 18-hole golf course was also famous for the Link's Bar & Grill where charcoal grilled steaks were one of its specialties. The Link's Bar & Grill was opened to the public and not just for members of the club. With any luck he would be able to miss any long lines that might occur nearer to dinner hours. In the conservative Midwest, old habits, like maintaining the dinner hour between five and six p.m. had not disappeared from the routine. Whether his final choice was right or wrong, it would be the best choice for a hearty meal, and he would have to risk it.

Fortune smiled upon Richard as he entered the restaurant. A friendly, young head waitress indicated the waiting period would be a short one, perhaps only three minutes. In less than that time frame, Richard was being escorted to a small table for two that gave him a clear window view of the comings and goings of both vehicular and pedestrian traffic. Perfect abstractions for a tired, hungry, disconsolate traveler. Although he brought with him the briefcase carrying the secrets of the unfolding universe, he did not plan to open it, or to do any work. The abstract mathematical figures, symbols, formulas, might attract uninvited attention to him.

A very pretty, cordial, middle-aged waitresses approached him in short order. He selected a cup of black bean soup, Caesar's salad, baked potato, and a New York strip steak, prepared medium rare. He was pleased to know that he could have a glass of Cabernet Sauvignon wine as well.

The wine came first and two quick sips were just what he needed to prepare his pallet for the greatly anticipated first course of his meal. He continued to gaze out the window, noticing a young couple holding hands, laughing and frolicking as they crossed the parking lot. He smiled, perhaps thinking of his own longings to be in the company of a female. He watched a formation of three geese, making slow, elegant circles, as they headed toward the central part of the city. Richard realized they must have been making for the large pond near the park. The black bean soup and then the Caesar's salad soon arrived and he devoured both in short order. Then it happened!

" Hi, Dr. Stedman! Remember me?" Richard's head swung nearly ninety degrees both left and right attempting to determine whom and where the vaguely familiar voice was coming from. "It's me, Stanley Davis. It's been a long time and I know you probably don't remember me. I hope I'm not interrupting. I just wanted you to know, I would remember you any place or time."

Richard instantly rose to face the voice coming from directly behind him. He did not immediately recognize his old friend Stanley. "Too many sunrises have taken place." He thought. After all they had not seen each other in several decades. Mercifully, recognition finally came to Richard.

"Stanley! Stanley Davis! You ole dog you. I haven't seen you in years," Richard said, jumping to his feet and giving him a huge, sincere hug. Their raucous greeting was such that other patrons in the dinning room turned as one to determine who this odd couple might be.

61

"Please sit down Stanley, and tell me what you've been doing. I lost track of you after you went off to college. I'm genuinely glad to see you."

Sliding into the booth opposite Richard, Stanley hurried through his greeting, "Richard, I don't have much time, they should be calling my name for seating shortly. I'm having dinner with several of my associates at the University. I want you to know that I, along with many other townspeople, are all deeply saddened by the passing of your father. I hope you know how I respected him immensely. In those days, it was not easy to welcome a poor, young black waif into ones house and treat him as one of his own, but he did. And I have never forgotten that. Do you plan to remain long in the city?"

"I hope not," Richard said. "I will be burying my father in two days. Then I plan to remain here for perhaps another three weeks at Stedman Woods. I want to sell the old farm. I intend to put everything in place for the sale while I'm here, then I must leave. I'm working on a very important project."

Stanley, recognizing the awkward and difficult moment chose to take a few more moments to engage Richard in polite conversation.

"I have been reading about you and your work in the new physics. Not everyone gets their latest physics papers written-up in prestigious magazines, and journals, like Scientific American and Time Magazine, you know!" Stanley put his hand on Richard's shoulder and gave him several pats of affection.

"Well, I have been working very hard lately. Perhaps too hard. I'm very close to something very, very important, Stan. But, enough about me, what are you doing now?"

Richard did not want to go any further with his project and wanted to change the subject. Looking closely at Stan, all the time with a quizzical expression on his face. It was an attempt at sudden recall.

"Let me take you back a few years and quickly bring you up to date on what is going on today in my life. My lousy golf game not withstanding." They both chuckled. "You remember, following high school, I had a scholarship to Morehouse College in Atlanta. When I finished my under graduate work, I went to Harvard, where I received my Masters degree in Philosophy. I guess I didn't want to work and make an honest living yet, so I attended Indiana University, Bloomington, where I received a Doctoral Degree in sociology. I wanted to live in the Midwest and was fortunate enough to land a job at DePauw where I became a full professor. I'm now Associate Dean in the Liberal Art's College. I guess I have been quite lucky, because I arrived on the scene at the perfect time. It just so happened the University was looking to bring some diversity to their teaching staff. Admittedly, it would take a person years to attain tenure and become a full professor at most colleges and universities. But being in the right place at the right time never hurt, you know. Now I teach sociology, religion, and philosophy classes. I've also done a great deal of writing, including three major books. I'm in the process of writing another, which I believe will be my best work. I think! You wouldn't like it much because part of my thesis, is that our science and technical achievements are out stripping our social development. It is my firm belief that science becoming a real danger to our future. Scientists know how to invent things, even explain how most of the universe works. But seldom do those scientists offer any social or spiritual answers; any direction or conclusions that make us change for the better. It is like trying to assemble a highly technical piece of equipment with no directions. But that is another story and too detailed to go into here. I know such things pale in the wake of your achievements. It appears it will be a few more minutes before they call my name. What about you, Richard?"

Richard seemed quite perplexed by his statements about current science and the work of scientists but he thought better of pursuing it any further. It was neither the time nor the place for such mental hand wrestling. Instead he thought he would placate his old friend by giving him an abbreviated version of his recent past.

"You might recall," he said. Our long chats about the direction we should take after high school. You know of my love for science and research. I always felt an adrenaline surge when an experiment went well, or if a new discovery was made, no matter how small. Well. I decided to make a career of science and research. I finished undergraduate work at DePauw in mathematics, and went on to MIT for a Masters in theoretical physics. I was lucky enough to work with Sheldon Glasgow, who later shared a Nobel Prize in physics. Then it was onto Berkeley where I received a Ph.D. in thermo dynamics in physics. All kinds of boring stuff to most people, really. But, I do enjoy my work."

Richard finished his steak dinner, wiped his mouth with great relish, and slowly sipped from his nearly empty wine glass.

"You know Stan, you might find it hard to believe, but I often think about our days spent together fishing, swimming and just talking by the pond on my dad's farm. Those were the good ole days. A lot of my friends in college found it incredulous when I told them my best friend from childhood was Black. After the riots in the late sixties, I often thought the world would be a better place by now. But sadly it isn't. Perhaps you are right about one thing, much of the science and scientists ignore their social responsibility."

It was nearly one half hour before the head waitress approached Stanley and told him his table was now ready. Both Stanley and Richard rose as one.

64

"Richard, I've got to go now. I'm glad I got to see you. I plan to attend your father's funeral. Say, by the way, a group of us get together over dinner once a month to solve the world's problems. We rotate the dinner meetings among our respective homes. Our next meeting is scheduled soon. Why don't I find out exactly when it is and give you a call at the farm? I'll have an answer for you tomorrow so you will be able to plan accordingly. I think the next meeting place is at the home of Dr. Jessica Harrington. Not only is she a great cook and a supreme intellect, but she is gorgeous and single as well. I tell you what! We've got a lot of catching up to do. You probably will need a break from intense involvement and this will be a great opportunity to meet a few of our professors and others from various backgrounds and perspectives." Richard shook his hand firmly. I will see what my schedule is and how I feel. I've suddenly developed some real zinger migraine headaches and I haven't been sleeping too well. I've still got a lot to do, and a great deal of the project depends on my work. But perhaps I will see you later."

When Richard looked out the window, he realized that he had to get a move on, if he was to reach the farm before darkness fell. The shadows were already beginning to lengthen. It was now seven eighteen. His driving time would be about twenty minutes elapsed time. It would definitely be dark in less than half an hour. Richard paid the check and gave the waitress a handsome tip. He felt a lot better, physically. But, was anxious to get to the farm and determine how he would muster the strength to endure the next several days.

CHAPTER 5

Evening
Return to
Stedman Woods

Outside the restaurant, dusk was coming on fast. Richard got into his car and began the final leg of his journey to his family farm, located southwest of Greencastle. He would be traveling on highway 231, past the county fairgrounds, Oakridge Estates, and big Walnut Creek, then on to his home, affectionately known to Richard and the surrounding community as Stedman Woods. He knew that the next few days would tax his mental and emotional fibers to the limit. He also knew he would be running a near dead heat with nightfall and he was not anxious for that to happen. He did not want to be driving the tiny country roads in the dark although he had some familiarity with them, of course. But wanted to get settled in at his home and relax. Richard felt somehow at ease as his eyes embraced the familiar landscape of rolling hills that harbored an abundance of cottonwood and oak trees, nestled in small pockets along the country road. The chalk-white farmhouses shuttered in greens and reds resembled the quaint cottages in travel brochures. They seemed to welcome him back to the land of his birth.

After some twenty minutes of travel, Richard noticed in the distance the familiar three-story farmhouse of Stedman Woods. It was built nearly fifty years ago. During his younger days, in the late 60's, he helped his parents plant summer flowers in the large flowerbeds surrounding the circular driveway. His mind conjured up the grapevines clinging to the twin arbors in the rear of the house. He had also helped his father construct two forty-room Martin birdhouse apartments, which he hoped, still stood majestically atop 15 foot poles, like twin sentinels guarding the house and the fields beyond. Although the sun had disappeared on the horizon there was still enough lingering light to see green fields with corn just sprouting through the surface of the field. They looked like a glorious green carpet. "Spring rains must have been good for the fields." He thought.

About a mile from Stedman Woods, Richard could barely make out the four acres of dense woods. He knew a half-acre pond lay nearby, which provided an excellent refuge for the varied species of wildlife. He recalled that he and Stanley Davis had caught many a large catfish from the pond on lazy summer afternoons. "Skinny dipping" and diving from a makeshift diving board was a great substitute for excitement when the fish were not biting.

As Richard tuned into the driveway, he noticed a gray Chevrolet van parked near the entrance to the front door. The lights inside the house were already turned on, although the faint light of dusk still hung low in the western sky. It would probably be another twenty minutes before total darkness would envelope the land. It wasn't really necessary, but Richard knocked on the front door with the bronze clapper anyway. It slowly opened revealing the dark silhouette of a tall, slightly gaunt figure. It was Jeremy Jarvis, his father's best friend.

Jeremy gave Richard a warm and hospitable greeting as he stretched out his arms to embrace him. He would be nearly 65 years old by now, but Richard could feel the strength, which still remained in the slim and slightly, bent body. Jeremy's face, once olive colored and smooth, now looked puffy like paraffin, but still had a hint of youth. His intelligent eyes peered out of the thick tufts of hairy eyebrows. His nose was slightly bulbous, and a full crop of graying hair sat majestically on his finely sculptured head. Jeremy was wearing a pair of brown corduroys and a red and black-checkered shirt, the kind backwoodsmen wear.

"Young Richard, my boy! It's so good to have you home again. I'm so sorry that it has to be under these circumstances. It's so sad that you had to get the message about your father the way you did. I could scarcely muster the courage to call you when it happened. I know it's been a really difficult time for you. You know, your dad was very proud of you and talked about your many achievements. Yes, you should know he followed your career from the day you left. He may not have acted as if he cared much about your leaving the farm life for an academic career, but he was happy for you. I want you to know that Mr. Stedman did not suffer in death. I was with him at the very end. Your dad was a very strong individual. I should know; we spent a great deal of time together over the past fifty years. We were like those two men in the movie, Grumpy old men. Richard knew that Mr. Jarvis was genuine in his expressions of sorrow. It was obviously painful for him to express himself adequately in the presence of his friend's son.

"You've been more than a friend to my family, especially to my father and me. I suppose one of the greatest scourges of mankind is suffering. To suffer alone is possibly the greatest indignity of all. I want to thank you for being there for Dad through the years and in his final moments, I will be eternally grateful.

"When I heard that you have been staying at the farm for the past several months, I wanted you to know that you are welcome to stay on as long as you like, eat least for the next several months, or so. It may come as a surprise to you, but I've given myself a few weeks here at Stedman Woods to get all of the paperwork completed to sell the estate and then return to Berkeley on a permanent basis."

Jeremy was visibly shaken at this unexpected prospect and staggered slightly, as they both walked to the large sitting room area. As Richard looked around the room, he was pleased with how comfortable the old homestead really was. "You must be tired, starving and emotionally drained from your long trip from the coast. I've prepared fried chicken, macaroni and cheese, and green beans for supper. All of your Dad's favorites. It will take me only a few minutes to heat the dinner for serving. I'm still a very fair cook, you know." Jeremy was beaming with pride.

"No! No! I can't eat another thing. I stopped by the Outback restaurant in town. I had a huge steak dinner and a couple of glasses of wine. I couldn't eat another thing. Obviously it didn't compare to your wonderful meal. However, I'd be happy to take a rain check for tomorrow. I have several things to do and will probably be eating on the run during the day."

Richard could tell by the blanched look on Jeremy's' face that he was greatly disappointed in his answer. He had probably spent several hours preparing a typical Hoosier meal. He was doubtless lonesome and wanted to talk. Richard decided the next best thing to eating would be to chat for a little while over another glass of wine.

"I'll tell you what Jeremy, will you join me in a glass of wine from Dad's old wine stock? As I recall, he had a fairly decent selection of dinner wines at one time. I particularly like the Merlots'. Do you? All of the good wines are not grown in the famous wine country in Napa Valley. Indiana does pretty well in the wine making department too." Jeremy's' face and eyes brightened. "Yes! I will be happy to join you. I'll go fetch us a bottle of one of his finest Merlots', and a couple glasses from the kitchen. I'll be back in a minute." Richard smiled as he asked to himself in thought, "Don't all Californians drink red wine?"

"Sure, Merlot is fine. I know where everything is. You to relax in your Dad's recliner.

Richard's eyes slowly took in all facets of the room. He saw so many memories. There were the pictures, and portraits lining the wall. On his father's work desk, Richard noticed his picture taken in his high school graduation cap and gown. He eased out of the easy chair to get a closer look at several pictures above the fireplace of faces long forgotten. On the far wall were two treasured portraits of his father and grandfather. His instant thought was, "Why such portraits make the individual they are portraying look so stem and void of any particular human values, such as happiness or surprise. Men always look as if they know everything; and nothing in the world is left to doubt. Only scientists felt that way."

He laughed at the thought. He had such fond memories of his grandfather. He remembered him as a happy-go-lucky, hard working, family oriented man. "Work in the hill and farm make men," was a familiar quote of his grandfather. These were the only thoughts that held any permanence about his grandfather.

The photos of his mother, Elizabeth, stood in stark relief to those of the menfolk. She was dressed in a flowery, red skirt, with a navy blue halter-type blouse that was more than revealing of her tawny physic. Her long, curly brunette hair framed her full red lips that showed only a hint of the difficulties life presented those who survived the rigors of life at the turn of the 20th century. A temporary lump of sadness caught in his throat, as he stared long and hard at her picture.

Richard's eyes now caught row upon row of books on all manners of subjects. Some read, others ready to be read. He had read or reread most of them at one time or the other. As he turned to walk back toward the easy chair, his mind played a cruel hoax on him. He thought he saw his father sitting there, crossed legged, reading the evening newspaper. A blue gray stream of smoke trailed upward toward the ceiling from the large pipe, he held tight in his teeth. Richard blinked once. His father was still sitting there. Only the entrance of Jeremy, with -the tray and its contents caused the apparition to disappear.

"Ah! There you are" said Jeremy. Getting reacquainted with your home, eh?"

71

Richard blinked one last time at the empty, easy chair.

"Now, I know I need to relax. Hallucinating is getting a little too close to the edge for my well being," he breathed to himself. He continued in a philosophical vein."Yes, memories, if they are good ones, provide one with a safe harbor against life's tumultuous storms."

" Another anchor against storms is a smooth glass of wine, Jeremy cackled. I found an aging bottle of Merlot, Jeremy said."

They both settled into their chairs, and Jeremy began the evening's conversation.

"You mentioned you wanted to sell the farm. Have you thought about its potential for large financial gains in just a few short years? I've heard talk recently about new commercial and residential developments coming this way. If you analyze what is happening in Indianapolis, you will see outlying cities like Danville and Plainfield becoming bedroom communities of Indianapolis. Their growth is creeping toward our area. People are not opposed to commuting some distances from their jobs in Indianapolis. They say there will be no more large cities in the next century. They cause too much negative environmental impact and offer a poor quality of life for their inhabitants, and certainly they are not good places to raise and stimulate family values- too much crime, poor schools, drugs and rudderless youth. The youngsters know that. But to build homes you need land that is less expensive than land near large cities. Yes! You've got to have land and lots of it." "You could sell, lets say 200 acres and keep the rest for yourself, including the homestead."

. "I like the direction this conversation is taking." Richard thought to himself; "nothing too heavy." He took two long drafts from his wine glass and made himself more comfortable in his chair and looked directly at Jeremy.

"No! There is no question about it Jeremy. You've got a good point. But, to be honest with you, few people who have an alternative chooses to return to their hometown do so. Especially, once they have had the opportunity to see the world, as I have. The whole world, and perhaps beyond is now the stage in which one must do collaborative science, religion, and commerce. Once you have cast your lot - tossed your hat into the arena- it's virtually impossible to retrieve it and run for the cover of a quaint life. You become trapped in the high stake velocity world of a global player."

Richard felt pleased with his nimble ability to play a major card in the conversation, without really trying. He had no intentions of bruising Jeremy's ego. He again sipped slowly from his glass.

"Another point, my good friend, is to realize that Berkeley, has more Nobel Laureates from all over the world on its staff either as full professors or visiting professors than any other major university in the world. It is important to my career that I remain in that kind of environment. You probably have a microcosm of that right here at DePauw University."

Both Richard and Jeremy were nearly finished with their first glass of wine. They simultaneously reached for the bottle to enjoy the warmth of another drink.

"That's just my point, Richard. With the powerful, multifaceted capabilities of desk top computers, Internet, satellite hookups, and the advancing communication highway in place, there appears little one cannot do to manage ones entire affairs right here at Stedman Woods." He flicked a finger in the direction of the computer sitting on the mahogany desk, just to the right of them.

"As a matter of fact," Richard said, "it would have been impossible to manage or make any money from the farm without this technology and Mr. Jarvis, his farm manager. Mr. Jarvis had gone to many seminars at Purdue University to learn about how to run a successful farm. It is my understanding that without this new knowledge we would have long since courted bankruptcy. Dad told me that they were using satellite images to learn when to plant, water, and harvest their crops. Computer information data advised them when and where to sell their cattle, to maximize profits. Other computer programs told them how to manage live stock feeding consumption and other variables to establish a controlled environment for bringing them to market at the most opportune time. Technology has certainly revolutionized the farm as it has almost all other aspects of our lives and with little labor output.

"Another example of the kind of professor taking advantage of less work is young Jessica Harrington. She and her talented research group in Atlanta's Center for Disease Control are reported to becoming close to finding a cure for AIDS. She is a professor, right here in this little town of Greencastle.

"Whoa!" thought Richard, "That's the second time in less than three hours he had heard that name." He decided to let it pass without further comment. Jeremy dashed ahead with his conversion attempt to keep Richard at home.

" Dr. Harrington is not the only famous professor to walk the hallowed campus of DePauw. Dr. Percy Julian, a Black man, was another world famous scientist who came to DePauw. He was born in Montgomery, Alabama. He was a chemist, professor, and industrialist. His research was on the identification and synthesis of hormones and steroids, the chemical composition of soybean proteins and oil, and the chemical nature of adrenal cortex steroids. His contributions to science earned him the prestigious Spingarn Medal. He eventually formed his own company called Julian Laboratories, Inc. and became president of that company.

My point is that DePauw University has an impressive record of distinguished professors far beyond what one would normally believe. I think that is very interesting, don't you? By the way Richard, what is the nature of the work you are currently doing at Berkeley? Don't get too technical with me on this. You know, I taught science only at Greencastle High School."

Richard thought he detected a stealthy grin creep across Jeremy's face, accompanied by a glint in his eyes that showed he might know a great deal more about modern science than he would readily admit. This conversation was now heading down a road he was not anxious to travel. He laughed at himself when he guardedly glanced over his shoulder to his briefcase, brooding in dark silence on the end table next to the fireplace. He would have to answer guardedly. Richard reached for his glass of wine . . . It was empty . . . again! He clumsily reached for the bottle and filled it near the brim. He tried to curb any slurring of words as he attacked the subject of his current research.

"There is a great revolution in science, particularly cosmology and physics, to attempt to understand, how the universe is made and works. It's called, The Grand Unified Theories, or "GUTS." The aim of "GUTS' is to completely unlock the secrets of all matter. It will enable us to understand the elementary particles within atoms on the micro scale, to the largest astronomical structures. All will be incorporated into a single conceptual framework. The ability of physics to unify all these mind bending, strange forces about us can hardly be put into words. Man will become Godlike, with unfathomed energy potential lying before him, once these secrets have been uncovered. It will be like the creator handing mankind a mystical gift, as we enter the 21st Century."

Richard started unknowingly to speak louder and with a heightened edge of excitement in his voice. His face was contorted and appeared maniacal. He rambled on.

"But, pretty much alone among the sciences, physics claims to be an all encompassing discipline. That is why their formulas, brain busting mathematics, and hard to understand jargon make people stand in awe of their research findings. Take quantum physics for example. There exist a bewildering array of particles, already discovered, that has a tendency to make other people, not exposed to physics, believe we can do anything. The trouble is: Perhaps We can! Einstein's Unified Theory and its equations are already unlocking mysteries that will eventually lead man to a whole new branch of science for the next century. I can guarantee you more astonishing events are assuredly just around the corner for mankind, achievements that will make splitting the atom from E=MC2 looks like child's' play of primitives.

"Just think, as early as 1916, Einstein was busy exploring the possibility that gravity is not really a "force" at all, but rather one of the observable elements of "space-time" itself. The force that controls all the other forces in what we consider to be the Universe as we know it. He further discussed that what we know as matter is, in reality, only a phenomenon displayed as areas of high-energy concentration. Einstein's' Unified Field Theory was completed in 1927. During the next four decades, until he died in 1956, when he was seventy-six years old, he spent all of his energies refining the theory. Some observers believe he failed. Others believe he withdrew it because he became convinced by mankind's' use of power against each other we would destroy ourselves. So, he withdrew it, claiming mankind was not yet ready for it.

"One thing he never altered was his basic premise that gravity, could be proven mathematically to be directly related to other forms of energy, including electromagnetism. Einstein announced what he referred to as "highly convincing results of mathematical proof of electromagnetism and gravity. The strength of his theory was a string of very difficult mathematical equations, which few men had, even an inkling of what was required to have even a slight understanding of them.

"Despite his premature guilt of failure, virtually all major technological achievements of this century have proved to be extensions of his General Theory of Relativity. Things like microwave ovens, televisions, computers, involve interactions between electricity and magnetism and they work for us with awesome power. But, to answer your question. I've been working on "GUTS" at the University, and I think I have . . . Good God." Richard said to himself in total amazement. "I can't believe I have gone this far in this discussion. It must be the headiness of the wine." He took another sip anyway, grateful that Jeremy had cut him off at mid sentience. He assured himself that he would absolutely sidestep any further inquiry about his work. He was thankful Jeremy continued his own meandering.

"Richard, I'm sorry to cut you off, but all the time you were talking about Einstein, and his theory of General Relativity, I was reminded of a bizarre incident reported to have taken place in the Philadelphia Naval Yards in 1945. It also involved one of your father's friends at the time. His name was Dr. Morris Jessup. I'll begin by telling you what I know of this fellow as a result of conversations I have had with your father.

"Dr. Jessup, among other things, was a very strange man. Don't get me wrong, he was by no means a "crack pot," but many of the people surrounding him would make him out to be one. He just happened to be one of the central figures involved in one of the most amazing tales of this century, or any other. It has been called, "The Philadelphia Experiment." A dozen books and articles have been written about the affair. Morris Jessup, supposedly did a great deal of research on the subject. Have you heard about it, Richard?"

"No! But, I do remember Dr. Jessup coming to our home. He and Dad would spend many hours, in this very living room, having long and muted conversations over wine. Not unlike what we are doing now. I would pass by the sitting room door on occasion and could hear them talking, but I had no idea nor could not understand much of their conversations. Once, when I brought them some cookies mother had freshly baked, I overheard your name associated with the words "Alien Abduction." I felt it strange, but a deathly silence pervaded the room when I entered. They both were looking very curiously at me. Richard felt greatly relieved that the conversation had now shifted from him. He had already talked too much about the nature of his project. He welcomed the relief. But he was not sure where Jeremy was going with the conversation. "What was his purpose in telling me this tale? I must remain vigilant." He thought to himself and he decided to do so by having another long sip of wine. Jeremy did likewise, as he hastened to continue his story.

"The incredible story begins by conceding that very little is known about Dr. Morris Ketchum Jessup, other than those rare moments he would see him at the Stedman house. I do know he was an astrophysicist. But he also was a researcher, astronomer, mathematician, lecturer and author. He was a quiet and reserved man. His uncle, a railroad executive in the late nineteenth century, gave him his name Morris. Dr. Jessup was born March 1910. He grew up in the quaint city of Rockville, Indiana. Rockville, as you know, is world famous for its natural beauty. The city is nestled among gently rolling hills. Many of the streams are forded by ancient-covered Bridges, now restored to their bright red colors of yesteryear. They could easily accommodate horse and wagon in the last century, but no vehicular traffic is allowed on them today. Some twenty are now restored and remain in the area. They provide great settings for artist- looking to capture the nostalgia and beauty of rural America."

Richard did remember Rockville from his youth. He knew that each year when nature shows off her dazzling colors of reds, purples, orange, greens and browns, thousands upon thousands of nature lovers flock to the city for a two week period of celebrating the arrival of the fall season. The gathering is called the "Rockville Festival." The town square looks like a Persian marketplace during the festival. Farmers and their wives sell country clothing, food, and memorabilia of another time and place."

Jeremys' voice seemed to trail off and his eyes began to glaze over. He was definitely reliving moments at the town square. A crooked smile played across his lips. Another sip of wine seemed to settle him, as he continued his reverie.

"Most of the food is prepared on the spot for the tasting and purchase. Huge, black caldrons, filled with piping hot navy beans await devouring by eager patrons. They are sold by the bowl along with chopped Bermuda onions and golden cornbread with homemade apple butter. In another spot in the town square, fresh sausage is made and cooked by proud farmers. Biscuits and fresh honey await others standing in long lines. Still others stand in line to savor morsels of a huge pig roasting on a giant spit. All this is accompanied by squeals from the young children as their parents await the signal that it is fully cooked. After gorging, families jump in their cars, with maps of the "Covered Bridge" locations, and take to the back, dusty roads that wind throughout the countryside. Once they arrive at a bridge, they all hop out of their cars for picture taking. This, then was the city that spawned the likes of Morris Jessup.

Jeremy now began to choose his words more slowly, and very carefully, as if taking great delight in the rapturous attention Richard had given him to this point.

" Now permit me to retell the saga of "The Philadelphia Experiment." In a nutshell, it was a project of the United States Navy. It was reported that Einstein was present when the Navy performed trials of making US Navy ships "Invisible" to enemy ships. It would be a perfect camouflage if it worked . . . And it did! "Reports say it happened one day in October, 1943. It was also rumored that they were using pulsating energy fields. A ship was made to disappear from the Philadelphia Navel Yard and reappear hundreds of miles away at the Norfolk Navel yard. Then it reappeared at the Philadelphia Navy Yard within a few minutes of elapsed time. As I mentioned the experiment worked. But, for the men on board . . . It didn't! It was a horrifying nightmare for the sailors and military brass.

" The effects of the pulsating energy field used in the experiment, were of various descriptions and were temporary, others were not. Some men saw double. Some began to hallucinate. Some became disoriented. Some claimed they had passed into another dimension, and had seen frighteningly strange alien creatures. Some died. Many survivors were summarily discharged from the military, under unspecified disability causes.

"Then enters an assortment of weird and charismatic characters, such as Jessup. He tries to uncover the truth behind the alleged Experiment. Following the publication of his findings in a book, Jessup received a letter offering more details and first hand accounts with further potential leads, guaranteeing that if he should follow the leads he would get to the bottom of the incident. Then came a mysterious Dr. Carlos Miguel Allende. He reportedly lived in Kensington, Pennsylvania. Jessup had long since left Rockville, Indiana and was living in Coral Gables, Florida. Jessup and Allende began corresponding with each other and to paraphrase Alice, In Wonderland, " when she explored the other world and its people, "This story became curiouser and curiouser. After years of detective work and coming close to solving the mystery, Jessup became more and more depressed at the startling implications of his research findings. Having been led down blind alleys, through the maze of government, and most troubling of all, the dark and murky world of government secrecy and cover-up, Jessup was a desperate and lonely crusader. He was at the end of his rope.

"In the end, Morris committed suicide by carbon monoxide poisoning, April 20,1959. This death to was fogged in mystery.

Taking his own life, I mean. Some say he was murdered by secret government operatives, because he knew too much. National security was at stake. The "Cold War" with the Russians and the Chinese was raging, and it had to be won by the West at all costs. His life story and the Philadelphia account have been captured in book form under the title, The Philadelphia Story, by author Charles Berlitz."

Richard was more than happy to see that Jeremy was concluding his amazing tale of intrigue surrounding "The Philadelphia Experiment." He was tired and admittedly, slightly intoxicated.

"Well, Jeremy, that was quite an interesting story," said Richard. "I had vaguely heard about the experiment, but I never knew there was as much research and detailed information about the case. You are to be congratulated on your research. I think I would like to obtain a copy of the book and read more about it in detail."

What Richard was most concerned about was the dilemma Jeremy had earlier talked about that had consumed Einstein. The part that bothered him was his point that Einstein knew the secret of electromagnetism and it's relationship to gravity, but failed to give it to the world. He was bound and determined that it would not happen to him. After all hidden away, in his briefcase, was the nearly completed write-up of his discovery. However, he continued to wrestle with the ethics of the issue.

"Since when did scientists concern themselves with the outcome and practical applications of their discoveries. Mankind must make choices of what to make out of his discoveries. It certainly won't happen to me. After all, just ten feet away from me lies the greatest discovery in human history." Just the thought of it made him exhausted. He was ready for bed.

"Jeremy, I promise that over the next few days, I will think more about the ramifications of selling the farm, as outlined by you. As a matter of fact, I'm meeting with lawyer Ernest Flownery in the morning. Which reminds me I had better move along now to bed. Hand wrestling with lawyers is something one wants to do when one has a good night's sleep."

Richard glanced at his watch. It read 12: 25 p.m. Considering the time differential, it was very, very late. He needed sleep badly, and he rose awkwardly from his chair. He had not given sleeping arrangements any thought. He assumed Jeremy was sleeping in one of the two spare bedrooms, upstairs.

"By the way Jeremy, which bedroom have you been using? I assume my old bedroom will be ok with you?" Jeremy nodded in the affirmative. "Yes," Your bedroom is all prepared. As I discussed with you over the phone in California, your father's instructions through the years were always the same. No one was to sleep in your room. It was to remain as it was when you left for the final time years ago."

Jeremy moved closer to Richard, lowering his voice to a barely distinguishable whisper.

"I forgot to tell you that I was able to locate the keys to your father's safety deposit box and the passbook for his savings and checking accounts. They are on the night table next to your bed. I have also made arrangements to store enough staple food items and frozen food dishes to supplement your meals when you chose not to eat out. I have laid out your father's burial suit on the bed in his room. We should get it to the mortuary as soon as we can. Do you need any help with your luggage, or can I get you anything else before calling it an evening'?" "Yes," said Richard with a grin much too wide. He thought his lower lip had split in two places, adding a third one. It was just the sudden flexing of facial muscles he hadn't used for a while. "It's the wine he thought," as he wiped his mouth with his sleeve. He was pleased there was no visible, crimson residue for Jeremy to see. "I'll put the glasses away, and then if you can carry one of the two pieces of luggage upstairs, I'll get the other one."

He rose on stiff knees, steadying his body for the launch toward the kitchen. Somehow he was able to carry off the feat without falling. When he returned from the kitchen, Jeremy had already gone upstairs with both pieces of luggage.

Frantically, Richard's eyes darted around the living room like a snake. "Where did I leave my briefcase? The briefcase containing the blue print for a new future of mankind far into the next Millennium." He was glad he only mumbled the words out of the earshot of Jeremy.

He laughed a maniacal laugh, as he realized he had brought it with him. It was right where he had left it, on the stand, next to the reading lamp. His mind was now shrouded and heavy as if a synaptic overbalance had short-circuited his brain, making his thinking muddled.

Picking up the briefcase, he dragged himself up the fourteen steps to the bedroom. He opened the door and immediately noticed there were no changes to the room at all. Everything remained the same as he day he finally left home for good. His heart quickened. He knew if he permitted it to happen he would sink into the throes of powerful fears and phobias. He would not let that happen. He freshened up for the night, and sank into bed. He pulled the covers up tight around his shoulders, childlike, turning out the lights all in one movement. He knew sleep would come quickly. But that may not be a blessing, for creeping up, not far behind, would be the . . . Dreams! The beckoning lights! The half-shaped human forms. Or worse!

Earlier that evening, after showering, Jessica had gone to the Marsh grocery to replenish her dwindling food supplies. She prepared a dinner of creamed chipped beef over biscuits, a small garden salad, and a scoop of vanilla ice cream for desert. Later, Jessica unpacked her luggage, tossed her undergarments in the washer, and watered her indoor plants that were beginning to look dehydrated. She was determined to retire early but stayed awake long enough to watch the late television news as she prepared for bed. As she half listened to the usual reports of fires, carnage and mayhem committed across the country and around the world, she listened intently to a reporter giving the local news that reported a story of "Strange Lights" seen in the skies over the western quadrant of the city for the past several nights. She found it curious that monitoring radar at Indianapolis International Airport verified the sightings but could offer no explanation for the dancing UFO lights. Jessica could only shiver at the words, Unidentified Flying Objects.

Jessica felt absolutely exhausted and collapsed into be, not giving the UFO story another thought. But she knew they would probably return in her dreams, sometime before the night would end.

The next morning, Richard did not gently emerge from his slumber. He was awakened only by a loud rapping on his door. It took several seconds to figure out what it was and where the noise was coming from. His mind whirled as it did a data search of its information banks and quickly identified the source. It was Jeremy Jarvis making another of several attempts to awaken Richard.

"It's nearly seven-forty five, Dr. Stedman. Time to get up! Remember you have several very important things to do today. And it looks like it's going to be a nice day to do them too! By the time you shower and shave, breakfast should be ready."

Richard could only mumble a greeting and acknowledgment of his wake-up call. He was too busy gathering strength to shove aside the last wisps of shadowy creatures, eerie lights, indecipherable formulas and symbols, all emanating from unknown sources, save his hellish dreams. It was moments like these when he feared he was losing his wits. "What could be their meaning" was all he was ever left to ponder?

Later that night, after showering, and eating a creamed chipped beef over biscuits, a small garden salad, and a scoop of vanilla ice cream for dessert, Jessica watched the television news and prepared for bed. It was a curious thing but as she was in the kitchen washing dishes, she thought she heard a reporter on the news, presenting a story of "strange lights" seen in the skies over the western quadrant of the city, for the past several nights. Monitoring radar at Indianapolis International Airport could not verify or offer any explanations for the dancing lights.

Jessica felt absolutely exhausted and collapsed into bed, not giving the "dancing lights" story another thought. They would be waiting for her in her dreams, sometime before the night was done.

CHAPTER 6

Day Two
Office of Ernest Flownery
Attorney at Law

To the local citizenry, attorney Ernest Flownery was known as just plain "Ernie." Although he tried not to show it, he liked the sound of that name. He even insisted that strangers he met for the first time call him "Ernie." In many ways he looked like an "Ernie," if such a stereotype exists. The name conjures up the image of the youthful "Ernies" we all knew in grade school. They were talkative, playful, mischievous, bright, and "on stage" at all times.

Ernie was 56 years old with a slight but athletic build. He made a concerted effort to stretch his five-foot seven-inch frame by standing very erect. Ernie's' close-cropped, reddish brown hair covered his large, round head like a doormat. Because of his constant, rapid fire speech and overall hypertonic state, his face was tinted with a shadow of red patches. His eyes darted quickly in all directions at once. But one was drawn like a magnet to his perpetual smile. His large, full lips hid large even, white teeth. He had a penchant for over dressing in expensive suits, ties, and shoes. Ernie looked out of place for a small, country town like Greencastle. He would have blended in perfectly with the "Mad Hatters" of Wall Street.

This was the man Richard would meet in just a few minutes. He locked the car door and strode briskly toward the red brick building that housed the law office of Ernest Flownery.

Ernie greeted Richard warmly, offering sincere expressions of condolences at the passing of his father. He quickly got down to the business at hand, mostly out of respect for Richard and his no nonsense approaches to the scientific doctrine. "Richard, I don't see any major problems in finalizing your father's estate. It is simplified by the fact that you are the sole heir. As I see it, we have just a few matters to accomplish and they are mostly routine."

"I'm glad you see it that way." Said Richard. He leaned forward in his chair, invading, on purpose, Ernie's territorial space.

"As my Dad's personal lawyer for many years, I assume his last Will and Testament, which he discussed with me nearly a year ago, has not changed? As I recall, he told me about his intent to leave a sizable amount of money to the local Community Hospital. My best recollection is that it was to be $75,000 dollars. A like amount was to be bequeathed to DePauw University. And, $100,000 dollars to Reverend Donovan's church. He and my mother were life long members there.

"Yes, that's a fair assessment and pretty much what I recall him telling me, as he drew up the will, said Richard.

"Nevertheless, Richard, I suggest we go to the bank and review the contents of his safety deposit box. I suggest we do that right away. I will first have to file some paper work at the courthouse that establishes me as the attorney of record and you as the Executor for the Estate. Personally, you stand to inherit a sizable amount of money and property." Ernie paused and took a deep breath. His face became a death mask. Then he spontaneously began to laugh, as he slapped Richard on the shoulder. "Of course, there will be sizable estate and inheritance taxes to pay. You also told me over the phone that it is your wish to put the farm up for sale, as soon as possible. If that is till your wish, I will begin such proceedings right away." "You know Richard, your friend and your Dad's life long confident, Jeremy Davis, told me, not long ago that the farm, with its extensive acreage, may be a prime target for developers seeking residential and commercial sites. His thinking is that the International Airport, in Indianapolis may soon cause a population explosion of workers that will be moving this way. Many people like the quality of life in the small, outlying towns. Less crime, lower taxes, cheaper land costs for both residential and commercial. If all of this is true, Greencastle could become a "bedroom community of Indianapolis. It appears many people don't mind the thought of commuting to work for a distance of thirty or forty miles.

"You many want to give it some thought over the next few weeks, while you are home. Unless you need the money right away, it would do no harm to wait a period of time before making a decision. Holding on to it for a while might also serve as an additional hedge against inheritance and other federal, state, and local taxes."

"I don't know Ernie. I'm engaged in a scientific project of great significance to me, the scientific community, and to mankind. You can't possibly imagine what I have stumbled upon. I can only tell you this much. It's been there all this time, hidden in Einstein's General Relativity formula. The best physicists have been trying to find the key for six decades. The impossible. The unthinkable is now possible . . . boundless energy at our finger tips, time travel, going to other star systems instantly. All of this is now within our grasp. The answer came to me all of a sudden, in a dream. I don't mind telling you that I am in the middle of publishing my findings. It's going to cause quite a storm. I can envision a great deal of personal traveling to scientific communities all over the world, with immense media coverage. I just don't see myself having much time to be fully engaged in managing the estate or other affairs of my father's."

Richard could see a sudden brilliance surround Ernie. It appeared as a heat wave on a desert floor. Ernie made a game attempt to speak, but the only sound that emitted from his gaping mouth, was a croaking sound, like a dying wildebeest in the clutches of a mighty lion. Ernie quickly reached into the right-hand desk drawer, withdrew a silver whiskey flask, and gulped two mighty drafts from it. Red faced and smiling, with drivels of whisky at the corners of his mouth, he was finally able to mumble a weak, "That sounds . . . Fantastic!" Richard quickly changed the subject, knowing he now had the intellectual and physiological advantage over Ernie. "Dad's estate should provide me with enough money to ensure I can concentrate solely on what has to be done to further my work. My instant opinion is to delay the decision of selling the farm, at least for a few weeks. There is one more thing, Ernie. It's about my project. You are to tell no one about what I have just discussed with you. Even the little I have told you."

"You have my word." Ernie said. "As a long time friend of the family, and as a lawyer." "I'm not so sure about that last part, thought Richard. Nevertheless, he stood and graciously extended his hand to Ernie. He knew that Ernie was in a position to earn hefty fees for settling the estate. He is also positioned for extended opportunities to gain considerably more, if any protracted commitments are involved in selling multiple parcels of the farm acreage."

Richard knew he was right. He could see a certain amount of greed in Ernie's eyes as he rose from his chair to accept Richard's hand. Ernie's eyes looked beyond Richard's. One could tell his mind was moving a mile a minute. Opportunity was definitely knocking for him, and he could well afford to be gracious.

"Richard, I certainly understand your concerns. I don't grasp the full scope of your scientific project, and it is not necessary for me to know. But I hope you realize that I am here only to serve you and the best interest of your father's wishes. Now is probably not the proper time to finalize or to put into concrete any plans that may have long-term consequences for you. You will have plenty of opportunities between now and the time you leave for us to discuss such important details. It is my strong recommendation that you obtain the services of a good professional financial advisor. If you don't have one, I can give you the name of the one I use for my personal affairs. In the meantime we will dispatch the other issues involved in settling the estate.

"I know you have a myriad of other details to attend to of great immediacy. I will be in touch with you on a daily basis to advise you of how things are proceeding on my end. I'm sure I will have several important papers for you to sign within the next few days. Again, I want to tell you how sorry I am about your father's death. He will be greatly missed by everyone in the community."

"It is very gratifying to hear you say such pleasant things about Dad. I will miss him too. He was a great inspiration to me." Richard said as he moved quickly to the door and out into the parking lot. Although he had long held a certain disdain for lawyers, for some unexplained reason he felt he could dispel such feelings, and consider Ernie a friend. But only time would tell.

Day Two, Afternoon
The church office
of Rev. Donovan

Rev. Donovan succumbed to the peacefulness of his office. The church secretary was busy down the hall working on the church newsletter. There was enough distance between them for him to feel, essentially, alone. He had just returned to his study. He glanced nervously at his watch. It was only 2:15 p.m., yet he felt emotionally and physically drained. The day had begun early with his hospital rounds, visiting the sick. His final stop was the intensive care unit, where he spent a great deal of time talking with members of the Crabtree family. The two sons and daughters were understandably worried about their 79-year-old mother, Samantha. She had suffered a stroke two days earlier and was partially paralyzed on her left side, but was now able to speak and could recognize her children. Her doctors were guardedly optimistic for significant recovery.

Rev. Donovan had known Mrs. Crabtree for nearly forty years and he knew her to be a woman of strong faith, a devout believer in the power of divine prayer. She had demonstrated that power and strength of prayer when her husband of fifty years passed away years ago, leaving her to care for their three children. All three of their children were able to finish college. But the stress of working two jobs during that dark period had now taken its toll on her physical being.

Rev. Donovan next visited young Sarah Whittington, who planned to marry Jeff Davidson on the coming Saturday. He was very happy for the couple. Both were college graduates and strong, active members of his church. They worked tirelessly with the church youth mentoring programs. They appeared to be mature in many other ways that gave him great optimism for a long, loving, relationship in the future. He then met with two executives from the local bank to finalize a church loan agreement for $25,000. The money was to be used for expansion of the church day care center. It was vitally important to expand the nursery because that facet of the church's outreach program produced significant income for the total church operations. It also fulfilled his vision for keeping and attracting members to his church. He was pleased with the outcome of the agreement that he was able to negotiate an interest rate two percentage points above prime, the rate charged by the bank for their best commercial customers. Finally he had lunch with Frank Straight, a staunch member of his church, who also owned the local Ford Dealership. Frank wanted the Reverend. to accept, on behalf of the church, and for his own private use, a new 1999 Ford Taurus. It would replace his venerated 1985 Chevrolet that had threatened, on more than one occasion, to leave him stranded on the streets of Greencastle. Frank was a member of his church and Rev. Donovan quickly accepted the offer. But talking so much high finance and signing so much paperwork had given him a headache. As a matter of fact his old nervous habit of sucking his teeth was beginning to surface. He fought it as if fighting the devil himself . . . but he felt himself losing the good fight. He needed peace and quite for a few minutes.

Now, collapsed in his office easy chair, he decided to meditate for a few minutes before Dr. Richard Stedman would arrive for his appointment. He tried to make the office as dark as he could. He was a strong believer that when a person comes to the inner sanctuary of himself, he comes to the center of his own being, and encounters the spirit of God. He also believed that all of the answers we spend a lifetime seeking have been hiding just below the surface within us. He was totally convinced that truth lies within, and it can be discovered only by each individual person. No authority, or "quick fix" books on mental health will win the day. Except, of course, the Holy Bible.

Rev. Donovan continued in his reveries and meditative state, thinking anew with forgotten youthful eyes, his thought turned briefly toward the 21st Century that lay just ahead. What would it bring? His conscious stream of thoughts continued. "When we really examine Homo Sapiens from its elevated position in nature, he thought, what is currently observed is not very flattering. One sees pretty much what he has always seen, mans inhumanity to man, as evidenced by two world wars. A "police action" called Korea, Vietnam, Desert Storm, Bosnia and hundreds of small bloody wars in between have killed nearly one hundred million souls"

But there was another perplexing question or which he must briefly dwell, if he was to offer any solace to Richard Stedman in just a few minutes. And that question is the same one that has dogged mankind since he abandoned the caves and peered outside his campfires, gazing in wonder at the stars. Does life have any meaning in such a vast and infinite universe? It still surrounds and mystifies us to this day. Each one of us sometime in his life gives pause to reflect and ponder his existence. This is true more especially when death claims a loved one. It seems pointless to man to live and die if we have no purpose or if we are not connected in some spiritual way to a greater and lasting universal whole.

But what else could he say to Dr. Stedman about the passing of his father that Richard, the scientist, did not already know? After all, a renowned physicist, Dr. Stedman knew things about the physical world as only few other men could. He knew things on the micro level: the atoms, electrons, positrons, the electro weak forces, quarks leptons, hadrons, and much more. He knew things on the macro level: The solar system, the stars, galaxies, quasars, and black holes, and God only knows what else. But, the Reverend felt he knew a few things himself As a man of God, Rev. Donovan felt it his purpose and mission in this life to offer a belief system to his flock that would come close to answering some of these questions. He was brutally aware of the fact that one could canvas the world and find as many answers as there are countries for every religion, cultural system, as to why we live and why we die. Yet, even the lowest peasant can figure out for himself that they all cannot be correct. Inevitable clashes result and millions have died holding fast to their belief that their belief is the only true belief. He held fast to the proposition that as our technologies and communications systems and economic forces draw us closer to a global village. These forces make it exceedingly difficult to hold fast to traditional values and belief systems. He knew that more human lives have been sacrificed in the name of righteousness over the past two thousand years to the sword, the gun, and the bomb, than all earthly calamities combined. Many answers to the questions of life and death used by the clergy have been for fear and control. Modern day logic prevents acceptance of much dogma, particularly for a man of science like Richard Stedman.

"It may be some comfort to Richard if I simply tell him his father was a spiritual being, whose purpose on earth was to gather greater understanding of his own spiritual existence as it

94

relates to its development and eventually, through death, his spirit contributes to the whole of universal creation and its infinite of unfolding.

"Science has brought us to the understanding that all life forms are energy, electrons, protons, all the elements present at the creation. Therefore, the deeper one goes into the nature of things, including ones mind and body, either alive or dead, the more we converge into the original source or the One. We come forth from the One and we return to the One. The Source. The Creator. Beyond our body, beyond death, there is the convergence at that point in time and space, where time and space are transcended and the resurrection, time and space are taken up into the infinity, and each of us will be in total unity with God. So, suffering and death is only a one-way station to God. Each one of us will experience oneness with God."

The Reverend was pleased that these thoughts and concepts had emerged to his conscious mind during his meditative state. He was now prepared to minister to his next appointment of the day. Rev. Donovan slowly continued his awakening from his meditative state to what he finally realized was the rapping sound of someone at his office door. He thought to himself that the person must have been there for sometime, since there was a considerable urgency to the sound. Rev Donovan called out, in a barely audible voice, that he was coming to the door. Rising awkwardly and sluggishly from his easy chair, he stumbled to the door and opened it. Rubbing his eyes with both hands against the sudden, blinding light, he recognized at once the youthful figure of Dr. Richard Stedman.

Nearly an hour and twenty minutes elapsed before Richard emerged from his discussions with Rev. Donovan. He walked out into the bright sunlight of early afternoon. Richard was dumb founded that the anxiety he had anticipated with the meeting with Reverend Donovan never occurred, despite the fact that he had to address and finalize many fine points of the necessary physical arrangements. It was necessary to pick up his Dad's burial attire approve the order and timing of the funeral service as well as other matters related to interment. He did not find the whole affair morbid or taxing. Even more heart warming and comforting was the simplicity of Rev. Donovan's approach to bereavement and consolation to those suffering the loss of a loved one. The Reverend was able to empathize with Richard's needs and was concerned that he would trap himself into what most pastors would offer as standardized, and packaged spiel to the bereaved. He remembered from his youth the zealous religious fervor that had been deeply ingrained in Indiana lore. It reflected the Hoosier need for simplicity, Richard thought. Or was it.

On the other hand, Richard felt that could not be the case. Rev. Donovan's' approach was too philosophical, too academic for a small town pastor. "Perhaps, I've been in California too long." He dismissed the matter. However, he did make a mental note to schedule a vacation away from the maddening pressure of the university as soon as he completed the write-up of his "GUT' Theory. He would go to Kentucky Lake for a week or two and visit several of his old fishing buddies who spent their summers there. He needed to get back in touch with "the common man." He desperately needed to connect with their hopes, dreams, their fears. He needed a reality check.

"This will be doubly important once the bomb shell of my findings explode upon the scientific community."

These were the thoughts as he reached his car door and prepared to visit with his lawyer. He smiled to himself as once again a warm feeling passed through his continence. He instinctively reached over to the passenger seat, stroked gently his briefcase, which seemed to emit strength throughout his physical being. Then he started the car engine and made his way

96

confidently through the tiny, sun drenched streets, toward the legal offices of Ernest Flownery.

CHAPTER 7

Day Two
Morning
Jessica's Home

Jessica welcomed a night of restful sleep. She was pleasantly surprised that no dreams, or headaches, greeted her at first light. She was also grateful she had no appointments, lectures, or meetings for the day. After showering and eating a light breakfast of fresh, sweet, honey dew melon, a slice of toast, and a glass of low fat acidophilus cold milk, she felt amazingly alive. She leisurely read the morning paper, the Greencastle Herald. Jessica had the feeling of reversing times arrow, as she became aware of the fact that the paper carried no stories of the sordid affairs of mankind's journey into the abyss. There were no glaring headlines of murder, rape, scandal, or political struggle. She found that fact a refreshing respite from the tawdry ilk found in the California papers. The headlines in the Herald concerned the debate over how to fund a new gymnasium for the local high school. There was, however, a front-page story about "strange lights" seen in the western skies near the city limits. Several credible witnesses, including the county sheriff, swore the "lights were "UFO's" She smiled, acknowledging the fact that the long shadow of evil would not touch her life this day. Bond issues and UFO's, she could handle . . . or could she?

Jessica thought it was strange, but as her eyes glanced again at the word UFO a slight shudder rippled throughout her entire body. She quickly turned the page. It was definitely not a subject she wanted to think about. Not now!

After browsing through a week of accumulated correspondence, mostly junk mail, and bill statements for her many credit cards, Jessica accessed her telephone recorder to review her audio messages. She found nothing of major consequence there either. Only one message caught her attention, and it was from Dr. Stanley Davis. He acknowledged that he would be attending the next dialogue meeting at her home this coming Saturday. He stated he would bring as a guest "The famous, young handsome physicist, Dr. Richard Stedman." She felt herself blush. Stanley continued. "Since Dr. Stedman is so handsome and dashing, you should wear that slinky, body-clinging red dress I like so much. Of course it wouldn't hurt your chances for an extraordinary evening, if you go to extra lengths and prepare one of my favorite dishes, spaghetti and meat balls."

Jessica snapped off the power button to the recorder. She put her hand to her chin and began pacing the room. She fell into a deep reflective state. "I could use a little excitement for a change." She said aloud. "I've not had a date in months. I've been working too hard on that AIDS VIRUS vaccine project, but I'm too dammed close to slacken the pace now. What I really need is some vigorous exercise to relieve some of the tension I've experienced the past several weeks. I think I'll take an early afternoon jog through the campus grounds. I seem to get into the fountain of pure thought when I run. Inspiration comes without demand at such times. Answers gush forth, mostly by serendipity; requiring little effort. It's almost as if I'm being prompted, coached by an invisible person or mind. Experience has taught me that the best way to get great ideas is to succumb to the gift, accept some and throw away most of them; as someone once said, "If you throw a lot of mud on the wall, some of it is bound to stick after a while. I'll just store that thought in my memory bank along with a similar thought I had before leaving California."

She recalled at that time, a strange but elegant thought drifted into her conscious mind, an idea about making cells "stealthy" to the AIDS VIRUS, similar to the military B-2 bomber and the F-117 fighter planes. They are invisible, but deadly to any foe. Why isn't it possible to "Trick" the virus into the open and cannibalize it after the cell spews out false DNA signals that prevent its mutation capabilities?" She cloaked these thoughts into inactivity and turned her mind to making a list for the items needed for preparing a spaghetti and meatball dish. Later that after noon, dressed in gray sweat pants, black jersey, and red headband, Jessica jogged across the DePauw campus grounds. She was nearly half way through her two-mile jog set for the day. The weather was lovely, with the temperature near 80 degrees and a slight breeze that tugged at her hair. A few cumulus nimbus clouds moved lazily across the sky, occasionally hiding the sun. The campus seemed to be teeming with students coming and going in random directions. She let her mind do the same. It settled on nothing in particular for the moment. She began taking deep breaths as she slowed her run to a walk. She noticed the comfortable, waist- high retaining wall that framed a lovely, landscaped area, fronting the Percy L. Julian Science and Mathematics Center. She decided to make it her rest stop and observe the students as they scurried about. Jessica gulped in deep drafts of air. As she rested against the wall, she tried in vain to control the many thoughts welling up from her subconscious . .

"The air we breathe contains thousands upon thousands of bacteria, pollen grains, spores, viruses and germs of all descriptions. Even tuberculosis, the disease which science thought it had conquered, is once again pandemic. In 1995 and 1996 alone nearly six million lives were lost.

"....Most people would be totally shocked, dismayed, and disheartened to learn just how little we do know about what diseases viruses can cause. Researchers know even less about what other, more rare, more lethal plagues lie just around the corner. Unlike bacteria, many of which are harmful but most are beneficial to mankind, viruses must infect a cell before they can reproduce. Some of my colleagues believe we understand only a small percentage of the viruses lurking in the air, in trees, and in many lower animal forms. Unfortunately though, far too many seek us humans as a host. As a microbiologist, I'm afraid my colleagues maybe right. I sometimes wonder how the general public would react if people really knew more about other viruses besides the AIDS virus are already waiting in the wings, waiting to strut onto the stage as a pandemic world-wide outbreak. Oh, most know what terrible, ravaging effects the AIDS VIRUS is causing. But perhaps more frightening to many of my colleagues is the ascendancy of mounting proof that the one time little known, Ebola virus may be capable of airborne transmission. That would be a tragedy of the first magnitude." The avalanche of thoughts continued.

"....The Ebola virus is one of the deadliest pathogens on Earth. She knew the Ebola is transmitted mainly through body fluids and for the time being rages only through Africa. It is believed that in 1989 or 1990, an outbreak transmitted by monkeys, may have become airborne and spread in Reston, Virginia. Some evidence shows that it is possible that there may be a separate strain of the virus that uses airborne transmission as the desired means of seeking its hosts. Like the AIDS Virus, Ebola, does not bode well for mankind as we entry the 21st century."

Jessica knew only too well the 1999 figures released by the World Health Organization on the infectious disease that reflect a simple fact. Mankind has dangerously miscalculated the threat posed by bacteria and viruses to millions of lives. The prospect of containing future outbreaks is decreasing. Just six ailments, the report said, Aids, Tuberculosis, malaria, measles, diarrhea, and pneumonia, killed 90% of those worldwide who died before their 45 birthday in 1998. The report further stated that resistance to antibiotics is adding to the toll.

She further recalled that TB drugs no longer work effectively in one in five patients in Eastern Europe, malaria drugs in Asia and African are learning to survive in the presence of mankind's deadliest antibiotics.

She knew the trend would continue at a torrid pace until the nation places more attention on the problem than has deliriously sporting it is in Washington to attempt to bring down presidents in disgrace, extol stardom on Howard Stern, mindless talk shows and their idiot hosts. All of that is to say nothing of how we greedily worship reformed drug addicts, movie stars and tell all books shamelessly hawked on network television. How disgusting, she thought.

As these morbid thoughts faded away, Jessica became aware that she had cooled off considerably from the first half of her two-mile run. If she was going to complete the other half, she would have to get moving quickly, or her muscles would tighten up. She did a few quick hip and leg flexes in place, then with long elegant strides, she ran toward the far outer boundaries of the campus. All the while, she strived to still any more disturbing thoughts.

Day three
1:30 p.m.
Tanner Cemetery

An early morning shower had given way to warm bright sunshine. Only a few scattered, high altitude cirrus clouds remained to march slowly through the blue skies over the old Tanner Cemetery in Greencastle. The cemetery had been developed before the turn of the century, but it was serenely beautiful and meticulously maintained. Giant sycamores bent low, as if to embrace the hundreds of headstones. Scattered throughout the grounds were brightly colored bouquets of spring flowers, neatly and reverently set next to the tombstones by loved ones.

At the edge of the gravesite of Harry Stedman, mourners huddled silently in small clutches. They stood as primitives, in awe at the eventual specter of their own death. Richard was thankful that his childhood friend, Stanley Davis was at his side, along with Jeremy Jarvis, who was visibly shaken by the moment at hand. Several other mourners who were distant family relatives and other long time friends from his church and community were also part of the gathering.

As Richard stood next to the gravesite, he began to experience the feeling of a person in a hypnotic state. He could scarcely hear the voice of Rev. Donovan, who began the last rites.

" Friends, we gather in God's Name to mourn the passing from this life of our beloved friend, Harry Stedman. We mourn him in death, but we celebrate the life he lived and will continue to live, as his soul migrates through levels of eternity, seeking oneness with our Creator. We mourn the life and death of Harry Stedman here on earth. But, the prophets of long ago promised each of us that we would find a greater reward in the after life, if we would do God's bidding. We know that Harry Stedman will receive that reward, for he was known for his generosity to his friends and his devotion to his family and to his church. Especially, his church. Let us pray.

" Healing God, we ask, in your name, that you would save us from our distress at this moment. We are sickened to the point of total anguish. In solitude we discover that life is not a possession to be defended, but a gift to be shared. As a church, we ourselves seem to be dead, dead to the knowledge of our trespasses against you. We are afraid to embrace the changes that come with death and the new life you offer. Our very souls cry out to you in our troubles, in our pain, and in the death of our loved ones. May you give us the strength each day to live our lives, not as one who would gather, but one who would sow. Now! We humbly beseech you to watch over the soul of Harry Stedman as it traverses the levels of eternity. We ask these blessings in the name of the Father who taught us when we pray to say . . . Our Father who art in heaven.."

As Father Donovan recited the Lords Prayer, Richard's mind flashed back to the days long ago, when his father and mother were young and he was a mere boy. He regretted the times when his father was unavailable for play and for the kinds of activities with him that other fathers did with their boys. Things like playing basketball, baseball, and going fishing down at the pond.

"I suppose it wasn't his fault. He worked hard managing the farm, plowing, sowing, cultivating, and raising livestock. The hours were long and difficult, but he endured without complaint. He never expressed much emotion, but, in his own way, he loved my mother and me. I can tell by the way he appeared content in his home. There was never any sniping among us. He did not smoke or drink. He enjoyed reading, watching television, and going to church.

"He was the master of his manse, the patriarch of the family, and there was little doubt about that. He did not rule by harsh words or the paddle. He ruled by his dominant character. Mom adored him, although he was not openly affectionate. I think it was because of his quiet strength. He was not a big man by the usual standards. Dad was five foot eleven and weighed about one hundred and seventy-five pounds. He walked ramrod straight with a gait that translated into one who left no doubt that he knew what he was doing at all times. His face, even in his advancing years, appeared to be finely chiseled. His hair was curly and remained that way until his death. He didn't smile much, but when he did it was quite disarming. It was strange, but the last time I talked to him on the phone, he seemed unusually compassionate toward me. He seemed to be brooding, as if he knew that something dire was going to happen either to him or to me." Richard's mind returned to the prayers of Rev. Donovan.

"Death is going home. Home to be at the side of the heavenly Father. We have heard this many times from many sages in the past, but no one is anxious to leave this earthly plane. Who would not prefer to remain as long as possible here on earth? Even the most eloquent portrayal of the hereafter cannot take away the sting and fear of dying. Yes, death is still a great mystery.

"Yet, Jesus came to take the mystery and sting out of death. He came to earth to assist us in the recognition that there should be no fear in death. Death only leads us to the place where the deepest desires of our hearts will be satisfied. It is not easy for us to believe that, but Jesus has given us his promise that, one day, we will be with him forever and ever.

"Yes! We must all die one day. That is one of the few things we cannot escape. But the big question is, "What can we still do with our lives and the time we have left to live on this earth? How can we prepare for death, so that our living will not be in vain? How can we live so that we might continue to bear fruit for the generations that will follow us? The answer is childlike in its simplicity. We should daily live our lives the way the way Jesus told us we should live, by, "loving one another." `So, we lay to rest, Dr. Harry Stedman, who leaves behind, in sorrow, his only son, Richard. But, I say to you, strange as it may sound, you can choose joy over sorrow. We can say to you, Richard, that weeping may linger for the night, but joy will come in the morning, with the sure knowledge that your father is without pain, in eternity with our heavenly father . . . Amen!"

All mourners now moved slowly to their automobiles, returning, once again, to their own struggles, their own joys, their own fears.

Richard, heavy of heart, joined the procession as it left the cemetery grounds amid limp hand-shaking and expressions of sincere condolences that followed him. He tried to be polite as he refused invitations to go to private homes of friends for refreshments. His soul could endure no more. He hastened to his car and drove home to Stedman Woods.

106

CHAPTER 8

Day Four
Jessica's Home

The early morning dawn broke over the rolling hills of Putnam County. It found Jessica stirring from another night of complete restlessness. The strange dreams had returned. The dreams took the same form of eerie ghostly lights. And for the first time in her many dreams, several shapeless forms were bathed in the light. They beckoned to her. They should have frightened her, but they didn't. In the past, she would awaken from the dreams like a frightened dog, hiding under the porch as a storm approached. But, gratefully, the golden sunlight, streaming through her bedroom window, released her from their icy grip. She had the distinct feeling she had been in a place where time and space were warped. But this time her dreams did not linger in the form of white-hot fear, although her body was drenched with perspiration. Jessica knew, from past experience, that a severe headache would follow the dreams, and they were coming on fast. But this time she was determined to fight their advance with all her mental powers. She also knew that it was not going to be easy. Jessica could sense the bony grip of the headache beginning to form at the base of her skull, spreading to the parietal area. She began deep breathing exercises, taking in huge gulps of air and exhaling slowly. All in an attempt to hurl the headache back to wherever headaches go after they finish tormenting the souls of their victims. "The power of mind over matter," she said to herself, as she began deep breathing exercises. At each point of exhaling she repeated, "I can whip it. I can whip it." Jessica felt herself gaining control over the pain. She was grateful to discover that a wave of distinct calmness was inching its way throughout her body. She was winning . . . this time!

After Jessica had gained full control over the pain, she reviewed slowly in her mind, the activities of the previous day.

107

Yesterday, after her exercise run, she felt physically energized. She had cleaned the house, and spent several hours reviewing scientific literature for the latest articles pertaining to the AIDS virus. Jessica then decided to turn her attention to the upcoming dinner preparations. She made a final mental check of attendees. It came as no surprise to her that all members would be present; they usually were when it was her time to be the hostess.

"Do they like me, or do they like my cooking? I won't waste my time conjecturing whether or not they respect my brain. I guess they must. I'm the only woman in the permanent group. Ha! Ha! Stanley and I are the only token minority members." She smiled inwardly at her feeble attempt at humor and reread the guest list with a heightened degree of interest. Not only do I get the full complement of the group for dinner, but for the first time in a long period, there would be more than one guest. Why would Stanley think some stuffed shirt theoretical physicist named Richard Stedman, would bring any thing to the picnic? He will probably try to steal the conversation of the evening by talking about smashing the atom down to the particle wave function, or "ghost particles," charms and quarks. And how did Stanley have the nerve to invite some rancher from Texas? The least he could have done was to leave the person's name on my voice mail machine."

She smiled at the thought of her dear lawyer friend, Ernie Flownery, who would be bringing a female guest, a philosophy professor from the east coast. Her addition would make a lot sense. Surely, he would bring a great deal of stability to any aspect of the debates that would have undercurrents of human values and ethics.

" Knowing Ernie, and his penchant to surround himself with beautiful women, she will probably be young and a knockout beauty."

The final guest would be Reverend Donovan. She really didn't mind his being in attendance. She always enjoyed his company and the group needed him too. He brought a sobering but highly charged presence to any gathering. However, she had noted of late that he seemed to be struggling with certain aspects of modern day religious dogma. Seeing his friends would be good for him. Normally, the group interactions were laced with some playful arguing, some skillful debate, and a great deal of sniping at each another. Especially, during mealtime. And yet, for some unknown reason, Jessica had an uneasy feeling that the discussions at this particular dinner were going to be highly unusual and intellectually demanding.

She recalled from the previous meeting that Stanley was given the challenge of coming up with a listing of issues for discussion, and sending it to each member in advance of the meeting. When she read her mail, upon returning to campus, she had opened a letter from Stanley, containing his suggested working list for discussion. She remembered being very much impressed with his initial effort. In fact, it was on her nightstand. It was the last thing she had read before falling to sleep last night. She reached for it again, and reread the contents that were under the general heading:

BEHOLD A VISION FOR THE 21st CENTURY. BUT, OF WHAT?

"HI Jessica! Just wanted you to know that although the above title is not very original, it adds a certain structure to my assignment. As you will recall from our last meeting, I was [elected] to structure several topics for our upcoming discussion meeting. The consensus from our last meeting was that the country has no definable vision for the New Age, the 21st Century, no vision that would redefine us as a people or reduce the paralyzing negativism and general malaise that prohibits our facing the challenges of the future with optimism. We agreed that we are left with the confused imagery of the past. We are

109

not thinking globally about, What? And How? About the trajectory our nation should proceed in defining a sane course for itself In short, no one is talking about anything of substance. Not our political leaders, our clergy, or our educators. And the media is most shameful of all. In the main, their programming content is focused on the brutishness of man's nature.

In that regard, please find listed below what, in my view, are the defining issues begging for immediate attention as we enter the next millennium.

1. How can we best manage the miracles of science and technology? Are the scientists too far ahead of the general populace? Are they lulling us into a false sense that they can save us from all of our follies? Are they, in reality, controlling us on an individual basis? Are they relieving us of any participation in forging our own destiny, leaving us rudderless, powerless, and alone.

2. Why is it that the Social Sciences have not given us insights into ourselves, comparable to the insights that the Natural Sciences have given us into the rest of nature?

3. What is the relevancy of current religious thought in society? Can theologians reconcile science and technological advances with religious dogmas that are not in step with the reality of what we already know of the nature of the world and the universe?

4. Why isn't more of today's brain power working on bold new social systems whereby the individual in our society doesn't feel it is necessary to destroy his neighbor by hate, fear, or other behavior that goes against accepted mores?

5. Why are we abandoning our children and denying them any hope for a decent quality of life? What new system models can we put in place to ensure that all children are given the

opportunity to learn, compete, and adequately provide for themselves and their families in the New Age?

6. What should be the nature of our cities? How can they be made more livable, offering a better quality of life?

7. How much do we really need from all of the information we are being bombarded with on a daily basis? Does too much information cause us to over or under react to life's challenges? Does too much frivolous information foster individual paralysis, fatalism, and loss of spirit?

8. How can a capitalistic, democratic society accommodate the needs of other political systems worldwide? Avoid wars, global warming, and the "greenhouse effect." And, at the same time, assist in the growth of these merging nations?

9. Are we humans any closer now to laying bare the secret of life, and the universe? And what psychological effect will such knowledge have on our society as a whole?

10. Does such a secret even exist? And if it does, what difference does it make in the grand scheme of things? {I think this topic would be of special interest to Dr. Stedman.}

I have taken the liberty of mailing advanced copies to all participants and their guests. You will also notice that I have accommodated my aversion for uneven numbers. So I struggled mightily to come up with ten issues. [Smile]

Please don't consider them as listed in a priority order. I'll leave the format open as to where to begin, and how many of them you believe we can successfully cover in our allotted time. I think spillover debate will eventually touch on most of them anyway

Finally, I hope you got my phone message about preparing my special order for spaghetti. And by the way, don't forget to wear the stunning Red Dress!

Your friend,
Stanley

CHAPTER 9

Afternoon
Jessica's home

Jessica did not look like a full professor at a prestigious university. Her hair was in a halo of large, pink rollers. She was wearing a gray T-shirt that had emblazoned on the front the phrase, "Don't Even Go There!" Sloppy jeans and dirty white sneakers completed her domestic work outfit. She had worked hard all morning house cleaning and was grateful she was not recovering from her usual companions of headaches . . . and dreadful dreams.

The day had finally arrived for her to be the hostess for the dinner and dialogue sessions of selected DePauw professors and their invited guests, if any. She had just completed arranging the place settings at the dining table, the final touches for the day. Despite the frenetic energy she had expended, Jessica felt strangely exhilarated. Guests were coming to her home. It seemed ages since she last entertained. She would be among friends and she would be meeting several new people, as well. It would be a welcomed change of pace from the strenuous brainwork she had faced for the past several months. Not that she wasn't pleased with the progress being made on the Aids Virus project; she was, but she knew there were many months, perhaps more than a year, before her animal trials might provide a breakthrough. "Yes, tonight will be special." She thought." I'm looking forward to an evening of good conversation, and of course, my very special spaghetti and meatballs dinner." She began to hum softly as she prepared the ingredients for the sauce.

The aroma of sautéed onions and green peppers wafted to her nostrils from soft pillows of steam, the mixture sizzling in the aluminum saucepan. She next added diced, plump tomatoes con Basilica, and chilies con queso. Finally, she added the secret

113

ingredient that Stanley Davis found so special about her sauce, a dash of Zalarain's Remoulade sauce. As an after thought, she added two pinches of salt and pepper. With a flare, she dipped her wooded stirring spoon into the sauce, withdrawing it to make a chef taste test, with her fingers, of course. After adding another pinch or two of salt and pepper, waving her hand back and forth quickly to get one finally whiff, she smiled contentedly and put the lid on the sauce pan for additional simmering. "I'll give it about twenty more minutes on low heat," she said approvingly and began to take stock of what chores remained.

"Lets see. I'll add the meatballs I've already prepared, to the sauce in a few minutes. I don't want them to be over cooked. The Caesar's salad will be easy. The desert will be simple as well: Ice cream and pound cake. That ought to do nicely.

"I'm really proud of myself. I'm nearly finished with every thing and I still have more than three hours before my guests arrive. I have only to go to the liquor store and buy several bottles of Merlot and Cabernet wines. These snobby red wines sing to the palate and have robust, full-bodied character." She laughed at the word "snobby," hoping it didn't describe some of the unknown guests who would be coming to dinner.

Jessica decided it was time to begin preparing herself for the evening. "I hate to wear the red dress I wore on the plain, but Stanley told me in his letter that I should wear it. So, I suppose I will. Nobody who will be present tonight will know that I wore it only a couple of days ago. I'll just take a nice, leisurely bubble bath, before getting dressed. At least I will feel different. Yes, Jessica, I think you are going to enjoy this evening immensely." Her smile was devilish as she glided toward the bathroom, seductively disrobing as she went. Another funny thought entered her mind at that moment. "The guests must entertain the hostesses after being well fed, and they will be well fed. It's the accepted mores of the gentle class." She laughed at the boorishness of her musings.

114

Day Five
5:30 p.m.
The Gathering
Home of Dr. Jessica Harrington

The final dinner preparations completed. Jessica sat languidly on her chaise lounge, relaxed, beautiful to behold. She sipped wine from a long, fluted glass. The haunting lament of Rachmaninof's First Piano Concerto, floated lightly throughout the living room. Such a blissful setting made her feel a sudden ripple of nearly forgotten desires. For several minutes, sensual longings haunted the landscape of her brilliant mind. It was yesterday once more. Many memories of the past still slept in her mind. But they would have to remain there. She was much too dedicated to the work that remained to be done on her project. Jessica allowed herself the luxury of several philosophical thoughts that suddenly popped into her head.

"Everyone has a need to love and be loved. Without love, life is like sailing on a vast ocean. No markers! No signposts! One knows the miles are passing by, but there are no sights. No sounds to mark life's passing. Still, other mysteries remain. Nature seems to require all things to evolve from pairs. Heaven, Hell! Man, Woman! Right, Wrong! Positive, Negative! On, Off! Young, Old! Ying, Yang! Etc. All such groupings lead to sweeping effects in our society, manifesting themselves in our technology, and religions. Yes, two's are . . . The doorbell chimed again, and again!

"How long had someone been ringing it?" She thought as she jumped to her feet, nearly spilling her wine. Gathering her composure, she walked briskly, but elegantly, to the door. She flung it open wide to welcome her first guests of the evening. It was Rev. Donovan and "Oh no! It can't be!" She choked back a scream. It was the stranger, Clay Haskins! Her seatmate from the flight from San Francisco. Her body started to go limp.

115

"Good evening Dr. Harrington," Rev. Donovan said. Ignoring Jessica's glazed eyes. "We're a bit early. But I wanted you to have an opportunity to get acquainted with my guest for the evening. Clay Haskins, meet Dr. Jessica Harrington."

Jessica's knees weakened again and started to buckle. Her eyes began to roll upward like those of a drunken sailor who had just lost a bar room drinking contest. Only the quick reflex reaction of Rev. Donovan kept her from falling in a heap. Nothing could save the wine glass, however, as it arched high, in slow motion, and then came crashing to the tiled floor of the foyer. Mercifully, recovery was quick for her.

"My God . . . It's you!" She began to laugh, embarrassingly.

Forgive me for being startled, but I had no idea at the time Rev. Donovan informed me he was bringing a guest, a long time friend from Texas, that it would be YOU! Trust me. I don't greet everyone at the door by making such a scene. Welcome to my home. Come in. It's good to see both of you again. As I recall Clay, the last words you said to me as we left the plane were, "Perhaps fate, sooner or later, will bring us together again. And soon I hope." With a broad grin and an engaging laugh, Jessica said, "Looks like later has definitely become sooner."

Rev. Donovan broke into the conversation, to save Jessica further shock and embarrassment. "I see you two have met before. I'm glad to see that it was on friendly terms. Let's do the introductions again, in a more formal way. Dr. Jessica Harrington, meet again, my good friend from Texas, Clay Haskins. While you two are getting reacquainted, permit me to remove all traces of the accident, As you know, the good Lord drank wine, but it is intended to be savored, not hurled at unsuspecting guests."

They all laughed heartily, as the Reverend went directly to the kitchen pantry to fetch the broom, dustpan, and a cleaning towel. He returned, and with a few deft swipes with the broom and towel, erased all evidence of the mishap. His swift action gave Jessica a chance to recover gracefully.

"Rev. Donovan, and you too Clay, come with me while I pour both of you a glass of wine. It looks as if I'm going to begin the evening at least one drink ahead of all of you. Or does it count if I spilled the first one?" She laughed as she flung her hair back, then took them both by the arm and led them into the living room. She asked as she poured the wine. "So, Clay, how did you become acquainted with Rev. Donovan?"

"Well, actually we go back many many years. Rev. Donovan knew my uncle. Remember on the plane, I told you about Uncle Clay? Well, Uncle Clay and the Rev were quite the roust-abouts before the Rev. went away to college. My uncle went to the University of Texas. And, as I recall, Rev. Donovan attended Southern Methodist. Many times, when they would go fishing, they would let me tag along. Some of the stories I would hear led me, early on, to believe the ministry would be a good pursuit for both of them.

"Any time I'm in the Midwest area, I make it a point to drop by to see the Rev. I had some time to kill before I move onto Chicago, so I thought I would spend a day or two with him. He told me about the dialogue sessions you people have and that he was entitled to bring a guest. I thought to myself, why not? You have doubtless learned from our plane trip that I do like to talk. So, here I am. Obviously, it came as quite a shock to me too when you opened the door. I just wasn't as dramatic when I recognized you. Are you sure you can stand my presence a little longer?" He took another sip of wine. He couldn't resist looking at her, deeply, as if for the first time.

"You're quite beautiful, Dr. Harrington. I wasn't paying much attention to your physical attributes on the plane. It was

117

my misfortune. Do you prefer I call you Dr. Harrington, Ms. Harrington, or Jessica?"

Jessica blushed, her cheeks nearly matching the color of her dress. "Whatever you prefer. We try to keep our meetings quite informal."

"Well, young lady, we Texans have a reputation for putting women on a pedestal. Down home, women are to be honored. So, I think I like Dr. Harrington for the present. It seems very becoming to such a lovely young lady. I've never known a lady Ph.D.

Rev Donovan rejoined them, having completed the clean up "I see you two are continuing where you left off on the plane. Jessica, I think I can use that glass of wine now, if you please. Did he tell you I have known him since he was a young whippersnapper? He was a lousy fishing buddy though. Especially, for a lad who grew up on a ranch with large streams and ponds." Jessica poured the Rev. a glass of Cabernet, as Clay began speaking again.

"Tell me Dr. Harrington, how do you like it here at the University and living in such a small town as Greencastle? One might suspect a brilliant scientist like you would seek a much larger working environment. You know what I mean?"

"To tell you the truth, I like it here very much. I'm not very keen on nightlife, anyway. My work occupies most of my time, but there is a great deal to do on campus. There are a great many plays and musical performances to attend. Believe it or not, Indianapolis has a great deal to offer in the way of cultural entertainment as well. It is only a pleasant, short drive away. The Eli Lilly Company is located there, and they do a great deal of valuable research. I know several of their research scientists, and it makes for easy peer group dialogues."

118

"I see," Clay said. But . .
.

The doorbell chimed again. "Excuse me gentlemen, I see more of my guests have arrived. There is a tray containing a variety of cheeses on the credenza, help yourself I'll be back in a minute."

She scurried toward the door. This time she was not carrying her wine glass. She opened it. Standing there was Ernest Flownery and his guests. Ernie burst through the door like a balloon releasing air.

"Hi Jessica! Hi everyone!" He gave Jessica a fond embrace. "You get lovelier by the day. And don't you look marvelous in your red dress!" He held her at arms length, admiring her. The California sun has only added to your beauty."

"Everyone! Meet my guest for the evening, from New York. Miss Margaret Ginsberg.

Margaret is a Professor of Philosophy at Columbia University." He gently took Margaret by the arm and began the formal introductions. Jessica went to the credenza for drinks. The men looked admiringly impressed by Ernie's taste in women. Margaret looked gorgeous. She was wearing a black evening dress. She was in her mid thirties. Her olive skin formed the perfect base for her ruby red lips and shoulder length, black hair. Her long eye lashes, hooded large, sleepy dark eyes. She greeted them all with a disarming smile.

Ernie began talking immediately, centering on his many trips to Berkeley. He followed up quickly by asking mundane questions of Clay Haskins about the scandal involving certain Dallas Cowboy players and their extra curricular activities.

Jessica chuckled to herself, knowing there would never be a dull moment or lack of dinner conversation with Ernie Flownery present. Her thoughts were interrupted again by the doorbell, announcing the arrival of her final guests for the evening, Stanley Davis and Richard Stedman. Jessica was anxious to see Stanley, but frankly she was more than a little apprehensive to meet his friend Richard. She set her wine glass on the credenza and floated to the door. When she opened it, she was glad she had set her glass down. For standing in the opened door way, next to a grinning Stanley Davis, was a familiar face, looking handsome and smiling in a self-assured manner. It was the man who had caught her fancy at the San Francisco airport. Feeling faint, for the second time that evening, she gulped two deep breaths and offered a beguiling smile that revealed her brilliant white teeth and moist red lips. She extended a sweating hand to Richard. "Come in, we've been waiting for you."

7:00 P.M.
Dinner at Jessica's

Over the course of the next forty-five minutes, Jessica was a veritable honeybee seeking nectar. Flitting here, flitting there, lightly touching down there, as she administered to her guests' every need. Things were proceeding, uncharacteristically for her, as planned. The only real glitch so far to her well-planned dinner was only slightly embarrassing. She nearly burned one batch of sliced garlic buttered French bread, but, not to worry, no one appeared to notice. They were thoroughly enjoying chatting with one another and her spaghetti dinner.

Jessica was devilishly sly in designating the seating arrangement for her guests, and it was not by accident that she seated Richard next to her. She could tell by the ease and sincerity of his conversation, his body language, and his fixating gaze upon her, that the magnetic attraction they experienced at the airport in San Francisco just a few days ago still gripped them. Jessica was deliriously happy, and she didn't care if it showed.

The conversation in such a short time span had gone far beyond the usual conversations of two strangers. The usual probing of family, education, careers, and hobbies. Instead, they laughed easily at each other's jokes, scarcely paying any attention to the easy banter taking place around them.

They discovered they both had "invisible playmates" when they were young. Their parents only scoffed at their playful conversations with these invisible, imaginary friends who would appear at their bedsides, bathed in a blue haze of enveloping light. They would tell their respective parents of tiny, child like figures that beckoned to them. Their parents dismissed their stories as imaginary manifestations of dreams. This point was made manifest when they also discovered that both, to this day, have intermittent dreams of tiny entities entering their room at night. They discussed whether these apparitions were some type of dysfunction that they both had in common? Both had read Whitney Strieber's book, Abduction. In his book he revealed that, throughout his life, he had been whisk from his home by alien beings. Richard and Jessica feared they were victims of alien abductions as well. It seemed incongruous that they were willing to discuss such strange and aberrant behavior in their lives, especially, on first meeting.

Meanwhile, other dinner conversations were light and easy to track by the other guests. The only out of the ordinary subject broached was one raised by Stanley. He had read recently in the Indianapolis Star of unusual lights in the nighttime skies over Greencastle and Putnam County. Undoubtedly, no one wanted talk about the matter. Rev. Donovan quickly changed the subject by observing the obvious coincidence that so many of the people at the table appeared to be drawn together by a strange set of circumstances. Everyone had a reasonable explanation for being drawn together, except Jessica and Richard. They had shared glances in a crowded airport a few days ago in San Francisco; now here they were, sitting next to one another, thousands of miles from their original encounter.

121

Jessica smiled proudly, but with some embarrassment, when Stanley reached for a second helping of spaghetti and meatballs, exclaiming aloud as he did, "My friends, we have been waiting for Jessica's cooking for months. I would like our guests to know that the only rival for good home cooking in our fair city is "Mom Mayes" soul food restaurant. In fact, I asked Jessica if she would prepare this dish for us this evening, knowing we would be in for a special treat. I might add, she has out done herself. The food has been just great.

Taking his cue from Stanley. Richard was the first to express agreement. He rose from his chair, and with wine glass in hand, prepared to offer a toast. All of the guests raised their wine glasses as one. "I believe our hostess has three outstanding talents, "Richard said. "She has beauty, brains, and the extraordinary capacity to appease the most ravenous appetite of my good friend Stanley. I should know. I have been a witness, since our early childhood, when he would come to our house for dinner. He always asked for seconds." Everyone had a good laughed. "So, I offer a toast to Jessica Harrington. It's an ancient Sumerian toast dating back thousands of years into antiquity, Jessica. It was offered only to those who opened their homes to guests and treated them as one of the family. So, it is now that I offer it to you with all sincerity and appreciation of a most sumptuous dinner, "May Your House Be Safe From Tigers!"

"Hear! Hear!" Was the resounding chorus of all of the dinner guests.

Jessica rose, politely, clanged her wine glass with a fork, to get their total attention. She proceeded to thank her guests warmly for their generous expressions of appreciation for the extra effort she expended to ensure that they would all have an exceptionally good time.

" I appreciate your thoughtful expressions. It pleases me so very much, that all of you have enjoyed yourselves thus far. But it is now time to move into the living room and make your selves comfortable, as we begin my favorite part of the evening, the dialogue sessions. There are plenty of beverages next to the credenza. I will join you in just a few minutes: I first have a few tidying up chores to attend to in the kitchen."

All of the guests went immediately into the living room. Stanley hesitated a few seconds while he downed several more bites of the spaghetti. Richard remained behind briefly as well, asking Jessica if there was anything he could do to help in the clean up. She thanked him for his generous offer but took him gently by the arm and led him into the living room to join the others. It is very sweet of you to offer to help, Richard, but, I can manage. She leaned over, kissed him gently on the cheek and whispered softly, "I'll be but a minute. Be a dear and save me a seat next to you." When she completed tidying up the kitchen, Jessica rejoined her guests, just as Stanley was finishing his preamble to the discussions. She noticed everyone appeared eager to begin; they maneuvered to find comfortable positions in their chairs.

"...And so we decided we were becoming too narrow, too one dimensional in our focus as scientists and as individuals. As a group we felt that, in many ways, we were closer to an interrelationship in our respective fields than any of us every thought was possible. Still, it was our concern that as we enter the 21st Century, these relationships will be coming ever more important, if we are to find a greater relevance to our work and in our lives. Unfortunately, no one seemed to be talking about any matters of consequence, and this disturbed us greatly. There abound great and bothersome questions that are receiving little attention, not even by our greatest thinkers, the politicians, the media, nor from the pulpits of our churches.

"Where are science and technology taking us? Why are families and individuals so dysfunctional? Where is self-fulfillment in a land of plenty? Why do we look to TV gurus for answers when they are content to feed us so much pabulum?"

"My assignment for this evenings dialogue was to put a list of potential topics together for our discussion. I have given each of you a copy of that list. It is my suggestion that we begin our dialogue with the question, "Where are science and technology taking us as we enter the new millennium? That question is broad enough that we may be able to exhaust some of the other topics at the bottom half of the list as the evening progresses. For the newcomers, the rules of these dialogue sessions are simple. All views are welcomed no matter how outlandish or far-fetched they may be. Disagreement is encouraged, but personalizing, and invectives directed toward a particular individual are not. We want to leave as friends." All laughed haltingly, as they anxiously awaited the individual who would speak first. The highly charged atmosphere suddenly cooled as Jessica made her entrance with a flourish.

CHAPTER 10

7:30 P.M.
The Dialogue Begins

Stanley . . .

"Ah! I see our famous Midwestern culinary artist, and research scientist extraordinaire, has returned. Jessica, I've given everyone the check-in-drill. I have advise the newcomers that the dialogue sessions, think tank if you will, is the brainchild of Jessica and myself and that the newcomers should feel free and relaxed, and personal-revealing is the order of the evening. Personal attacks are out of order. I have further advised the group that I will issue "white papers" to each participant on the subjects covered this evening. They are to be used in public symposiums, academic lectures, and other venues as you deem necessary and appropriate. We are now prepared to address our agenda. But first Jessica, can you give us your famous five minute version of what science is, and where it stands today as a discipline? I think it might be helpful to our non-scientist friends to have a working knowledge of what we mean by scientific discipline. I don't think I am putting you on the spot, because I have heard you do it before . . . at one of your lecture series to DePauw students interested in pursuing a career in science."

Jessica . . .

"My five minute version huh? Ok, here goes. Someone with a watch stop me at the exact five minute mark."

She laughed tauntingly as she tossed back her slightly disheveled hair from her dancing eyes. Jessica settled softly into an easy chair, next to Richard. Scanning the room for someone on whom to focus her attention, she settled upon the baleful gaze of Rev. Donovan. She then began to speak slowly . . . and with deliberate authority.

Jessica . . .

"Today, the sun rose over the eastern horizon, as it has done for billions of years. Below it, some four billion people were doing the same kinds of things they have been doing for thousands of those billions of years . . . trying to keep body and soul together . . . All in a vain attempt to make sense out of their internal and exterior world. Many succeeding, many were not.

"Thousands of years before man learned to write, science began. No one knows who the first individual was who discovered fire, invented the wheel, developed the bow and arrow or tried to explain the parade of stars across the heavens . . . the rising and setting sun . . . the origins of the clouds and the rain . . . All we know for sure is someone did. Ever since then mankind has added incremental knowledge to these beginnings right up to the current time. But there is no scientist who stands alone in his knowledge . . . no matter how powerful his or her intellect may be.

"Today . . . Science covers the broad field of human knowledge and is concerned with facts held together by rules . . . or principles. They test these facts by the scientific method. They feel that any subject which man can study by using the scientific method can be called science. advances made in science, scientists still recognize many unsolved problems. Many of them may never be solved. Some of those unsolvable problems are the reason for these meetings. We gather together not so much for solving them. But to think about them . . . and in turn . . . perhaps the general public will do so as well. We will doubtless touch on this point as the evening progresses. But for now, let me give just a few examples of the unknowns. Physicists have not yet produced temperatures needed to control atomic fusion. We don't know, despite what some may say, how photosynthesis works. What, and where does the conscious mind lay? How did life originate? What is God? What causes cancer and mental illness? How can we cure the AIDS virus? Is War

126

inevitable? Why are our cities rotting?...Is it possible to combine the Grand Unifying Theories of all nature [GUT] into one grand, elegant theory? Is it possible for humans to live in harmony? Is there a potential for the conscious mind to live on after death? How many dimensions are there to space, and time? Is there other life in the universe? What is the enigma of UFO's? I could go on, but there you have my five-minute drill. No, it was less than five minutes, because no one raised his hand giving the five minute signal."

Jessica turned to Richard and smiled. It was a smile of one who has just produced a batch of homemade cookies that made her mother proud. She was really looking for some recognition of his approval or disapproval about her statement that the "GUT" remained undiscovered. There was none. His eyes averted hers. But he had appeared to be visibly shaken at her mention of "GUT".

Ernie . . .

"I would like to make a quick observation regarding the comments made by my new found friend, Jessica. I'm sure we will address the issue in more detail as the evening progress. But it is perhaps important, that we place it on the table now. It is my opinion that too many of us are falling into the trap that the gateway to all of our fear, woes, obstacles, and future awaits only some unknown, or as yet desired, untested technological breakthrough. I would submit that a great question to be debated is why are we not getting the payoff from the natural sciences that we get from physics, chemistry, biology etc.? I say it's because scientific laws can explain trees, grasshoppers, and computers. But human beings have the capacity to ignore such boundaries. Humans have a conscience. They have free will. They can choose to take either fork in the road. They can choose not to rape, murder, take drugs, love, or hate. The laws of nature, however are immutable."

127

Stanley . . .

"Thanks Ernie for those purposeful and insightful propositions, Ernie. I'm sure many of your points will be revisited before the night is done, and thank you Jessica. As usual . . . It appears you have mastered scientific inquiry better than most. You made clear the meaning of science for our non-scientific guests. I'm sure it will be well for us to remember those tenets as we continue.

"I'm interested now in a deeper question or questions regarding the current status of the relevance of science. I suppose I really have several questions rolled into one. In particular, I'm interested in where physics, philosophy and religion will be taking us in the coming millennium. Given the tremendous advances in understanding of the micro world of the atom and its workings, and . . . With our tremendous understanding of the cosmic universe, is there still room for God?" "Margaret, would you begin the inquiry by giving us an overview of where the philosophical community stands. I would suggest that Father Donovan and Richard enter the dialogue at anytime they feel they are in agreement disagreement with Margaret's positions."

Margaret . . .

"Before I hurl myself into "white water" in an attempt to answer your very daunting questions, let me make a few extraneous remarks. I want every one to know that I feel very fortunate to be here this evening. It has been such a long time since I have had such a lovely evening. As an outsider to your group, I have been made me feel so much at home. I admire what you are doing with your dialogue sessions. They embrace the best of different scientific fields and coalesce the current views and standings of the various sciences as we enter the "New Age." I was told I would enjoy the evening, and I certainly have. I must admit however, that I didn't know I would be asked to participate in your discussions. It's very strange, however that I don't feel I'm being put on the spot. Let me now, in the briefest way, address your question, Stanley. First, it may be well to say a few things about what philosophy is and what it appears to be becoming.

"The classical definition of Philosophy is literally the love of wisdom, Philos. It aims to understand the moral aspects of one's life according to reason. Especially, as reason relates to the sciences and the universe as we know it. I want to say more about this later, if it is appropriate. But, for the moment, it may be worthwhile for me to say few words about why I studied philosophy. Since my childhood I felt attuned to the beauty and infinite expanse of nature's being-her many wondrous forms of animals, plants, earth, sky, stars and galaxies. Then there was my overwhelming sense of the relatedness of them all. Some visible and real, and other aspects hidden from our conventional sense of reality. I don't mind shooting an arrow at my field. That's how we will get better and wiser as we pursuit our craft. During my many years of study, I have noticed how much of the classic philosophy has changed. The original quest for reason seems to have gone out of style in the modern world." Since the time of the early Greeks, the search for the answers to humanities great questions, has been pursued, Answers to such questions as, what is truth? Goodness! The soul? The after life. Mans inhumanity to man. The sacrifice for the greater good. The transcendence of life beyond ourselves. These things seem to be lost concerns especially, in this century."

Stanley . . .

I think I understand the basic tenets of Margaret's ideas about where philosophy may have gone wrong. I now would like to ask Jessica how science and virtue are viewed by your contemporaries. Perhaps more specifically what authority holds scientists together as an entity of scholars? What virtues are held in common by them?

Jessica . . .

" I see Stanley that you are just intent on getting me into "white water" this evening." She tossed back her head and gave a long purring laugh. "But, I will give your word virtue a go of it."

It may come as a surprise to some, but a scientist does not cheat, nor make wild, unsubstantiated claims; they do not try to persuade at any cost, they are not prejudiced as their disputes being discussed are outside race, age, sex, or class standing. As individuals they may live less than a virtuous life, but they are trained to avoid any form of persuasion except fact, or what is perceived to be facts. .

Stanley...

It appears then, that what you are saying about the scientific fraternity and its virtues mirror what a democratic society should be all about, free inquiry, free thought, free speech, and tolerance toward others and their opinions.

Margaret . . .

That is quite true. The brilliant author, scientist and humanist, Jacob Bronowski, believed that a democracy can flourish and grow by the tension, the give and take between dissent and respect of the opinions and views of others, and tolerance for them. And in the long run making all of us more deeply human. And I might add just what is needed in the world today.

"I now see, what many philosophers neglected to consider, the relevance of science to our field of philosophy. Especially, the new physics of the 20th century. I'm speaking now mainly of the outstanding leaps of intellect of Albert Einstein, Heisenberg, Stephen Hawking, and Schrodinger, and the other prodigious

130

architects of the Quantum Theory. Thanks to such men, many answers to the awesome vibrancy of the cosmos, black holes, worm holes, other dimensions, and the like are now known and widely accepted by the scientific community and the general public. I have now embraced the physical sciences but it may come as a complete surprise to you that I also embrace the mysticism of the Eastern sages. Particularly the Dalai Lama of Tibet. Particularly their view that nature is a single reality that can be experienced on many different levels. So, I think we now stand at the threshold of a new understanding of reason for being a part of nature and most important, able to understand a great deal of the deeper meaning of it. Is it now possible that just perhaps, science, religion and mysticism, are but different approaches to our understanding of nature?

"I think this view was adopted by the great Albert Einstein. Einstein realized in his early childhood by reading books on science that most of what he had been taught about religion could not possibly be true. Nevertheless, throughout his adult life he believed that a strange, divine order existed in the universe and wondered whether or not divine order was a necessary cause. He has often been quoted with his phrase, "god doesn't play dice with the universe." In other words what we see in nature is not by happenstance. To the non-scientist God is associated with the God of Miracles, miracles of faith and healing of the soul. The God of Miracles intervenes in our lives, destroying sinful cities and sinfully wicked enemies like Pharaoh's armies, thus making way for the righteous.

"Yet, it is fair to say that, for most scientists, that their propensity to talk around or over the heads of non-scientists, discarding miracles, if they in fact occur, as non reproducible or outside science is a copout. It is true that one might rightfully ask why we humans cling so tightly to our respective religions through irrational arguments when religion has been historically used to mask vicious wars and unspeakable crimes against others not holding specific religious views. Holy wars throughout history have perpetuated the worst crimes ever committed against others.

"Nevertheless, Religion is to be found universally in every human culture. All speak, even primitive tribes, of an "origin" myth that addresses where they came from. Most of these myths speak of some connection with a Being or Beings from the stars. So it would also appear that religion binds individuals and societies together, offering a shared destiny. It enables "faith" to be the great attractor, even though it may suspend common sense and gives purpose and meaning to life. As we philosophers are fond of saying, is it necessary to understand why the Robin sings at the break of dawn. Perhaps it is as simple as they were created for singing and singing gives them pleasure?"

Rev. Donovan . . .

" Margaret, that was wonderfully put. I think you have given us a good start to the exploration of Stanley's difficult agenda subjects. It is just as difficult for me to admit, coming from a small Midwestern city, and being the spiritual leader of a small church that it may be irresponsible for me to discuss such intellectual issues. We are simple people in our church, on a simple journey of life. But I realize that we religious leaders must change our thinking in order to be more relevant in the 21st century. We must rid ourselves of old paradigms, if we are to offer our followers a more meaningful existence. Perhaps someday it will be necessary to make a radical change in our approach to preaching to the flock. In many ways science is destroying their belief systems as we learn more of what science and technology today have given us..

"Perhaps it is time for we religious leaders provide more than temporary spiritual nourishment. Science, religion and the mystics of Eastern thought may have a common pursuit that might even enhance each other in ways that we have not explored in the past. The sages, as you call them, of Eastern thought believe in the experience of oneness with the whole of nature. One may say that science, particularly physics, sought to hammer away at matter and the atom, to determine its ultimate boundaries. Mysticism, the unboundedness.

"To expand on Jessica's excellent definition of science, I would agree with her that science wants to understand the nature in all of its full detail and to unify it in one all in compassing equation. Although, taking things apart into small and smaller components has been its strength, this process could be a great weakness, as well. By stripping away layers of nature, science loses a sense of the whole. In particular, meaning, unity, wholeness, and oneness, and objectivity are lost in the detail and data." It is very curious, but just as science can become more expansive through acknowledging a formal relationship with mysticism, so mysticism can become more expansive through science."

As an outsider and non-scientist, Clay had been listening intently, slowly sipping from his half-filled wine glass. If the others had been watching him, they would have noticed his eyes darting among them. He had wanted to speak for some time. As the evening wore on his nostrils began to flare: he was not going to be intimidated by all of the geniuses in the room. And he was intent in proving it. Now!

Clay . . .

"Hold on a second. I think we are dancing around a real and sensitive problem here. Many people see things through different eyes on this subject of the relevance of science, religion, and philosophy. As we enter the 21st Century, I don't need to tell you that there is a host of people who believe that science is too far ahead of religion. In the past, humankind remained observer to nature and its wonders. Now, we have the capability to manipulate nature. We stand fascinated and terrified as we witness gene coding bionic parts for humans, germ warfare, hydrogen bombs, computer economics, space vehicles traversing the solar system. Global economics is collapsing societies that have held together for thousands of years. Now it is taking only decades for systematic world change. But, religious dogma has not changed. It's out of step that many young people claim [God is dead.] It is a point of fact that many of the prayers of the church faithful appear disjointed, self-centered, even depressing. A strange situation of being rudderless appears to be developing. All the while, sincere leaders of churches doggedly debate the ancient fine points of religious doctrine. Sadly enough, many of their parishioners urgently grope in vain for a new understanding of reality and of the purpose of their lives.

" For hundreds of years the dogma of churches was rarely challenged. Any person who did so would likely receive harsh punishment, including banishment to dungeons, even death at the stake. We all remember what happened to Bruno the scientist who said the earth was not the center of the universe. This proclamation did not set well with the theologians. After all, let us not forget that God at the time, and often still is today, was supposed to hold forth in the heavens. Poor Galileo was spared death if he would denounce the wonders discovered by his telescope. He was forced to spend the rest of his life under house arrest anyway. It is astonishing to me that the vastness of space, beauty of the moon, planets, stars, has been given its rightful praise by poets, philosophers, ordinary mainstream individuals, yet and religious thinkers ignore such truths."

It was obvious to all present that Clay was expelling thoughts he had been struggling with for some time. Now that he had a platform of distinguished listeners, he intended to maximize the moment. His cheeks began to turn the color of ripe peaches and his voice rose several octaves above normal as he continued to press on. His eyes darted and flickered toward each of the participants. They returned blank stares that told him nothing of what they were thinking. But he remained unflappable as he continued.

Clay . . .

"People are willing to praise reformed athletes, rock singers, movie actors, fallen politicians, drug addicts and alcoholics, but they give little thought to what is being discovered by scientists. Scientists are cloning sheep, enabling women to have mega births of children at one time, discovering "black holes" and planets, restoring all manner of organs and limbs to our bodies, transforming our lives with computer technology, using the Hubble telescope to peer to the farthest reaches of the Universe, even to the time of its birth. One would think that our priests, poets, philosophers would be the first to either embrace or damn these wonders in our culture and throughout our society. After all, didn't some psalmist long ago attempt just that when he said, "When I consider the heavens, the work of their fingers, the moon and the star. What is man that thou art mindful of him? . ."

Ernie . . .

"You're absolutely right Clay. It is hard to look back on those events from the vantage point of today's world but in many ways things have not changed much. Blind obedience is still required in many branches of splinter churches. We all can remember the tragedy of Jones- town. Such leaders realize that religious faith requires strict obedience to their particular dogma." The mother church has not forgotten that religious faith makes people less discontent with their lot, less envious of their neighbors. Most churches taught that advantages in life were to do the " will of God. " A teaching which too many were and are willing to accept." With declining influence of churches that could do no more than they are doing to reduce jealousy and hatred because they cannot explain to the satisfaction of many of today's disconnected, discontented younger generation, why there are so many sorrows, problems, and frustrations. Too many

135

of us have to wrestle with dreary, difficult and brutish lives. It happens in the home, away from home, around the world. For most of us the 'American Dream' must remain an out of reach dream.

"In reality, our own lack of personal skills and or lack of preparation for the competition of others more qualified or more skilled at manipulation, reduces our own chances for achievement. It is my view that is the reason too many of us are too willing to let others do our thinking for us. Talk show hosts, movie stars, athletes, and newscasters become the new heroes and bearers of truth. It leads to a sad state where the young seek the safety of opiates, and alcohol to escape the demons within. "It seems a certainty that the myths and dogmas of yesterday, which our parents and forbears took for granted as living truth have all collapsed. Even some philosophers seem to have accepted this position. Many seem so devastated by the collapse of religious beliefs that they are paralyzed in their thinking. Except for our distinguished philosopher friend Margaret, few original thinkers have emerged on the academic philosophy stage in more than a hundred years.

"Despite the obtuse frontal assault on religion and philosophy, Margaret and the Rev. Donovan remembered the admonition made by Stanley at the outset, [Challenge to individual thinking is permissible, but personal challenges are not.] Neither of them expected to be so involved in the evening. Margaret said nothing for the moment, as Ernie continued.

Ernie . . .

"Physicists, scientists seem to be the only ones favorably grasping the sorry situation, probably due to the tremendous successes they have had since the turn of the century. This success does not mean they do not empathize with the dismal state of much of the world's inhabitants. Scientists believe that the successes made in the understanding of the atom, and galaxies give them almost limitless optimism in developing a whole new set of beliefs in how human beings can again look to one another and the universe and find our soul."

Jessica, who had excused herself to retreat to the kitchen, now appeared with a tray filled with cake and ice cream and began to serve her guests. Most appeared to welcome the brief respite, but left no doubt they were eager to continue the dialogue. Especially, when it was Margaret who resumed the previous discussion.

Margaret . . .

"You raise some interesting points about the relevancy of religion and philosophy. I particularly like the fact that you excluded me from the ranks of philosophers with their head in the sand. But I would hasten to add, the future may not be as bleak as many believe. There has been a great deal of thinking over the last decade about the interlocking of the ideas that have come forth from science that elevates the stature of both. The new thinking embraces much of the recent discoveries in quantum physics, eastern religion, and a renaissance of philosophy. Let me see if I can summarize briefly some of the thinking along these lines.

"It is my belief that early in the next century man will eventually return to God through the greater understanding of such knowledge that will be revealed to us through scientific proofs. Physics and cosmology will lead the way. We will come to the understanding that we are one with all of nature, or essence, or creator, or God. The names may differ but our understanding will be universal. We are nearly there now but we just don't understand it because too many long held views must be swept away."

Rev Donovan ....

" You seem to be pointing your finger in the direction of a familiar biblical truth. "For everything its season, and for every activity under heaven its time. . Whatever is already, and whatever is to come has been already, and God summons each event back in its turn. "Ecclesiastics: I, 15"

"Permit me for just a second to see if I can attack a very difficult line of biblical reasoning. My approach may seem awkward to some of you at first, but let me try anyway. I want to objectively look at my own discipline. After all, I should defend my own domain. Right?"

He laughed, but it was more of a cackle, as if he were not too sure of the depth of the water he was about to plunge into. Rev. Donovan took the leap anyway.

"When inquiry approaches the ultimate question of our existence, religion, physics, metaphysics, science and philosophy, the lines become blurred. It has always occurred to me that it is profoundly significant that individuals who live on a tiny blue planet have come to understand so much about our universe. Therefore, 1 would be terribly surprised if some equal or greater intelligence than our own did not emerge in many places in such a vast universe. The same Creator who made it possible for us to be here surely could have been the creator of life elsewhere."

Margaret....
"This may be quite revealing because as it is quite easy for the general public, particularly the younger generation who feel so disconnected from aspects of their lives that living offers no relevancy. Perhaps Richard will help me out in this discussion because a great deal of the new philosophical thought is based on the physics and mathematics discovered in the 20th century. Both are closer to a spiritual reality than is believed. Perhaps it was not the most propitious time for such thoughts."

Richard . . .

"At the risk of commanding too much of the remaining time. I would like to make just a few more points. Strangely enough, one of them begins with mathematics. Mathematics, one of the few disciplines that have resonated down through the ages of time, seems to be mystical in nature.

"Mathematics, which has no physical material nature seems to be a compelling, integral part of matter. Yet it is invisible. The mathematician, like the mystic, believes in sudden insight. Sudden insight by our mathematicians and whose formulas have enable us to peel away the structure of matter, revealing the ultimate beauty in nature, leaving the scientists humble after their discoveries.

"When one looks into matter it is so subtle it is beyond anything physical, as we know it. This point is a little difficult to grasp, but when we explore matter as far as it can be explored, is it be matter or something unknown to us? I think I know what the New Age religious view would be. They would say it is beyond matter. Ultimately it is impossible to put such transcendence into thought, so any proper definition would have to lie somewhere between transcendence and order of some unknown form. That unknown transcendence or form many would call God.

" Sir James Jeans who is believed to have said, God is a mathematician, basically was saying that all modern physical proofs have been discovered in mathematical formulas. Since mathematics can be discovered as pure thought, is it a form of nature? Or is it spiritual in form? According to 20th century physics the only things we know about matter are the equations. If the equations are formed correctly, for some mysterious reason, they will come out giving desired results that expand our understanding of reality. It bears a great deal on Eastern mysticism. As a matter of fact, many of the early scientists who worked on the quantum theory had strong eastern philosophical views."

Jessica . . .

"Margaret can you give us a one or two sentence view of what mysticism is?"

Margaret . . .

"Yes. Mysticism is the general belief that the only comprehensive way to approach the ultimate reality, essence, or God, is to become one with all nature. Unity is the operative word."

Ernie . . .

"If I understand correctly what everyone has said so far, and that is doubtful, isn't it true that the physics, through mathematics, strives to uncover the essence of things? Now I am to understand that it is mathematical order, or something deeper, a spiritual actuality that is subtle and transcendent that the physical scientist is striving for? They are searching for an underlying unity. To go one step further, the mystic and the scientist see in all matter something that is transcendent, once one gets to the smallest of the smallest? If that is possible. "

Margaret...

"That is very good. The mystic sees within all things the divine. Where the disconnection between physicists and mystics emerges is that the mystic cannot prove his views. He can only discuss them."

Clay . . .

"But, isn't it true, that it is now virtually impossible at this stage for physics to prove much more in the laboratory or in the linear accelerators? So doesn't that leave the scientist and the mystic groping blindly in the same "bone yard?" And isn't it true that we have lost our connection with myths and mysteries. Modern science continues to demystify much about our modern world, leaving us with not much in its place. DNA cloning, our solar system, black holes, the universe are not so mysterious anymore."

Stanley . . .

"Whoa! Let's slowdown for a minute. Let me make sure I'm getting this fundamental question about mathematics and the mysticism correct. Is it true then that those who work in particle physics, astronomy, or cosmology are all attributing profound meaning to mathematics? And the equations are predicting everything? Einstein's E=MC2 for example, or Planks Constant which is the earliest seconds after the "Big Bang" or the mathematical proofs found in particle physics that led to the discovery of quarks, leptons, and hadrons are bordering on the essence, or godlike characteristics of all of nature, or God?"

Richard . . .

"It certainly appears so. But there are those who feel philosophically that mathematics may be just one level of ultimate reality. There may be others. Einstein is reported to have said, "The whole universe is mysterious. Ultimate reality is mysterious." This is close to what eastern thought says. He was probably correct in his statement by the way, because many physicists feel they are glimpsing something beyond reality, some kind of truth heretofore unknown, when they get close to understanding all the constituents of the atom."

141

Margaret . . .

Isn't it true and what we have been saying all along this evening, that the mystic is thinking and believing without language? He feels the essence, transcendence, and believes that anything can trigger it. A walk in the forest. A stroll by a lake. A beautiful sky. A solitary moment. The unity with all nature begets the communing with nature. The meditation is made manifest through focusing the mind and blacking out all things that would interfere with deep perception. The mystic goes deeply into conscience and the physics into matter. Is it possible they both have arrived at the common denominator? Nature is then revealed. They both can now operate at a higher level?"

Stanley . . .

"That sounds miraculous. But hasn't the mystic been saying this for thousands of years? If I understand my good friend Richard correctly; modern science would lead to the conclusion that the mind is never absent from any form of matter. I have read Capra's "The Tao of Physics," where he attempts to make the same point. The book was an international best seller, which would indicate that human kind is somehow ready to make the next leap to integrate the two disciplines in the near future. Do you accept that proposition, Margaret?"

Margaret . . .

"Yes I do, but surprisingly enough, it may come from a different viewpoint. It seems theologians feel they can do no more than they are doing to reduce crime and punishment. We haven't discussed this, but I'm thinking now about Reincarnation, a gift from our Eastern friends. So thinking coupled with science and religion may be the new wave of the 21st century, extending to the Western world. It certainly offers more hope to the skeptic of Western Religion. In fact it holds out a great deal of hope for the alternatives of some dogmatic religions.

142

"Eastern religion speaks of a previous existence of a past for which the only thing we humans can understand is that life presents in different stages of a long development. We are all in different stages of an individual and cosmic personality. Since there are not accidents of birth, the environment in which we start life is the result of our past and the opportunity or tests we need for this stage of our earthly development is the recognition of life's continuum. In other words, by our actions, or inactions, in a previous existence, we have made our life. And, if we wish, we can construct our lives by molding them to our own desires."

Clay . . .

"Jessica, from your position as a microbiologist, isn't it true that one of the most significant discoveries in recent times, even though it has been widely ignored, is that the material in the human body is constantly destroyed and then renewed? It has long been known that we are constantly renewing blood supply. Isn't it true then whether we accept the idea of reincarnation that literally we have often been "reincarnated" in our present lifetime, when most of the material of our bodies and brains has been replaced with fresh material?"

Jessica . . .

"That could very well be true. Most of the material we are composed of, protein, is frequently renewed. Even the bone matter is renewed on a cyclical basis. It is a continuous, ongoing process, taking some six months to complete in its entirety. And what is more difficult to believe is that there is a complete turnover of brain cells about three times a year. However, only the physical body structure changes with our growth or age, and at death. No one knows the mechanism that controls this elaborate recycling. Even amino acid must not be out of place while this recycling is taking place. What we do know for sure is that the eggs, plants and animals we eat turn out to be us.

"Some scientists feel the controlling mechanisms are electric fields. The interesting thing about life fields is that they can exist outside matter and travel through space, instantly. They are of themselves non-material. They appear to be of an "organizing" nature, i.e. electric fields are literally the basis from which all living things spring. These human fields are complicated, but they can be and have been measured in the laboratory. Many paranormal events suggest our ability to tap into such fields with our minds. Much of the mystery of life fields remains just that- a mystery. But there they are just waiting for concentrated study in the next century."

Margaret . . .

"I want to follow up on the point of fields and reincarnation proposed in Eastern thought, and how it may have the potential for grist for the theologians. Reincarnation, the rebirth of the "soul," can offer a reasonable explanation of the inequities and injustices of human existence. Since the mind and memory are eternal, man is eternal. Modern discoveries of electromagnetic fields and their properties demonstrate that logically and scientifically they are possible.

"There is no question that some of the greatest thinkers of the West and of the East accept the proposition that reincarnation as fact. In addition modem physics accepts the law of conservation of mass and energy. Since humans and all matter are made of energy, we can never go out of existence, even after death. Especially, if we are part of a grand universal energy field.

"Probably, just as important as any thing reincarnation as a concept is compatible with the widespread belief in a just God. It gives new meaning and purpose to life. We can happily endure and overcome the travail of this existence. We can use the next life simply for improvement.

"One of the great problems faced by the prospect of reincarnation is the same one that plagued Darwin's theory of evolution. We must face our own weakness. We cannot blame anyone for our failures. The reincarnation concept of our bodies, brains, race, parents, society as a whole are under our own control is scary proposition because basically means we are in control of our own destiny.

"If we discard our excuses, we advance to the stage that our mind and conscious can exist in space, apart from the body and that its purpose is to seek a higher evolutionary, and intellectual plane of existence."

Stanley . . .

"I have no quarrel with the concept of reincarnation Margaret, but I have the feeling that in the near future people will look back on 20th century science, with all of its wonderful advancements, and ask why in fact we missed the answer to some of our toughest questions when Eastern thought tried to tell us all along what the ancient philosophers knew thousands of years ago. I guess my question is the same one we began with. Is science ahead of religion and is God dead?"

Jessica . . .

"That is not necessarily true, in my humble opinion. It doesn't have to be that way. Perhaps both disciplines are intertwined. I think scientists are catching up to religion and are closer than we think, as Margaret has so eloquently portrayed In a sense, religion realizes that God and religion can claim to be far ahead of science.

"For instance, most religions teach that man has an immortal soul, independent of his mortal body, but cannot explain what a soul really is. But contemporary science is getting close and early in the 21st century, we many have a satisfactory answer, provided we are willing to accept the best these disciplines have to offer and dismiss a great deal of negative religious dogma."

Clay . . .

"For my own clarification, let me see if I understand correctly what we have said so far. At this period in time we know that or conscious memory survives changes of the material brain and thus must be independent of it. If it survives the constant changes of material make up, then logically survives physical death. And research has shown that the human body is constructed, maintained, and controlled by electric fields that in turn can be over-ridden by the mind. Mind then must be the soul or spirit as recalled by religion. Therefore, we can make the leap then that religion provides answers to the potential for the validity of prayer, faith healing and the best answer for going to church."

Stanley . . .

Great job! As far as I'm concerned you deserve another glass of . . .

Looking directly at Jessica, Ernie was about to drop a bombshell into the discussion. His main target was Jessica's field of microbiology. He took a sip of wine to fortify himself, hoping no one would notice the nervous gesture. Ernie began to grimace and then chuckle, stopping abruptly.

Ernie...

"No one has ever seen one DNA molecule discussing something with another molecule." Ernie felt a sense of pride in his sly attempt at humor. He did not succeed. His captive audience was not anxious to hear more from him. But they could tell by his crooked smile that he wasn't done yet. Not by a long shot.

Ernie . . .

"I guess I will have to go along with that business about our bodies being recycled every 6 months. It reminds me of Miss T. In <u>Alice in Wonderland</u>. She said, "It's a very odd thing-as odd as can be-that whatever Miss T. eats-turns into Miss T.""

The group remained silent except for Margaret who stifled a laugh by putting her hand to her mouth. Ernie hastened on with a sense of purpose. He felt compelled to demonstrate his intellectual side to his nature.

But on a more serious note I want to go back to the discussion of electromagnetic forces that drive the body's actions and reactions. Richard or Jessica may want to comment on this but it is my understanding that an electromagnetic field is when something occurs somewhere in space because something, somewhere else occurred, somewhere else in space with no visible means producing the effect. The two events stay connected by a "field." You cannot see or feel this force that controls our bodies. I read in <u>Discovery Magazine</u> some time ago that scientists have measured such fields with a human subject, a vacuum tube and a powerful voltmeter with high resistance. A certain Dr. Burr spent decades studying such fields from human, animals, and even trees. The "fields" were always found in each of these forms. His results were verified by other scientists many times. If we would only seriously consider such findings, it would open future fields of study for science in the 21st century. Particularly as it may influence radical changes in medicine. Patient healing by bio-feed back is just one such possibility. One my rightly say that biochemistry is in the same infant stage as physics was before the reality of the quantum theory.

Margaret . . .

As I have indicated before, it is logical to assume that the nature and purpose of human existence is to learn and develop into a higher form of existence. The more we learn the more freedom we can enjoy. Perhaps this is the real meaning of Christ injunction to "Lay up treasures in heaven."To many the injunction has more rational meaning than the "heavens" promised my most religions. Conversely, if we fail for various reasons to improve are minds and bodies we are doomed to "hell" and must repeat our lives in another time as promised by the prospects of reincarnation. Or as the epitaph written of Benjamin Franklin:

"Lies here, food for worms, but the work shall not be lost. For it will appear once more in a new and elegant edition revised and converted. Surely it is easier to believe that the man writes his own "penalties" and that it builds, in its infinite memory, its "hell" or "heaven" out of its own experience and out of thought it has aroused within and externally with others."

Since the "fields" are no physical one might be expected to be unaffected by extremes of heat and cold, without a body it would not require food, water, or oxygen. Thus without effort or discomfort the soul would be a space explorer at the death of the body. To many this would be a better alternative than the "eternal rest" promised by the churches.

As we have already seen, many thinkers in the East recognize that Karma and the doctrine of a rebirth the only reasonable way to explain why many souls are destined to exist in this life in crippled, diseased deformed bodies, or in insane asylums. Their belief is that in the next existence they will be made whole again.

Stanley . . .

"In essence then, our state in our present lives, whether good or bad, is the result of what we have done or learned in a previous existence, and what we do in this life, will determine conditions in the future."

Clay . . .

"It might be of interest to know that many distinguished historical figures as Plato, Pythagoras, Virgil, Ovid, Shopenhower, Edison, Henry Ford, and General George Patton believed in a pre-existence. But Christian leaders still regard the subject as not fit for discussion. This is strange because Christians believe that Jesus Christ existed, as the Son of God, before he incarnated in human form.

"Again we know that the soul can exist in space apart from a body and that its purpose is to learn and gather experience. And it can do this despite the constant turnover of the materials of the brain and we can continue to do so anywhere without a body. Two thousand years ago, Jesus Christ taught that we are "children of God." And that the kingdom of God is within you."Luke XV11; 21. Perhaps this was the only way he could explain, to the uninitiated, electromagnetic fields or what we now understand as modern physics."

Margaret...

Many people today believe that science is ahead of religion and religion is out of step and irrelevant. But, I understand electromagnetic fields, and I believe I do, then there is strong reason to believe that Science is catching up with religion and offering experimental proof to support what faith has known for centuries, that the Essence or God is the organizer, the prime mover and the basis for the mind/electromagnetic energy that supplies direction for everything as it relates to the human body and the DNA is the messenger. Thus, religion can claim to be far ahead of science.

Clay . . .

If indeed religion teaches that man has an immortal "Soul" independent of the perishable body but cannot explain what "soul" really is. Modern research into electromagnetic energy fields offers a new and much more rational explanation.

Ernie . . .

And you might add that there currently exists a strange dichotomy here. While well-meaning Church leaders discuss the finer points of ancient doctrine, the 21st century research into the properties of mind and thought can be very helpful to religion. The potential for new insights into the nature of prayer might offer more effective faith healing and offer a powerful reason for going to church. In theory religion should be the dominant science with the other branches of science complimenting it. All of this is possible, but first, religious leaders must study more science and learn as much as possible about modern scientific research about modern "physics." In short the theologian should cease to think of modern science as an enemy and welcome a new alliance between the two.

Richard . . .

"It cannot be emphasized enough that if religious leaders would become more familiar with the current thinking of theoretical physics, including the quantum mechanics discoveries made during the first half of this century, they will find it much easier to accommodate the new science of tomorrow. As an example, cosmologists have now proven that planets exist around distant stars. This proof will doubtless lead to the conclusion that other life forms in the universe do exist. The cosmology that has proven that planets exist around distant stars, may very well prove one day soon, other dimensions in the universe beyond the ones we are so familiar with. To say nothing of the fact that someday soon science may prove that UFO's actually exist and may come from dimensions unknown to us. What will theology do then?"

Jessica . . .

"I find myself in agreement with Richard. If one follows his views about the potential scientific proof of other dimensions, then the theologian can rightly say that the biblical saying, "In my Father's house there are many mansions," has a ring of plausible scientific truth about it. What causes me greater concern is the direction my field of microbiology is taking. I believe the experimental advances being made have profound implications on the belief systems of mankind. A good example might be the amazing advances by our scientists in the area of recumbent DNA experiments. Many say that it will be possible, within a decade following the new millennium, to clone human beings. Then, through genetic manipulation we can be anyone or any thing we choose to become. We will become as Gods. Jurassic Park will become a reality. Rogue scientists around the world, with their own agendas, are currently taking snippets of one species and combining them with another species. Who is wise enough, as an individual, or as a group, to guide, monitor and bring this work to the world for the greater good for all mankind?"

Clay . . .

"As far as I am concerned, religious leaders, philosophers, physicists should stop thinking modern knowledge is evil and welcome it as an ally. The next millennium should be very exciting for new ideas that will truly permit the soul of man to soar. We should be doing our best to become prepared for it."

Clay was not sure by the vacant stares of uncommon silence that his pontifical speech left any kind of favorable impression upon his newly found friends. He did know that he suddenly felt emotionally drained.

The time was now approaching nine forty-five p.m. It was Stanley who reminded the guests that past dialogue meetings ended at eleven p.m., and it was his intent to adhere to that schedule. He further indicated that he was highly pleased with the trajectory of their progress to this juncture and that he was now prepared to take the group into further mind-bending territory. He explained that he would like to spend the remaining time discussing relevancy of the "New " physics in the coming age. The group began to stir as one, in an attempt to correctly position themselves in their seats. Most reached for another sip of wine.

Stanley could not help but notice, in particular, the sudden rigidity of Richard's body. He looked like a man bracing for a frontal blow. His apprehension was for good cause because Stanley was about to put him on center stage.

Stanley . . .

"Richard, we are very honored to have a person of your reputation and respect in our presence this evening. As a long time friend and admirer, I know you have a tendency to remain quite detached in a group setting, but I would now like for you to provide us with your views on where physicists are in its current understanding of matter and the universe. I've even heard that a Grand Unified Theory of matter is possible in the immediate future. The key to the universe, no less. Wasn't it Sherlock Holmes who said something to the effect that, "When you eliminate the impossible, what remains is the truth?" "I can't help but believe that the latest understandings of physics will coalesce and help bridge the existing gap between science and religion. It just might be there exists a power assist from the

"New Age" physics that the general public should know more about. Even a sophomoric understanding of the new physics just might give us the anchor we have been looking for to make sense of life's crushing challenges that lie ahead in the coming millennium."

It was strange to see Richard rise slowly, with hands to his chin, as if he was about to launch into deep thought. It was evident he was more comfortable standing and moving about as a professor in a large lecture hall. Visible tension filled the air as if electric wires were everywhere in the room.

Richard looked at Jessica. She caught his eye and that wasn't good. He knew that having information at his fingertips was one thing; getting a group of intellectuals to understand such a difficult subject matter was another. He didn't want to embarrass anyone by speaking beneath them, nor did he want to be too technical by speaking in a physicist's jargon. He began in a slow, halting voice.

Richard . . .

"I apologize for being so reticent in withholding verbal comment to any great extent. I guess I have been too impressed by the honesty and intensity of your varied points of view to get too involved. Many of the points raised this evening have a direct bearing on mankind's understanding of his place in the universe. The average person does not have time to spend immersed in such philosophical thought, but he should, even if he learns only a few of the salient views physics is engaged in.

"As the 20th century dawned, it ushered in a plethora of new ideas that shattered many of our notions of reality which stood unchallenged for centuries. Many such long held beliefs were swept away. Physics was compelled to rethink models of reality. Two profound theories rocked the very foundations of our basic understanding of ourselves and the universe we inhabit. One was

153

the Quantum Theory, which uncovered the strange, almost mystical realm of the micro world. The other major advance was the Theory of Relativity, which combined space and time on the macro scale."

"A great difficulty people have in attempting to understand modern physics is in trying to fit abstract concepts encountered in these theories into common sense framework constructs.

"It is understandable that people have a psychological need to reduce things into simple, easily conceived images. I will try to make this point clear in a few moments when I discuss the scientifically proven Heisenberg principle of the duality of a particle. It is called the Uncertainty Principle. This is where a wave and a particle, and at the same time. They are like " Jekyll and Hyde" particles. The Uncertainty Principle has such profound meaning that this one principle has changed the potential of all science, including philosophy and religion. It all begins with our understanding of the micro world. The atom is a strange world that literally leaves our head spinning. Let me give you one quick example.

"Perhaps the strangest particles of all in the micro world are neutrinos. These strange almost mystical objects have no mass at all, and travel at the speed of light! They are nearly oblivious to solid objects. They can pass right through the earth without touching anything! A billion of them are going through you and me as we sit here. They pass through lead, planets, galaxies, without touching anything. They come as close as anything imaginable to being pure . . . nothing!"

"Astrophysics is another science where common sense reality is shattered. Especially gravity waves. Gravity waves have been described as "ripples" in space itself. They are not made of matter. They do have measurable energy and motion, however. One could say they are just rippling emptiness and them to can zip through anything.

"Gravity waves were discovered and made known by George Scoot in 1992. He and his colleagues at Berkeley had conducted the research from a satellite launch that scanned the heavens. Stephen Hawking called their discovery the "Scientific Discovery of the Century, if not all time.""

"Mathematical formulae have made such discoveries possible, just as you were discussing earlier. It describes the zany particles and they have proved logical and have a sense of beauty and elegance as well. Still what the formulas describe is bizarre. Black holes are an example and they have been discovered. Almost everyone has heard of black holes, and I hope to say a few words about them as well in a few minutes. But for the moment, just know that their immense, incredible power drives the universe and perhaps more."

Clay . . .

"This leads to the mystical, religious appeal you were discussing as well. But we must keep in mind that despite the wonders and mystical qualities of the "New Physics," a great deal of modem technology was brought into being by our present understanding of these difficult conceptual ideas." Ernest . . .

"I would like to digress for just a second to make another point that bears heavily upon our past discussion about the scientific method of experimental discoveries and new theories. I suppose it is really a philosophical issue. I'm not seeking an answer at this point, but it is something we all should hold fast in the back of minds as our dialogues continue. The issue is this. I find it quite surprising that discoveries are often made on the grounds of observations that have been known for sometime. For example, Copernicus, Newton, Einstein, Darwin, Heisenberg, Crick and Watson all made significant discoveries from inferences from know facts that awaited their exceptional, intuitive powers.

"Their discoveries or predictions were realized only years after the significance of the discoveries were made. They were reconsideration of prior knowledge, in a new way. It is as if the new concept was offering itself for discovery, just waiting until we could open our minds. We still have no clue of how discovery comes about. How does this understanding come about? The question may be asked, how can things not yet understood become capable of being understood?

"What or who guides the discovery from potential thought to discovery? We have described the scientific method, but that is a pursuit- a process, not sudden enlightenment- creation if you will. But, as I said in the beginning, we should probably keep that in mind as the evening draws to a close."

Richard . . .

"As I mentioned earlier, quantum theory and relativity are the corner stones of 20th century physics. The Quantum Theory offers a capstone for our current knowledge of molecular, atomic, nuclear, and sub atomic domains. The theory of relativity provides us with the current understanding of space, time, and gravity. The down sizing of distances and speed is recognized as the Lorentz Fitzgerald contraction effect, put forth by George Fitzgerald and Hendrik Lorentz and is a direct result of the theory of relativity. The effect is present near light speed, but it has been proven in the laboratory. The difficulty presented to us in our common sense thinking is that things and objects must, physically, be somewhere. We believe that atoms and particles must exist, somewhere. Our bodies are made up of such particles and therefore particles occupy a place of definite location, since a particle to exist must be somewhere. However, quantum physics dictates that this is not so. The reason for this seemingly impossible paradox is called the Heisenberg Uncertainty Principle. I mentioned it a few moments ago. The principle is named after the German physicist, Werner

Heisenberg who was a major contributor to the Quantum Theory in the 1920's.

"The theory states, in principle, that it is impossible to know the position and the motion of a particle at the same time. Whenever an observer seeks to find an electron, it can be found somewhere, but what we cannot observe, or know, is both the position and motion at the same moment. Now, here is where the incomprehensible, or unbelievable aspects enter. But it is a fact. No matter what ingenious methods we attempt, the very act of observing the electrons location interferes in an unpredictable way with the motion of the particle.

"Now again, what does all of this seemingly nonsense, really mean? Essentially it means that the observers, you and I, as we go about our daily lives, by our very existence, are active participants in all of nature, in all creation, if you will. Again, it has been experimentally proven that electrons can "tunnel" through obstacles and experimental devices by vanishing on one side and then instantly, reappearing on the far side of the barrier obstacle. This is weird. But it is the world of quantum physics, where the aspect of a particle being everywhere at once is nearly impossible to grasp. "Ghost" particles choosing all potential pathways only to emerge as a real particle when we observe it. Only mathematics and eloquent equations can reveal the subtleties involved. The uncertainty principal is such a foreign place. A place where other worldly things take place that we may never know its true understanding. We are like children in our true understanding of it.

"Let me now hasten on to just a few thoughts about the Theory of Relativity. It may illustrate a little clearer why it is that the stranger discoveries of science take us far, far afield of what we understand the universe, and our place in it to be.

"The Theory of Relativity, predicts distances expanding or shrinking, depending on the movement of the observer. It was proposed by Einstein in 1915. It includes gravitational effects. It is also geometry at work in empty space and time. But it is not the familiar geometry because it is warped or curved space and time. And it can be bent, distorted, shrunk and stretched. This was proven by observation of a total eclipse of the sun. It was observed that a slight curvature or bending of light by the sun's space warp could be determined.

"The significant point to this finding is that gravity bends space, and space can change or move. So particles are fuzzy and ghost like and so is space. A good word to use is "foam like." "Place" has no meaning as a common sense reality and the role of consciousness in the physical universe. Normal is not normal.

"Gravity also produces time warps. It has been proven that time moves faster at the top of a building on the lowest floors. The effect is very small, but it can be measured. In addition, on a clock placed on aircraft and rockets at high altitudes, time runs faster in space than on earth.

"All of us are familiar with the weird effect gravity has on stars several times larger than our own sun. It results in a "black hole" in space. A black hole is where neutron stars shrink in a time warp and curves space around it. Astronomers have discovered many "black holes" using the powerful Hubble telescope that is parked in deep space.

"So, these surrealistic effects I've been talking about, Quantum Physics, Gravity, and General Relativity have profound effects of our understanding of who and what we are. Behind them lay nether worlds that distort our reality and shift our perspectives of our known universe. Just as important are the questions, why and how did we get here, and perhaps even, where are we going?"

Ernest . . .

"It seems to me that what you are saying is that these concepts produce the possibility that the creation of the universe came from almost nothing at all. Well, practically nothing. It almost smacks of the biblical creation, exnihilo."

Margaret . . .

"To a scientist, or philosopher "almost" leaves a great deal of explaining to do.

Especially scientific inquiry. All unknowns amount to questions of "why." So, one is left with the domain of the philosopher and the theologian. Religion teaches that man has an immortal soul, but it has a difficult time explaining what a "soul" is. However, modern research offers a new rational way of explaining it. For instance consciousness and memory survive the constant changes of the material brain, and therefore must be separate from it and can survive death. It would be a great deal of comfort to individuals and families if religious leaders would explain as much to the bereaved."

Jessica . . .

"That's a good point, Margaret, and there is more good news. Science has also shown that the human body is under the control of an electromagnetic field. The mind can produce electrical changes in the field. Science research has produced startling evidence that the mind, the "soul" are realities, separate from the body. So, it is then possible to explain this new scientific proof to a disenchanted younger generation that is urgently seeking some new understanding of reality and purpose of life. Surely this is a more rational, exciting, and appealing prospect than the insipid dogmatic promise of heaven or hell cherished by most religions."

Richard could not help but feel a warm glow from the raptured attention he was getting. Nevertheless, he did not want to go much further in this vein because the thought processes of this subject can numb the mind. He did not have to worry because Clay raised a questioning gesture with his finger signaling a question for Richard.

Clay . . .

"Richard, you are to be commended for making such difficult subject matter understandable to a lay person such as me. Your thoughts lead me to return to a central question. Why don't religious leaders openly discuss, or think creatively about these gifts science has given us? They tend to exclude them as if they have no virtue of their own. It is as if the naked insignificance of man has paralyzed our imagination of such gifts as something too dreadful to contemplate and therefore should be ignored. It is a sad commentary that modern research offers no support for fringe beliefs, but as we have seen, it cannot only offer support for the great religions, it can also explain them in a new way, to a new generation."

Clay . . .

"Most of the world's past creation myths start with some type beginning of creation. Curiously enough, they all state some type of variation of "Let there be light." Light appears from the darkness of the deep, to paraphrase the biblical beginning of Genesis. Without light, the earth as we know it would cease to exist. As Jessica well understands, all chemical reactions rely on electrons and photons interacting with one another. Thus, without light, chemistry itself would not occur. I guess I should yield to Jessica for a better answer, but that is my understanding."

Jessica . . .

"You're on the right track. It is light that has such a vital role in the subatomic processes that could not have been there during the formative development of the universe. The presence of light energy and its properties for formation of matter appears to aid the biblical, "Let there be light" And subsequently, "Let there be earth."

Stanley . . .

"I see what you mean. From what you have just said, it is now possible for religious leaders to take this scientific knowledge and draw meaningful conclusions to track biblical text."

Richard . . .

"Permit me to be rather technical for a moment. Although the slope may be just a bit slippery to follow, it should be of benefit for us to make the brief effort. It should lead us to the same point of view.

"The latest models of atomic structure dictate that each atom has a number of negatively charged electrons. Encircling each atomic core are positively charged protons and neutrons. When excited by external light waves of the right frequencies, some electrons may jump to new positions. Some are closer, some farther away from the core center. Curiously enough some may instantly move to lower position. But, no electron can occupy the same space as another. This is called the Pauli Exclusion Principle. It serves the purpose of preventing them from all falling into the depths of an atom.

"Here is the final important part of this exciting drama. Each time an electron moves to a closer spot, it emits a photon or particle of light. Thus, light as we know it radiates and is

161

absorbed each time the transfer takes place. All chemical reactions depend on electron and photon transactions. Therefore, without light, chemistry is impossible. You could say, that is why God said, "Let there be light."

Ernie . . .

"Religious leaders one would think, would be attempting to embrace such scientific proofs and bring them into the forefront of biblical teachings. After all, I have heard nothing yet that would exclude any spiritual Deity. The psalmists have often told us of the wonders God has given us. The heavens, the moon, the stars, all of nature's grand plan. Wasn't it Genesis that spoke of darkness upon the deep? God said, "Let there be light," and there was light! It remains logical and much more appealing to the modern generation, that the "Big Bang "theory could be the birth of such light. The mystery disappears."

Jessica . . .

"I think we biologists have the same problem with physics and cosmology, as with religion. As Richard has pointed out, the exploration of the atom forced physicists to revise their general theory and thinking about the nature of the physical reality in a totally different way.

"In biology, the discovery of the double helix by Crick and Watson has not led to a universal law or theory about our true nature and place in the universe. They have not recognized how the basic biological phenomena of how organisms that are wounded in some way regenerate to the exact structures they had before. Nor is there any clear understanding of how the egg forms the organism.

"What is required to find solutions to these problems is to rid ourselves of past dogmas, old paradigms and look to new concepts. I hope that in the next few decades of the new millennium we will be able to do just that.

"It is my view that the direction that will be taken is to broaden, on a conceptual basis, the recent developments in modem science. An interplay with science, religion and philosophy, if you will. The adoption of such a holistic approach should produce wonders in medicine by forcing us to cure the whole person by finding the specific mechanism of disease control, rather than curing the symptoms of disease.

"Another example, if I understand Richard correctly, quantum theory states that we play an integral part in the universe's existence. As observers, we are able to manipulate all events in the universe. So, it would be my view that this mystical new reality of physics and astronomy should be appealing to those of a religious or philosophical bent."

Clay . . .

"Richard, permit me to ask a very elementary question. If the Big Bang theory is correct and star formation resulted from gravity coalescing such matter over a period of billions and billions of years, then all of us in this room are made-up of stardust. Is that not true? For some reason, when I look to the heavens at night I like the idea that we are stardust, created in a super nova explosion billions of years ago. So my other question then is, am I really billions of years old?

Richard . . .

"Ha! Ha! In a way of speaking you are billions of years old, since over time, matter is energy and can never be lost or gained, you can say that all of us are part of the beginning of the universe. I suppose this mystical appeal of the new physics and astronomy have a religious or philosophical bent for many people. "

163

Clay . . .

" I have another quick question. If gravity within black holes gobbles up planets, stars, galaxies, where does matter go that is eaten? Does it give birth to other universes? It leaves us with a universe with holes in it. The holes must lead somewhere. "

Richard . . .

"That is a very interesting point about where does the matter go once entering a black hole, There is a great deal of thinking that posits that if one could safely negotiate a black hole without being stretched thin as spaghetti, then one would indeed exit out into another place, dimensions or as it has been called wormholes in space. A wormhole is a physical existence in space where science fiction writers like to give faster than light speed to their rocket or space ships. The voyages of the Star Trek Enterprise make great use of such potentials."

Margaret . . .

"Evidently Richard, what you have been saying is that the macroscopic and microscopic worlds are intimately interwoven."

Richard . . .

"Yes, when someone looks at an atom, the atom jumps in a fashion that can't be determined. But the good news is that man has a place in the grand scheme of things. In other words the uncertainty is not necessarily fundamental. A deeper level of a description of reality must exist."

Ernie . . .

"So, when an observation is made, the quantum field progresses through stages, through the equipment, our sense organs, or our brain through our consciousness?"

Richard . . .

"We can state this proposition in another way, the vibrating energy patterns which have no independent reality of the whole entirety, which includes the observer. We must consider the fact that all matter and energy everywhere must have a unified existence. Symmetry could be the operative word. Symmetry is related to harmony and form. It remains the same unchanged. A sphere is symmetric for example. Science now believes all forces exist to permit nature to maintain the cohesiveness of all things in the universe. These symmetries are known collectively as Gauge symmetry."

Richard began to grow in his confidence that he had escaped thus far, and perhaps for the evening, any questions that might relate to his Grand discovery. It was not to last long, however. And it would be his friend Stanley who would, unknowingly uncover his facade. Richard's pulse quickened and his heart jumped as Stanley spoke.

Stanley

"Well, my friends, the time is now twenty-five minutes until eleven. I believe we've come a long way toward unraveling some of the great mysteries and problems left unattended and unsolved as we enter the next millennium. I also believe we have progressed enough in our overall understanding of science to ask ourselves the ultimate scientific question. Will the greatest discovery in the history of mankind, the Grand Unified Theory of all nature, and matter, ever be solved? And if it is, does it hold promise for all mankind? Are civilizations prepared at this time and juncture to deal with such a profound advancement in science? Will it bring us to the feet of God, or something beyond?"

Stanley pointed his outstretched hands in the direction of Richard, much as a circus ringmaster introduces some extraordinary, talented act. Richard took a quick sip of wine and plunged straight ahead with his commentary.

Richard...

"For nearly half a century particle physicists and other theoreticians have been hard at work, and with startling success, I might add, in furthering our understanding of the atom. However, it has been a long, long journey. A journey of nearly 2500 years, to be more exact. It is believed that it all began with the Greek philosopher Demarcus, who smelled bread baking and theorized that a prime, invisible particle might contain a building block of all nature. He called the particle the A-tom, "That which cannot be cut.

"Many of the elementary particles known today were discovered in the course of just such attempts to fill out pleasing, but incomplete constructs. We now stand at the threshold of the 21st century, unlocking the final secrets of the atom and the universe. An exciting rebirth of human understanding is at hand. We have, or soon will possess the startling theory of everything. Knowledge to jump-start the "New Age" The existing Universe is the answer, but what is the question.

"The question is, "Is it possible that all physical laws can be unified into a simple, mathematical law? "The Holy Grail" of how and why the universe is as it is, and why?

"It is not very interesting to explore much of what science knows about matter, but I feel everyone should grasp elementary facets of this knowledge in order not to be shocked and dismayed when science unveils this awesome finding. I won't try to overwhelm you with the daunting mathematics and formulas, but permit me to give you a very short dissertation of my views of where we are and where we are going.

"No attempt to explain the universe, either by scientists, philosophers, or theologians, can be considered successful unless it accounts for the coming into existence and going out of existence of matter. How do we reconcile a timeless God and his laws, yet a God whose universe changes and evolves? Perhaps it is possible that God didn't create the universe and just sat back, in an easy chair to see what man would make of it. Perhaps he did however, provide immutable laws for man and permit him to unveil them. To date several theoretical and experimental developments occurred that encouraged the idea that all unknown forces could be unveiled. Collectively these forces are known as Grand unified theories, or GUT's. The fundamental forces of nature, the weak, strong, and electromagnetic forces. This pioneer work originally done by Pakistani physicists Abdus Salam, physicists Steven Weinberg and the university of Texas, and Harvard physicists Sheldon Glashow. Let's take a closer look at the particles and the processes they were working with that led to these force fields.

"Particle physics is the bone yard where scientists study the interactions of what is described as "elementary" particles. There are many of these, among which are protons, neutrons, electrons, and others. The scientists use huge machines called particle accelerators, like the one at Fermi Laboratory, outside Chicago, Illinois, to smash particles into one another in an attempt to duplicate, on a small scale, the interactions that might have occurred at the time of the big bang.

"What science is eager to find is a unified theory which will explain all of the laws of nature in one set of equations. There are just two forces that are of importance to us. These are gravity and the electromagnetic force. Gravity, as all of us know it makes things fall on earth, permits us to walk without falling [most of the time], holds stars together, and plays a part in how the universe will expand or perhaps, collapse.

"The electromagnetic force is electricity and magnetism. Electromagnetism determines how light, radio waves, and other fields are produced and propagate. It governs the actions of electrons with the atom and the way they join together to make molecules. It is vital to chemistry and hence life, since living things are made up of complex chemical molecules.

'The other two forces, electro strong and weak, affect the behavior of other particles such as neutrons and protons. They determine how the nucleoli of atoms stick together and the way a neutron decays into a proton, plus an electron.

"The description I have just given you is the accepted model of the particle world of the proton and neutron. Although I must add for final clarity, that the neutrons and protons themselves contain much smaller units, called quarks. I will mercifully spare you of further agony, for now, at any rate, of any additional atomic breakdown.

"The weak, strong, and electromagnetic forces behave differently in the universe as we know it. Long ago, perhaps 15 billion years ago, at the time of the Big Bang, these forces were essentially the same as they are now.

"In 1949 mathematician Kurt Godel found a solution to Einstein's general relativity equations that indicates the universe is rotating and also implies that time travel is possible. This sparked a more than passing attention by the physicists and science fiction writers. Later, there were other models, supersymmetry, and superstring theories. These theories are speculative, but build on what is already known. Most good theories are verifiable with the accepted rules of scientific inquiry. Perhaps for the first time, we may be at a point where such theories may never be experimentally tested or verified. This may not be so as I hope to illustrate in just a few moments.

"Supersymmetry embraces a host of all the known particles and their antiparticles. It does two other important things. It

168

accounts for the quantum theory of gravity and offers an accounting for dark matter or missing mass that remains unknown, This missing mass may exceed ninety percent of what is needed to fill the known universe."

Stanley . . .

"Isn't that the way it has always been? The bearer of change or new ideas is rarely accepted, despite the comprehensive elegance of the Superstring and superstring theories present a daunting problem that has always existed. Even scientists with new theories and ideas are rarely greeted with open arms. Their theories must be tested and observed to meet the observer's prediction. Current particle accelerators cannot produce energy collisions powerful enough to confirm or deny this theory."

Richard . . .

"That may or may not be true. Other theories may offer more promise, such as the Superstring theory. Let's talk for a moment about Superstrings. It presents a description of all known forces, and gravity as well. It too is a theory of everything, all particles, space and time. Everything!

"The big surprise is that it requires ten dimensions: nine of space and one of time. We live in three observable dimensions. That is our only reality. Most of the matter created during the Big Bang may be completely alien to us, unknown and unseen by our eyes and literally beyond our physical reality and experience.

"Where are the other dimensions?? They are all intertwined in a point, according to this theory. The particles we have discovered are vibrations of the strings in an infinite variety of vibrating possibilities. One might envisage the potentials of a violin.

169

"The discovery by physicists of anti- matter with an electric charge opposite that which constructs our reality, cannot exist with known matter. If they ever collided with their positive matter counterpart, they would annihilate one another. On the Marco level it wouldn't matter much. But, any relatively large chunk of matter colliding with anti matter would result in an explosion of major catastrophic proportions. Could it be that the existence of anti-matter might lead to unknown, unseen dimensions and universes as well? On that sexy thought I will end my exploration of the exotic theories captivating theoretical physicists today."

Richard was emotionally drained, but was able to maintain his professional composure as he sagged into his chair next to Jamie. He was finished and would say no more about the "Holy Grail," the Grand Unified Theory. He had said enough to satisfy Stanley's charge to him. The guests appeared to understand most of his treatises. But he still knew what they didn't. "GUTS" had been solved and it was he who did it. Stanley rose to bring an end to the dialogues. His secret was safe, for the evening at least, safely tucked away in the briefcase at Stedman Woods.

Stanley . . .

"It's just a few minutes before eleven o'clock. I promised you we would adhere to past tradition and end our dialogue discussion at that time. Before we conclude, I want to make an attempt to "down load" a brief summary of what I believe we have said this evening. But, first I want to dispose of a few housekeeping chores.

"First, I would like to thank all of the guests for joining us this evening. I hope Margaret, Richard, Clay, and Ernie, have enjoyed the evening. I appreciate your contributions to our discussions. All of you have added immeasurably to what I believe was one of the most engaging, intelligent pursuits we've ever had. The millennium is just around the corner and like you, we are concerned about that is relevant baggage to carry into the

170

21st century. I trust you will go back to your respective places and remember with a greater sense of appreciation for what we regulars attempt to accomplish doing these gatherings. Don't be surprised if you see in print much of what you all have said. Several of us are writing books or scientific papers on the subjects we have discussed. I'm sure you will be given an opportunity for peer review and credits where appropriate.

"I would be remiss if I did not acknowledge the efforts of our hostess Jamie

Harrington. She certainly has gone to Herculean efforts to create an atmosphere conducive to the strenuous, mind awakening thoughts put forth this evening. The spaghetti dinner was par excellence, as usual

"Now comes the hard part. I have exactly three minutes to offer my summary. I was taking notes which I will have typed and sent to each of you. But, for now, here is my best recollection of tonight's salient points. If anyone strongly disagrees with my conclusions, write to me after you have had the opportunity to read my notes of the meeting.

"For tens of thousands of years man has slowly, but inextricably, produced a dazzling array of accomplishments though human thought. This evening our challenge was to see if we are coming to an end of comprehensive thought as science, philosophy and religion appear out of step with what society is willing, or capable of accepting from any of these disciplines if they continue to stand alone from one another.

"We have given examples of this grid lock. Science won't, or can't keep mankind safe from the alarms, rumors, demons abroad in the land. It creates through manipulation of technology an aura of self-assurance that only destroys our long sought after assurance and certainty in a world where there is no assurance of anything. Especially when we learned this evening that quantum theory says we, as observers, are partly responsible for all of the

171

observable behavior in our environment and in the heavens above. Most of us don't want that responsibility and are much too eager to turn it over to others, hoping our best interest will be taken care of. It is a false hope.

"In the twentieth century physics has led us to the view that the universe is no longer a machine made up of separate objects, but is an all encompassing whole. A conglomeration of interconnected relationships and infinite possibilities that include the human observer, in a very involved way.

"The new science provides the rational approach to the nature of things that can change the behavior in a positive way. It can provide the foundation for improved attitudes and values that we will surely need in the next millennium.

"It may be fair to say that Science has become like a talisman. Perhaps we may never be able to completely understand matter through the workings of a grand unified theory, but maybe it will be possible through some heretofore, unknown principle, perhaps the way physicists attacked the unraveling of the atom, we might uncover the existence of laws of nature that determine human behavior and nature in a new social theory.

"It is impossible to forecast where these approaches might lead, but interdisciplinary joining such as religion, philosophy, and sociology will come to understand and appreciate the mutual benefits of joining together for the overall benefit of mankind. It will be a new day dawning when we are able to discard the hand-waving denial of modem advances.

"Perhaps we will then come to recognize the existence of laws of nature that determine human conduct and human revolution. We will then develop the ability and capacity to better understand human nature.

"These brave, imaginative leaps provide us with beliefs in what our senses tell us and what philosophers, poets and religious leaders have known for a thousand years. That is the fundamental reality in our world is not to be found. Finally, there is probably no answer to why or what existed before the big bang, before time began. We believe it started from a singularity. A unique state. There is no answer to why such a state existed in the first place. It is probably a matter of where scientific explanation breaks down and God takes over."

Richard . . .

"Is this what astrophysics Robert Jastrow says, [He has scaled the mountain of ignorance? he is about to conquer the highest peak; as he pulls himself over the final rock, he is greeted by a band of theologians who have been sitting there for centuries]"

No one doubted that the evening had been very special, almost communion like. Jessica and Richard received the most attention as the guests filed out the door.

Richard was the last to leave, lingering only long enough to ask Jessica if it would be presumptuous on his part to ask if she would have dinner with him sometime within the next few days His body shuddered noticeably when Jessica smiled softly, drew near, and kissed him on both, blushing cheeks. She whispered in his ear that she would be delighted to join him for dinner and would anxiously await his call.

Richard was nearly beside himself as he tried to contain a flood of emotions, most strangely forgotten in the dim past. It had been more than a year and a half since he had enjoyed the company of a female. His nostrils still contained the alluring traces of the buttercup like scent of her perfume. He literally sucked in the night air, as he opened the door to his car. He glanced back to the doorway to see Jessica's long, graceful hand,

173

fluttering a final ending to an unforgettable evening. The darkness hid his Cheshire like grin and eyes that sparkled like newly polished diamonds.

It was nearly midnight when Richard pulled into the long driveway leading to Stedman Woods. The light from a nearly full moon cast eerie reflections through the giant sycamore trees lining the approach to his home. Somehow he felt a sense of comfort that Jeremy had left several lights burning throughout the house. For an instant his mind flashed back to an evening such as this when he arrived home late from his first high school date. His parents had stayed up late, too late for his promised time of return. He had been granted permission to drive the family car and that fact alone gave his parents great pause. They were anxious and less than impressed with his lame excuse that he had run out of gas. It was not a very inventive excuse. But they were happy that he had returned safe, and the matter was quickly dropped. Nevertheless, ever since that time, his father treated Richard with not too subtle degrees of regret.

Sadly, now, both of his loving parents were gone. A terrible feeling of loneliness made his entire body shiver. It registered on his heart that he was now, alone. "Loneliness must be the greatest burden a man can carry," he thought. Upon reflection, Richard had been feeling lonely and depressed since his discovery. Maybe! Just maybe! Jessica Harrington can make me feel alive again.

He quickly forced his mind to draw a dark curtain over such thoughts. Upstairs, in his briefcase was where his future lay. It contained a gift for mankind. A gift unimagined in the course of human history. He was to be the benefactor. Fantasy was about to become reality.

Richard went immediately to the kitchen, opened the refrigerator door, and poured a glass of milk to heat in the microwave oven. Through the years, warm milk had comforted him. Especially when he had spent long hours, and sometimes days, studying, in the research lab, or after arduous periods of intense thinking. The night's activity had been one of the latter.

Jeremy was asleep upstairs. Richard smiled a crooked, but plastic smile, as he read a brief note Jeremy had scrawled on a note pad, and placed on the kitchen table next to a bowl of brightly colored artificial fruit. It read, "Richard, in the refrigerator, on the second shelf, next to the condiments, I fixed a roast beef sandwich for you, with all of the trimmings. It's even on sourdough bread, your favorite. Bon Appetite!"

Richard was tempted to eat one half of the sandwich. Jeremy was right. It was his favorite sandwich. A slight tinge of hunger passed over him, despite the delicious, filling spaghetti dinner. "Not tonight," he thought. "If I eat something this late at night, I will never get to sleep. And I need a good night's rest. " Richard would be meeting the attorney, Ernest Flownery, most of the day, working on matters of his deceased father's estate. And he had promised Stanley he would have dinner with him tomorrow night. He slowly sipped the warm milk. His head was low, resting on his elbows. Suddenly, without warning, a feeling of total dread came over him. The hair on the back of his neck began to bristle It was like an unseen presence. The same feeling a person might get when his subconscious attempts to alert him to the fact that he is not alone in an otherwise vacant room. Jeremy was upstairs asleep. He had already checked on that. He looked over his shoulder and around the kitchen area. No one was visible. He now felt an extreme urge to sleep and to dream. His acute mind attempted to break through the veil of uneasiness, but to no avail. Somehow he knew that a restful sleep would not come easy this night. It was going to be another night of dreams of lights, and silhouettes of beings beckoning to him. He turned out the lights downstairs and trudged upstairs to his bedroom like a slave going to the dungeon.

175

CHAPTER 11

Day Six
Richard's home
Morning After Jessica's Party

Richard wanted to sleep late on the morning following Jessica's dinner party. Two enduring thoughts had haunted him during the night. First, there were the ever-present visions of the beautiful Jessica. She had crept into his dreams during the early morning hours like a cheetah stalking its prey. Even upon waking he wanted to reach back to hold on to her image. He wanted to dwell on the beauty of her countenance, her boundless energy that infected all those around her. But, it was her dark limped eyes that spoke of . . . things! He looked into the abyss of her eyes and found danger, mysteries, companionship, even lust, lurking there The second aberration that haunted him during the night was the prospect of finishing his project. He knows he must soon immerse himself in the pursuit of completing the write up of his discovery of the elusive, mystical, and exotic monopoly. Indeed felt he was cheating himself lately by not giving the matter his complete attention lately. He decided to devote the entire afternoon to the subject, but first he wanted to rid his mind and body of sudden, awful feeling of dread. "Why am I feeling such anxiety," he thought? In a few months he would be world famous, pursued by the news hungry press and his peers.

Richard also knew intuitively that something was close at hand. Something that would alter his life forever. He was certain now that the shadowy figures in his dreams were trying to tell him something. They appeared to be caressing his mind. Was it for good or ill? He did not know.

All he knew for sure was that they were beckoning, just beyond the curtain of reality. He had the creeping feeling that the entities were preparing him for some, as yet unrealized events of supreme importance. Would this be the day? Tomorrow? The day after? All he knew for certain was that it must have something to do with the onset of the morning's anxiety. The feeling was not sudden but appeared like the approach of a velvet fog. He was sure he was walking through some thick woods, being watched or stalked. The feeling had been with him for sometime, but now it was more intense, more threatening.

Richard was aware that the morning would be a hectic one. He would welcome the busy work. It would occupy his tortured mind. He decided that after breakfast, he would talk with his research team at Berkeley. He knew they had time to run another monopoly confirmation test by now, and he was anxious to learn the results. Richard was confident the data would again be positive, the same as the earlier runs. This would make five trials to date. All of the previous data trials were successful, certainly enough to convince his research team of the validity of his discovery. This brief reverie spurred him to get out of bed and into the shower. He turned the temperature nozzle to the point that would ensure the water would be slightly hotter than normal. And he intended to luxuriate in it. He scrubbed himself vigorously as if scrubbing thoroughly would cleanse away his feeling of dread. It appeared to work, temporarily.

The morning's agenda included lunch with Stanley. He looked forward to seeing him. Richard recalled the days of their youth when he would slip across town to the poorer section of Greencastle to visit his black friend. Their friendship had endured from kindergarten through high school, despite the fact that his father had moved several miles outside the city when Richard was twelve years old. After his mother died, his father had desperately wanted to leave the city and move to the solitary

178

life in the country. His search ended with the purchase of the country estate now called Stedman Woods!

Richard suddenly developed an enormous appetite for a big country breakfast. He decided to shave later and even forego dressing completely. Combing his hair and donning an all white terry cloth robe, Richard literally bounded downstairs. When he entered the kitchen, he found Jeremy had already begun preparing breakfast, busily stirring pancake batter.

"Good morning Richard! You look a lot better than you did this time yesterday."

"Thank you Jeremy. I had a wonderful evening last night at the home of Dr. Jessica Harrington. I met several new people, the dinner was wonderful, and I must admit I have never been engaged in such a stimulating discussion, excluding, of course, the many heated debates at symposiums and seminars I attend regularly. In many ways it was quite humbling, yet refreshing, to hear the passionate depths, and often, the negative opinions held by others. It was definitely unique since the dinner guests represented such varied academic backgrounds as physics, philosophy, religion, and sociology. There was even a person to represent the current attitudes of the common man. You should have been there to hear this person called Clay; he was an ordinary fellow from Texas. As a matter of fact, I think he was a rancher. But he seemed to know an awful lot about many things. He even stumped us with some of his deep questions about the relevancy of religion and philosophy. Quite honestly, he was a very strange man. I mean really spooky, in an engaging way. But, the most curious and intriguing aspect of the evening was the familiarity we could sense and feel among us, despite the fact that several of us had never met before. It was as if we had collectively experienced some strange and mystical journey together."

"Say, Mr. Jarvis, why don't I make one of my world famous omelets to compliment your pancakes?"

"Sounds wonderful to me! Two people in a kitchen at the same time never bothered me a bit.

"Tell me Richard, How did you get along with Dr. Jessica Harrington? She's quite a good looker, you know. I've had the pleasure to be in her company on only one occasion, but only. And chatting only briefly with her at the time but she was very impressive. The fact that she is not married doesn't hurt her attractiveness either."

He chuckled aloud as he continued to beat eggs into the seasoned flour mix.

"Well, hurry up man, tell me more about her. How did you two get along?"

"Strange that you should ask," Richard said with a sheepish grin. "It had been only a few days ago that we met. We only exchanged glances, as complete strangers, in the San Francisco Airport. Then a chain of impossible events happened. First, by happenstance, I met Stanley Davis, my childhood friend, at a local restaurant here in the city. He invited me to be his guest at the home of this unknown person. He told me her name, but it meant nothing to me. When she opened the door to greet us, I just stood there with my mouth wide open. Believe it or not, she nearly fainted as she dropped her wine glass. The total scene was unbelievable. We plan to have dinner tomorrow night."

"By the way Richard, when do you plan to return to the West Coast?"

Richard continued to dice onions for the omelet, but Jeremy's question caused a visible tremor to race throughout his body. He recovered quickly.

180

" Frankly, I haven't given the matter much thought. Perhaps in a week, unless something untoward causes a change of plans." A few moments of silence passed between them as they hastily continued to prepare breakfast.

Golden pancakes and a large omelet, which would be halved between them, magically appeared on a large platter at the breakfast table. Soon to follow were American fried potatoes, biscuits, milk and orange juice. Both ate as if they had been shipwrecked for weeks on a deserted island.

Richard was much calmer in spirit following their bountiful meal. They now enjoyed light conversation about random current and past events in their lives. The only disquieting moment occurred when Richard glanced at the morning paper, lying on the edge of the table. His wandering eyes paused briefly on a small caption of a front-page story. "Strange Lights Again Appear in the Night Skies Over Putnam County." He shivered! Richard diverted his eyes immediately. He was not interested in looking further into the story. It was almost as if he already knew its contents. Richard was beginning to think he knew why!

He rose from the breakfast table, politely thanked Jeremy for the wonderful breakfast, and went directly to his library study. Richard picked up the briefcase that had been his constant companion for the past few days. He was anxious to look over the first draft pages of his research findings that would soon appear in the prestigious scientific magazine, NATURE. But first he would call Jessica to confirm dinner arrangements for the next evening.

Richard sensed Jessica was genuinely happy to hear from him. He could tell by her relaxed, honey-like tones that greeted him. He seated himself comfortably in his armchair and with one leg draped lazily over one of its arms, he talked slowly and deliberately into the phone. A playful smile played across his lips. They talked for nearly an hour. They talked of their childhood. They talked about what drew them to their respective careers. Their breakthrough experiments. They discussed their longing to develop a special relationship with someone who could understand their passion to make a contribution to mankind.

For the moment, all the science, all the knowledge he had gained, the experience made him feel empty, like a butterfly that had just metamorphosed. The old became new again. He knew that he needed a companion like Jessica.

When Richard hung up the phone, he knew the moment was special. It reminded him of the time when, he finally built up enough courage to ask Shirley Miles, the most beautiful and popular girl in his sophomore class for a movie date. At that time it was an embarrassing moment for him. He had never dated before. However, and to his utter surprise, after an hour of stripping his soul bare, she eagerly agreed to be his first date. He regretted that he never actively pursued, in a more permanent way, the affection they both felt for each other. But his studies came first, leaving little time for dating or extra curricular activities. As far back as he could remember he had a thirst to read, explore, and discover new things. Especially, at the pond on Stedman Woods. To him, Stedman Woods was like "Alice's Wonderland," as he peered endlessly "Through the Looking Glass." He would find incredible treasures just waiting to behold. From that early laboratory he was led to wonder how things happened, and how things fit together. He noticed the birds, chipmunks, squirrels, and other odd creatures that crawled, scampered, and flew. He noticed the different species of trees and plants. There were moments when he felt an unearthly presence there. It would whisper to him, in his mind, he thought. It told of things he couldn't understand, then or now. He never told his parents, of course.

The morning was now going well for Richard. So well in fact that he allowed himself the luxury of thinking about his

"EUREKA" moment of discovery. It was that delicious moment that most scientists rarely achieve, despite years of rigorous study and research. He thought about that moment so rare, when a scientist suddenly learns what no other person on earth knows.

Surely it was the same for Newton, Maxwell, Salk, Einstein, Edison, Pasteur, and so many others down through the ages. Richard knew the lives of the average physicists are filled with pain, apprehension, hardship, anxiety, dread, even bouts of hopelessness and despair.

But, for him, it all changed three months ago when Eisa Chang his graduate student was running a trial on the monopoly Richard had designed a special apparatus to detect a monopole. His breakthrough came when, in a flash of brilliant insight, he decided to look to the heavens for a solution to GUT and not the particle accelerator. Richard knew that the biggest accelerators in existence and those dreamed of could never achieve the tremendous energy levels necessary to observe the monopole, if it did indeed, exist. The best and most widely held theories of GUT would remain forever untestable and proved by the standard method of observation and experimentation. However, with the aid of his friend and astrophysicists, Dr. Claudia Peters, at the Lick Observatory, she was able to provide his data from the Hubble Telescope on a peculiar galaxy known as M87. This system was known to be shooting out material at the incredible speed of light. The source of this violent activity at the center of M87 is a black hole, the ultimate energy producer. The energy it produced was the equivalent of billions and billions of watts of energy. In one second the energy produced is equivalent to all the energy potential put together of all the known galaxies. Obviously more than enough energy to produce, in vast quantities, the much sought after monopole particle. It remained a matter of utilizing the Vela Satellites that were arrayed secretly in orbit in the 1960's to determine the presence of Russian launched satellite weapons that could attack the earth from space. The Vela Satellites utilized Radio Telescopy, just what

183

Richard needed to detect the monopoly. It was an ingenious method that had escaped the best scientists of the day. Nevertheless, he could not escape a strong sense of ambivalence about the fact that the idea for this methodology came to him in one of those damnable dreams that were his constant companions since childhood.

It was amazing that the most powerful particle accelerators in the world could not detect the predicted monopole. After all it was the most complex technological machine ever built. It had enabled particle physicists to make amazing progress in discovering the nature of the atom. It had reduced matter, the atom, into quarks, hadrons and leptons. Essentially answering the question, "What is the universe made of?" But not quite! Actually he now knew why.

By the time he entered college the Quantum Theory was well understood and well verified. The unification of the weak and electromagnetic forces wed with the electroweak, carried by four particles, and the photon. Quantum chrome dynamics [QCD], which embraces the behavior of quarks. Scientists understood the field theories that describe the attempts to join QCD with electroweak forces which collectively are known as Grand Unified Theories. But, none had found the missing tau monopoly . . . yet! It was Richard's new and improved apparatus that enabled him to detect them in energy radiation from the depths of the sun.

Richard knew that there are two potentials for particles-real and virtual. Real particles travel from point A to point B. They conserve energy. They can be measured. Virtual particles carry force. They can be measured. They can borrow energy, but the more energy borrowed, the shorter the time the virtual particle can exist. A charged particle emits a messenger particle dissolving into a pair of opposite charged particles, for a second, and then restores them before they are observed. These virtual events happen to connect to all charged particles that exist.

The GUT predicts that, what in the past has been elusive, the tremendously massive particles X Bosons. They can appear as virtual particles and as a consequence, the wave decay of a proton. If discovered it would provide a source of untold, unbelievable energy. It would be possible that just a ton of water could provide all of the energy required by the United States for one day.

At one time, everywhere matter was the same, displaying perfect, beautiful symmetry. Through the passage of time it has changed, and spread throughout the universe into the many forms we recognize today. Essentially, Richard's discovery of the tau monopole permits research physicists to do two additional things. He knew the beauty of what his discovery would do to solve several other existing problems of modern physics. First it answered the question of the missing, invisible "dark matter," since theorists could previously only account for 10 percent of the necessary mass in the universe. Now the heavy monopole particle would make up that difference. Secondly, scientists could now "reverse engineer" what is known today about the splitting of the atom back to the time universe began, the widely held view of the origin of the "Big Bang." Only Richard understood how to put all the pieces of the puzzle together.

Richard's findings also solved the riddle of the "Fifth Dimension," and how time travel could be made possible. Heretofore, humankind had only been able to accept three dimensions of space, and a fourth dimension of time. Now, a fifth dimension was possible, one that is smaller than the nucleus of an atom, but all of us, including the universe were born inside it. But his secret would propel him far beyond that. Of all of the scientists on earth, he was the only one to complete the picture of how the universe began and will end.

185

Mid Afternoon
Jessica's House

Jessica rose early the next morning following her dinner party and dialogue session. She was feeling unusually energetic, despite the usual dreams of eerie lights and shadowy figures present during the night. This time however, the headaches that normally followed the dreams were absent. She had spent a great deal of time reliving the highlights of the previous evening. There was one aspect of the event that brought a worried look and wrinkled brow to her reflections: the improbable set of circumstances that drew the guests together. The odds against such an occurrence were astronomical she knew, especially, meeting Richard. Only a few days ago they were complete strangers barely exchanging glances, in an airport thousands of miles away. What did it all mean? What hidden destiny lay ahead for them and for what purpose? Jessica decided to leave the matter in the hands of the gods. She began to mentally plan her day's agenda.

Jessica decided to take advantage of her "feel good" physical state by leisurely having a light breakfast, running two miles around the University grounds, and completing the clean-up of her house, all before noon. It was her plan to devote the afternoon to her research, which had been totally neglected for the past few days. She needed to make several calls to her associates at the Centers for Disease Control[CDC], in Atlanta. She fondly called it, the Pentagon of the nation's disease fighting nerve center. She was proud of the fact that she worked at the CDC. The CDC was where the Hantavirus was identified. It was there that the Ebola, Crimean Congo Hemorrhagic Fever and South American viruses were being studied.

The research team she headed was getting very close to a testable vaccine against the HIV virus, and she didn't want to lose any momentum. After her follow up calls, she would spend the evening doing theoretical thinking about the virus. She also

186

wanted to spend some time reviewing supporting data she had used during her presentation at the Berkeley symposium "The Current Status of AIDS Research." But for now she was hungry and needed breakfast.

Jessica had finished breakfast and was now well into her two-mile run. The morning air was cool and fresh. She sucked it in and exhaled in soft, purring sounds. A gentle breeze tugged at her form fitting, powder blue jogging suit. The slight wind tossed her hair back along her slim, graceful shoulders, a lovely sight to those who glanced at her, and there were several who did. She became aware of, and even welcomed, the disassociated subconscious thoughts that kept drifting in and out of focus. Most of these thoughts dealt with her research work on viruses.

Strangely enough, her first thoughts were about Hemorrhagic diseases of which the deadly Ebola is a prime example. She knew that the virus attacks a cell and destroys it from within. The patient literally bleeds to death internally. It is a nightmare disease. Jessica knew that humans are not the natural hosts for hemorrhagic viruses. It is only when man stumbles into its normal habitats, like poor sanitation in developing nations and virgin jungles, that humans get into serious trouble. Fortunately, the virus withers and disappears when sanitation in the under privileged nations improves.

These thoughts led her to think about how the Western world had begun to relax attention from the AIDS scare. Especially, since the new drugs called, protease inhibitors became widely used in early 1996. The decline proved to be an unfortunate lull.

Jessica had warned her colleagues at the symposium suggesting to them that they could not lose sight of the fact that the best way to reduce AIDS is to prevent HIV infection. She recalled a visit by the renowned researcher, Dr. David Ho, to the

187

DePauw campus in early 1997. Dr. Ho, who received the "Man of the Year" award from Time Magazine in 1996, was recognized for his pioneering work in the treatment for human immune deficiency viruses. Dr. Ho discovered that when the HIV virus was attacked early with powerful new drugs, the virus disappeared in most patients. He had carried out his work at the Diamond AIDS Research Center in New York. He reminded his audience at the DePauw lecture that "It's not time to celebrate. The fact that HIV is undetectable doesn't mean it's absent." Her thoughts continued.

To most AIDS researchers, it has become obvious that drugs, no matter how effective, are not the solution to the world's deadliest epidemic, especially since drug treatments can range up to $20,000 a year. Therefore, it won't help the poor in America or in developing third world countries. For example, nearly 90 percent of the people suffering from the disease are in Africa, India, Thailand and Central and Eastern Europe, well beyond the ability to afford such drug treatment. Only the truly rich can afford such treatment. Private drug companies don't spend heavily on vaccine development because vaccines are less profitable than prescription drugs. In most countries vaccines are purchased by governments not by individuals. Since most third world governments are very unstable, their money goes toward standing armies and weapons of war.

She considered the immense credit that should be given to other researchers in the past who pioneered great discoveries in the HIV field. People like Irving Sigal, who convinced his superiors at Merck that they should look to a protein called Protease that permits HIV to copy itself. It was essential to the life cycle of the HIV virus. Then there was Flossie Wong Stahl, working in Gallo labs who discovered why HIV is so deadly. It rarely makes a perfect copy of itself, mutating into viruses that resist drugs and vaccines and rendering them useless. She shifted her research to gene therapy.

Jessica knew the worldwide scope of the AIDS pandemic. She mentally judged that in India alone it could be estimated that, by the turn of the century, from 15 to 50 million children in Kenya, Rwanda, Uganda, and Zambia will have lost their parents to the disease. Jessica could not help reflecting as well on the fact that in 1984, top AIDS Officials, including Margaret Heckler, of the Department of Health and Human Services, stated that an AIDS vaccine would be created in three years. To date, fifteen years later, a vaccine against the immune deficiency virus has been mainly theory and an unrealized dream.

She had thoughts about the many befuddled scientists who drearily predict it could be as much as decades away. Jessica knew better from the slow, agonizing, yet astonishing progress she and her associates were making. The team's progress to date had taken four years to reach the confidence level that they had achieved. But she still was overly cautious, just as Dr. Ho in the past had warned that other disease vaccines that nearly wiped out or brought under control- tuberculosis, mumps, rubella, polio, yellow fever, and small pox -were now making come backs in certain parts of the world.

In the 1960's, experts had vanquished tuberculosis, cholera, and malaria. These deadly scourges were being wiped from the face of the earth, only to make successful comebacks. Then came other diseases, Lassa fever, Legionnaire's disease, Hantavirus, Hepatitis, and Ebola. The Ebola virus outbreak began in the remote village of Gabon. Ever since the first mass outbreak in 1976, the virulent Ebola virus tops the list of the worst way to die. The symptoms are devastating- hemorrhage, bloody stools, and the literal disintegration of various organs.

Jessica tried, in vain, to shut out the dreadful thoughts about the Ebola and AIDS virus and to think about something more pleasant, but she met with little success. The veil once lifted would have to run its course.

189

She remembered how these viruses have stricken mainly people of color and those with aberrant life styles, such as drug users and the gay community. How could it be that far too many people in government and big business turn their heads and turn off the money supply for research? "It's not America's problem," they seemed to be saying. That type of thinking is so sad, she thought. Americans have forgotten that the flu virus that killed more people on earth than any other disease began right here in the United States. The 1918 flu virus killed 20 million people worldwide in less than one year. It originated from American pigs. Researchers have now traced it to an army private who died of the disease during the first world war. Using DNA analysis on an autopsy of his exhumed body, researchers confirmed the result. Two other flu viruses, spread world wide this century, Asian flu in 1957, and the Hong Cong flu in 1968, both mutated from pigs!

Jessica realized that throughout history diseases have made the leap from animals to human. Hantivirus, AIDS, and Ebola are only recent examples. But it has been only in this century that such diseases had the benefit of worldwide air transportation to leave the jungle or the third world cultures.

She was aware of the fact we knew that we are facing, in reality, greater problems than Aids or Ebola. For instance, untreatable infections in hospitals. She also knows that another flu pandemic is coming. It is just not known, when! Miracle drugs such as penicillin and tetracycline have been over prescribed and over used and caused the bacterium and virus to develop immunities. Relatively speaking, unlike Ebola, or Hantvirus, these viruses are not that deadly, but flu kills because it is so contagious that nearly everyone on the planet can get it.

Jessica stopped briefly during her run to do bending and calisthenics exercises. She acknowledged the greetings of "Good morning, Professor Harrington," of several students as they passed by. After five minutes of exercises, she trotted off briskly, as perspiration dripped lightly from her forehead, and chin. Yet, she felt powerful, and her spirit glowed.

As she crossed a wide meadow, her mind began to review the process of how the AIDS virus works in the human body. The virus is essentially a slice of genetic code, with a protein coating. When a copy of the virus contacts a vulnerable white blood T cells, it penetrates that surface. Once inside, it uses special enzymes to splice its genes into the host cell chromosomes. When those cell genes are activated, they begin producing more HIV. The trick is to intervene in this process where it is possible to block a reaction and prevent the HIV virus from breaking out of the invaded T cells. If they could, cripple the mutated cells to the point where they are so weakened that standard treatments would then destroy them completely. She knew that mutations themselves are copied by the replicating mechanism. Mistakes that cannot be copied. Such mistakes must be eliminated in some way. Faced with chemical errors, the copying system may ignore it and put in one of the standard codes. It doesn't matter what mistakes are made, as long as the end result is an alteration that can be copied faithfully in succeeding generations. She thought again about the nature of genes. Stripped of its complexities, nucleic acid, especially DNA, does very little except replicate and code for proteins and structure RNA molecules. Something must keep a gene and its material products together. This is done by keeping the genes and its products in the same way. It is called a cell and it is surrounded by a very thin, semi permeable membrane which prevents most of the molecules inside from leaving unless one is needed outside. Special gates and pumps in the membrane get food and other molecules into the cell from outside or let out waste products and other materials.

In her mind, Jessica flushed out in more technical terms, the T cell's role as Davis pins of the bodies' immune system. HIV must first attach itself to a particular protein called CD4, on the T-cell surface. Within a few weeks a person's infected body must receive a powerful combination of inhibitor drugs, or "cocktail" drugs such as, AZT, DDL, DDC, DHT, 3TC, and naviraphine. These drugs may temporarily thwart the virus, but there are survivors, and they go on reproducing offspring, unaffected by the receptor protease drug "cocktails." They continue to spread throughout the body.

Jessica thought about the fact that any cure must do more than clear HIV from the bloodstream. It must remove the virus from the lymph nodes, the brain, the spinal cord, male testes, and anywhere else that it may be hiding.

Where AZT just slowed down viral reproduction, the protease inhibitors shut it down almost completely. Unfortunately in the case of HIV, almost is not good enough. Sometime within a month viral particles mutate into a strain that is resistant to protease inhibitors.

As she made a turn past the university library, Jessica was on the final leg of her jogging circuit. Her mind turned briefly to the method that was driving her research team to the brink of discovering a method for vaccinating the world's population against the AIDS virus. She recalled the team decided, for the reasons previously going through her mind that radical but simple applications of new technology, in other scientific disciplines, just might hold the key to a breakthrough in her quest for an AIDS vaccine. New approaches were not thought possible even a couple of years ago. Why not? After all, nature seems to prefer to reveal her mysteries only to those who dare to think differently; only by using unconventional approaches will one be allowed to see glimpses of her secrets.

Jessica recalled asking her research team, at the time of its formation, to spend the first day asking nothing but "What if" questions. Not to answer the questions, but to formulate questions and to model what avenues seemed logical to follow. At the close of the day's session, they were to reduce the possible avenues of pursuit to five of the best candidates for exploration and deliver them to her for review. She smiled to herself as she recalled the potential solutions. In retrospect, the attack model they came up with as a result of the "What if" potentials, proved exciting. She could easily visualize the typewritten paper they submitted to her that held the potential for an AIDS vaccine.

"Stealth" Cell Model
By Dr. Juan Migel Allesandro, Et Al.
To: Dr. Jessica Harrington

The research team assembled in a three-day retreat for the express purpose of developing unconventional approaches to model an HIV cure, and our vaccine model is now prepared to submit its ideas. What follows is a distillation of our efforts. We anxiously await your return to the CDC to flush out additional details and understanding.

What if' we sent out "Stealth" chemically coated messenger proteins that track down, recognize, and warn the T cells of an impending invasion. Once alerted the T cells radiate signals that trick the HIV virus into revealing itself as it nears the T cell through angiogenesis, causing the virus to sprout its capillaries much too early to penetrate the cell wall. Then the virus can be vulnerable to attack by cutting off its energy supply by flooding the bloodstream with free-floating AZT and CD4 molecules. These molecules would also act as decoys and prevent the HIV virus from attacking T cells. The concept can be visualized if one thinks of over the horizon radar, or scouting planes that protect the mother ship in times of war. Better still, think of the now famous F-17 "Stealth" fighter of Desert Storm fame. Using the "Stealth" concept, the action steps would look like this.

1. Release AZT and CD4 molecules receptors at a distance from the T cell through the molecules CD4 = CO receptors, before the advancing virus has an opportunity to enter the cell and mutate.

2. Simultaneous to the release of messenger proteins, the T cell deploys external shields of angiogeneses inhibitors that would, potentially surround and starve the virus if it attacks the cell. A promising line of research already centers on a group of molecules called Chemokines, which can shield cells from HIV.

3. At the same time the cell detects penetration of its cell, it releases PPE [Purified Protease Enzymes], along with the release of integrate inhibitors to halt the viral DNA from using the genetic material in the T cell DNA from making its own RNA. If it does, it would be weakened, or attenuated for easy destruction, since the chemical switch that signals the HIV cells to reproduce wildly would be switched off.

4. In addition to the "Stealth" line of defense, the vaccine will have "one last card to play," It is a trump "Wildcard" Since there still may be a chance that bits of the virus, called proviral DNA, are locked in the chromosomes, unreachable with all but the most powerful drugs, the "Ace" is played. IF, the virus reaches the Protease enzyme stage and prepares to cut the viral proteins into pieces, so they are incorporated into a new virus, they will be destroyed by the Protease inhibitors.

Using this model Jessica's research team had made dramatic and breakthrough progress toward an effective vaccine. They had nearly completed test trials of the PPE vaccine on primates. The results to date were stunning. The primates were given powerful doses of the HIV virus, followed immediately with the PPE vaccine. Astonishingly, nothing happened to them. Could the virus regain its damaged genes? Or, worse yet, might it mutate into something else undreamed of? Could the vaccine harm people? The answers to those questions would be the final and the biggest hurdles any vaccine must surmount, human patients. She felt that even an imperfect, but suitable vaccine could buy valuable time now and a more sophisticated one later could be introduced. Is it possible? She was determined to find out!

Jessica was now entering her drive way. It had been the most exhilarating jogging experience she ever had. She welcomed the sensations of mild fatigue that had liberated her mind and body. She thought how wonderful it would soon feel to be taking a nice, long, leisurely bath. She thought to herself, the latter would be the time she would think about her newly found friend, Professor Richard Stedman. She began to blush.

3:30 P.M.
Same Day
Rev Donovan

Rev Donovan was full of joyous excitement. He felt rejuvenated, rejuvenated in spirit and in religious zeal. Reborn. His conversion followed the dialogue session. When he arrived home around midnight, he decided to read, and ultimately reread, passages from Geneses. His aim was to reconcile parts of it with the dialogue session that dealt with the "new physics, particularly, the relevant aspects of the Quantum Theory and Big Bang Theory. Nothing had inspired him more than to hear Margaret raise the point that the Vatican in Rome issued a pronouncement that the Mother Church should recognize the significance of the Quantum theory, and what it means to church postulates.

He felt as if a creeping fog had suddenly lifted. He knew that a little knowledge could be dangerous, blinding, but also exhilarating. For some time he had been struggling with how to make his sermons more relevant, more in tune with the seemingly endless stream of new scientific discoveries, discoveries in medicine, space, and astronomy. The young people in the church were turning a deaf ear to religious tenets

195

that were in seeming conflict with what is currently known and well understood by science. Perhaps what the Pope was saying is, "Can science discover super laws of nature and reduce them to some ultimate answer, perhaps God, or the Creator? At some point, perhaps sooner than later, we will have to acknowledge something or someone."

I know from casual reading that many scientists accept a position that there is something beyond our present understanding of reality. It is a reality that brings us closer, if only in a symbolic way to religious precepts. He had vowed that night to broach these subjects head on. After all, someone needed to prepare the young for the time when all mystery is gone- when the human spirit discovers that most of the mysteries and dogmas of the past disappear in the face of new scientific discovery. It is natural to be frightened by such things that we don't understand. We cringe at the thought of ghosts, spirits, demons, the bizarre phenomena of UFOS, new discoveries in our solar system and the heavens beyond, miracles of modem medicine, the mysticism of Eastern thought. All of these concepts are gaining prominence at the close of the 20th Century, and will certainly be a part of the baggage we carry with us into the 21st Century.

The 21st Century will certainly propel us beyond the banging of cymbals and drums to keep "evil knowledge" from our doorstep. Rev. Donovan wanted no more of the hocus pocus religion. No more appealing to peoples emotions rather than their rational thinking.

In the wee hours of the morning, his mind had raced with such thoughts. He had darker ones as well. He knew that nearly 100 million people were watching television ministers, as they soaked their faithful of hard earned dollars, so difficult to come by. After all wasn't it Oral Roberts who said just a few years ago that if his viewers did not make contributions totaling some eight million dollars for some building project within a few months, that God would call him home? Didn't Rev. Jim Baker's church organization fleece nearly 100 million dollars from the faithful?

All the while, he was being smitten by one Jessica Hawn. Didn't Rev. Jimmy Swaggart fall from grace, succumbing to the more carnal desires that affect mere, humble creatures of God? ? Weren't the mid 1990's riddled with cases of parish priests preying on their young, male parishioners?

The perception that we are left with following these wrenchings of the religious fabric, is that of pseudo priests and preachers, chasing money, power, and sex. What else could our young people think, as the electronic and print media captured every tearful moment to such tragedies? As the anchor to our past for stability in our lives, the church is being destroyed and many believers live with it. The results are predictable. A hostile environment at home, the workplace, the streets, respect for one another, all vanish in a state of paranoia. The wizard of Oz has been revealed . . . Again! People are left with a feeling of isolation and unable to cope. Individuals attempt to develop patchwork strategies for existing in such a world, but most are doomed to failure, left to survive in an untenable, unlivable situation, a situation in which they "can't win,"

Rev. Donovan was spiritually moved by the shear logic of Dr. Richard Stedman's science critique at the dialogue session at Jessica's dinner party. So much so that he decided the right way to proceed with his newfound conversion was to speed read a book on Quantum Physics. He was not interested in the formulas, calculations, and indecipherable mathematics but in a general review of the concept. Something he could read for himself, at his own pace, and have open discussions on such issues with his Bible study classes.

After breakfast he had gone to the DePauw University library. He headed straight for the science section. At the information desk he found a young student, perhaps a senior, from the physics department, since he fit the stereotypical model. He had an ectomorphic build, thick glasses, unkempt hair and pock marked face. Rev. Donovan greeted him cordially, but very directly.

"Young man, I need the definitive book on particle physics. The Quantum Theory to be exact. You know, a book for beginners, with no mathematical equations.

"I know you!" the young man said. "You're the pastor at the New Vision Baptist Church, in town. I've attended your services on several occasions. I must admit, your sermons are more relevant to young people than those of several others I've attended. I don't go to church that often anymore for just that very reason."

"Well, young man, visit my church again in a month or so, and see if I've made any improvement."

"I will, "said the young man. "By the way pastor, you're very fortunate, the two books I would recommend, "The God Particle," by Leon Lederman, with Dick Terest, and "In Search of Schrodingers Cat," by John Gribbin, were turned in just yesterday. I've read both of them, and believe me, they are must reading for the masses. Really relevant for today's generation, if you know what I mean. I would recommend that you read, "The God Particle," first. No pun intended. It's a really fun read." The young man broke out in a wide, disarming grin.

Rev Donovan produced his oft used library card, thanked the young man, and hustled straight to his pastor's study, where be began to read joyously. He stopped only to gulp down a ham sandwich and a glass of milk for lunch, which the church secretary had brought to him, along with an admonishment that he needed to take a break. Rev Donovan would have none of it. His mind was deep into another reality, a reality of the micro world of quantum mechanics. A world of electrons, protons, quarks, and neutrinos, and the deeper, philosophical question of man being an active participant, on a conscious level, of an ever evolving universe, or universes.

198

CHAPTER 12

Day Six
Morning.
Stedman Woods Estate

It was nearly 7:30 in the morning, the following day, when Richard began to stir. He remained in a dream state for several moments, pushing everything else out of his consciousness, even the golden rays of morning light streaming into his room. It hardly mattered to him. His head felt heavy, as if it were twice its normal size. The headache was there again! He knew it would be when he fell asleep the night before. His eyes were bloodshot, with veins visible like lines on a road atlas. His stomach had soured from too much wine at the gathering at Jessica's. For a brief moment, he had an unsolicited flashback of multi colored, glowing lights converging in the sky above Stedman Woods. The apparitions also appeared, but mercifully, quickly disappeared from his mind's eye.

He stumbled out of bed to the bathroom, daring not to look at his image in the mirror. Richard ran cold water into the washbasin, spending an inordinate amount of time splashing water on his face. Feeling somewhat refreshed, he decided to brew a quick cup of coffee before eating a light breakfast. He would shower and shave later.

As he descended the stairs, he could hear Ruben already preparing breakfast. He quickened his steps as he welcomed the heavenly aroma of coffee brewing and bacon sizzling.

"Good morning, Richard! Good heavens, from the way you look one would say that you thoroughly enjoyed your dinner last night. Perhaps too much?" He snickered. "Have some coffee. It's black as night and hot as hell. I'm also preparing bacon, scrambled eggs with Colby cheese and plenty of hot peppers, just the way you liked them when you were a boy. Your shower and shave can wait."

"Well, since you have gone to so much effort, I think I will," Richard said with glee. "It's very thoughtful of you to do this, by the way." For the next hour they enjoyed the breakfast and small talk. Richard recounted highlights of the dialogue session, stressing the unique nature of the individuals taking part. How by its conclusion they felt a strong sense of bonding. They exchanged thoughts of the bizarre coincidence of how the gathering took place. How it was that Jessica and Clay were seatmates on the flight from San Francisco to Indianapolis and reunited at the party. How strange it was that happenstance at the restaurant drew him together again with his childhood friend, Stanley Davis, when he first arrived in Greencastle. They discussed how fortunate they were that attorney, Ernie Flownery just happened to invite Margaret Ginsberg, the famous, well-respected Harvard Professor of Philosophy to the group, and how much she contributed to its success. Finally, but hesitatingly, Richard mentioned the beautiful Dr. Jessica Harrington and how they became instant friends, after just a fleeting glance at the San Francisco airport. It was curious but just the mention of Jessica made his headache disappear, instantly.

Jeremy knew by the intense look in Richard's eyes that Jessica not only was bright and lovely, but had somehow lighted a flame deep in Richard's soul. This pleased Jeremy because he knew that Richard needed female companionship in his young life, now, more than ever. Richard thanked Jeremy for the wonderful breakfast and excused himself from the table. As he hurriedly ascended the stairs, Richard began to experience a highly charged state, approaching unexplained fear. But of whom, or what? Somehow he suspected that before the day was done, something frightful, something grave importance awaited him. The feeling never abated, even through the

200

morning shave and shower. He dressed quickly and silently and haltingly walked downstairs.

"Perhaps I need some fresh air. Yes, I need fresh air," he thought and hurried out the door, mumbling a barely audible "Good bye" to Jeremy. He slipped quickly into his car, opening the passenger side windows and sped down the driveway into the morning's dawn, gripping the steering wheel as one being pursued by the hoary hounds of hell.

When he arrived at the office of Ernie Flownery he found the lawyer's secretary eager to see him. She was young, blonde in her late twenties, petite and full bosomed. Her body was lithe and athletic like an athletic instructor at a local spa. She greeted him with a wide smile as she held out her hand in greeting. It was warm, yet firm. Richard noticed that she let her hand linger longer than one would normally expect upon first greeting. He thought, "Another time and place I might explore further what that gesture meant. Richard decided to ignore any deep-rooted meaning. He merely stared at her, unblinking. She looked at him closely and her smile changed to a quizzical expression of curiosity.

"Are you feeling Ok, Mr. Stedman? You look a little . . . weak!"

"Oh, I'm fine, just a little preoccupied this morning, he said, not caring whether or not he was convincing."

"Well, Mr. Flownery is expecting you. He asked me to send you right in the moment you arrived. Oh! Ah, by the way, he asked me to hold all of his calls; he doesn't want to be interrupted. So, it looks like you two will be spending some time together. May I, uh. get you a cup of coffee? It, ah, may make you feel, ah, better!"

"Yes, thank you MS ...?"

"Sarah! Sarah Peters," she said, gathering her composure. Go right in. I'll be back with your coffee in just a minute.

Richard strode briskly into Ernie's office, where he found him sitting behind a large oak desk. Behind him was a large picture window that afforded a sweeping view of a grassy picnic area. Adjacent to the picnic area was a large pond, where some wild geese were enjoying its placid waters.

"Richard! Good morning. It's good to see . . . My God! You don't look so . . . Fresh!"

Richard replied in a muffled, strained voice.

"I... Ah . . . didn't sleep very well last night, I guess. I'm a little overwrought and jumpy this morning."

He slumped into one of two overstuffed, brown leather easy chairs. Sarah Peters drifted in, unannounced with two steamy hot cups of black coffee and left them on the oak coffee table, next to Richard. She left as quickly as she had entered, looking over her shoulder, she observed Richard, with his unsteady hands, welcoming the first sip of coffee.

Two hours later, Richard emerged from Ernie's office. They had spent most of the time discussing the previous evening at Jessica's home. Their conversation appeared to mirror his breakfast conversation with Jeremy. They came to no definitive answers, but seemed to agree that it was possible that some unknown, external source to the group somehow contrived the whole thing.

They also spent some time reviewing necessary estate matters. There was the newspaper notice to anyone laying claims against the estate; determining total assets, liquid and otherwise; obtaining a real estate appraisal for the potential sale of Stedman Woods; the signing of papers that made Richard chief executor

202

of the estate. Ernie estimated that it would take about six to nine months before there would be a final settlement. He also agreed that he would give Richard monthly progress reports. Finally, they settled the matter of legal fees that called for a substantial retaining fee.

With these issues settled, they shook hands again. Richard left the office, scarcely acknowledging Sarah's well-intended wishes that he "Have a good day."

Day Six
Cafeteria
DePauw University

Richard had completed his busy schedule for the day and was now driving along the highway toward home. He was anxious to get back to the comfort of Stedman Woods. He glanced at this watch. It was nearly six o'clock in the evening. The sun was completing its downward spiral toward the western horizon, presenting an impressive sight, as it hung suspended like a bright red balloon on a string. He suddenly realized that it had been a wonderful day.

The weather had been perfect for a late spring day in Indiana. The sky had been a gorgeous robin egg blue when he walked across the DePauw campus. The campus never looked more lovely and serene. He had enjoyed a very pleasant lunch with Stanley Davis. They had agreed, at Jessica's dinner party, to meet at the University Union Building cafeteria for lunch.

Richard was glad he had arrived a few minutes early for his engagement, and spent the extra time watching the comings and goings of the young students. He was surprised that he began to think about the perceived differences between the students at Berkeley and students at DePauw. The students on the West Coast campus appeared to enjoy contemplating things on the higher order. Such esoteric pursuits as making microchips out of

DNA, atomic physicists studying matter on the micro level, wondering why the Universe is as it is. All the while worshiping the sun and the seaside. Conversely many DePauw students concerned themselves with things as they are. They appeared to be more concerned with societal issues, like why can't people get along with one another? How can our institutions, such as the churches become more relevant to today's youth? They also concerned themselves with studying ways to preserve and rekindle, societal values and virtues of their parents and grandparents. Richard found himself agreeing with many of Stanley's propositions, discovering he was more Hoosier than west coast, after all.

Stanley had raised many such issues over lunch. He had mused about why Americans were so lonely in spirit and seemed so disconnected from the world at large, and lamented the point that many young people did not seem to care very much about anything of importance. "Perhaps," Stanley had said, "that is why so many of the young seemed to be more concerned about reading the latest sleazy autobiographies of fallen movie stars, professional sports bums on drugs, engaging in the latest scandal involving sexual and alcoholic deviant behavior. Too many young people glue themselves to talk show pariahs, that parade imbecile, emotionally bereft guests on stage. All searching for some aspect of life that will give them meaning and pull them back from the abyss."

Perhaps Stanley was right when he challenged me as a scientist to answer the simple question, "Why is life filled with so many questions and so few answers." He had countered weakly, by paraphrasing Steven Weinberg, one of the most celebrated theoretical scientists of the last fifty years, when he answered, "The most astonishing thing would be if it turns out that everything we think to be true about life would in fact be true." In other words, in searching for answers to our many painful questions, is it possible to come up with answers to difficult questions, if we would only believe it is possible to solve them."

He thought he had won the day with his spurious, but easily accepted argument. He was wrong. Stanley had countered again when he posed one of his accustomed tacit arguments.

"You know Richard," he said, "The real universe proceeds about its business without stopping to read scientific journals. The fact that one can come up with a plethora of answers does not mean they are correct."

He recalled his belly laugh as he gave Stanley a friendly slap on the shoulder.

"Touché" was the only response he could muster.

Richard was accustomed to such obtuse arguments from him. They had hundreds of similar debates in their youth, as they stood skipping stones upon the pond at Stedman Woods. He loved such exchanges and sorely missed them. He deeded it on this day as well. Stanley had continued on a philosophical vein as their sandwiches, soup and salad dwindled and disappeared. They had sipped coffee as they continued their conversation.
"Richard?" Stanley had said. "I did a lot of rethinking of old questions as a result of some of the issues raised at Jessica's house last night. I suppose that is the hidden beauty of the dialogues sessions. It has the tendency to heighten one's thinking about matters one doesn't think much about during the course of our busy lives. For instance, and I don't remember who made the point, but the essence was that science was not the end unto itself." He pressed the point that Science has provided the tools to equip the 21 Century generation with weapons of knowledge that will vanquish the terror of ignorance.

"Central to that knowledge," Stanley had persisted, " is the issue of whether our little corner of the universe is representative of the entire potential that may exist elsewhere in that universe or perhaps other universes. Perhaps there is another eternal question that begs an answer, and soon! It has to do with technology. The unsettling question is, do we have a choice? Western technology has unleashed tremendous forces. Even as we close out the 20th Century, it exercising great power. But, Richard, is technology to be the twilight or early morning triumph? Is not technology a creator of vast economic wealth? Isn't Microsoft's Bill Gates worth nearly forty billion dollars alone? Isn't space now the final frontier? Is it not true that atomic weapons are heinous? We can clone animals in test tubes and telescopes in space permits us to see to the far reaches of the known universe. These achievements would bring us great optimism as we enter the new millennium. Yet, science and technology have not prevented war. It has only made the world more dangerous. It has not enabled the races to get along in peaceful harmony. It ha not rid our society of cruelty against one another. It has not rid our cities of drugs, homelessness, property and despair for our young and old citizens. It has not educated our young children. It has not rid our political system of corruption and greed. No! I'm afraid it has only permitted all of these ills to be enhanced on a scale unheard of in human history."

"Whoa, Stanley," Richard remembered saying. He was getting a little perturbed at his friend's frontal attack on science.

" Perhaps it should not be necessary for me to defend all scientists and their work. Nor is it necessary to recount the scientific achievements that have lifted man from the brute to where he now stands at the threshold of god like powers, and the rational explanations for the universe is almost certainly possible. Oh, I will grant you the point that we may be ultimately barred from the Ultimate knowledge, but we must not stop trying. What man does with that knowledge, whether for good or ill is beyond the philosophical pursuits of the scientist. We provide only pathways, it is up to the philosophers and social engineers like you to show mankind which road to travel.

"We are all in this world together. We who are children of the universe are linked inexorably to that universe and must seek its secrets through our combined awareness.

"It is you my friend Stanley, as an expert in the social dynamics of the world's peoples, who needs the utmost attention. You said it before, and many times that what the world needs is an improved world in a manifest way."

"No," he had admonished Stanley, "it is not the scientist who created the developed worlds current destruction of our natural resources and the growing threat of environmental pollution. All can be traced to the developed world's thirst for power and energy." He beamed to himself as he recalled the waitress refilling their empty coffee cups, as he continued pressing home his points of view. "And how can we come to grips with the AIDS epidemic which the brilliant Jessica is apparently very close to producing a vaccine, even if she solves the riddle soon, will the real problem be solved? This disease, dreadful for those who are unlucky enough to contract it, is not fully understood by the general populace for its long-term threat. The problems this virus presents to the world have health authorities panic stricken.

" What worries the researchers the most is not that it is prone to occur among sexually active people in the West and in Africa, it is the point that AIDS causes religious fundamentalists to exhaust their self righteousness upon men and women. No, it is not AIDS that concerns them. It is the spread of AIDS. It spreads exponentially. The numbers double every year, which means that in less than three decades, everyone on earth will be infected. Fortunately, as Jessica well knows, things are not quite as simple as that. Those at greatest risk will die or change their sex habits. But the spread is still the great problem, not the disease. We have looked deep into the abyss and seen our own reflection. The AIDS threat is of Biblical proportions. We are sitting astride one of the pale horses of the apocalypse. We have

207

a World problem. Ships, planes, automobiles that cries cross nations and oceans are the true conveyors of the disease.

"It is we who have promoted the spread, we have done so as a result of political and economical struggles that put a stranglehold on the other nations who are sacrificing their resources in vein attempts to feed the brogdigidian appetites of developed countries. So once again Stanley we are all doomed if we point a finger at some particular scientific discipline. When one points a gun at someone, four fingers of the gun hand are pointing back to the shooter."

Richards' view of their pleasant but direct conversation was that it ended in a stalemate. Nevertheless, a subterranean thought had begun to creep into his mind. He had the feeling that the dialogue session at Jessica's and his luncheon conversation with Stanley were just a prelude, a brief exercise in preparation for a time, a moment that was soon to come.

Richard drove into the driveway at Stedman Woods: he decided he would postpone dinner. He needed to relax his mind from the day's activities. He decided he would change clothes and go for a walk down to the pond. It was something that he had not done for years and to his best recollection miraculous things for his soul could always be found there. He greeted Jeremy and advised him of his plans for a walk. Then he went directly to his room. Unnoticed by Richard was the quizzical and troubled eyes of Jeremy as they followed his slow, halting steps leading to the top of the stairs.

CHAPTER 13

Late Afternoon
The Pond at Stedman Woods

Richard disappeared from the rear door of his home. He had changed from his dress suit and tie . . . and was now clad in a blue denim shirt, khaki trousers, Converse tennis shoes that were well scuffed from age and frequent use. He had snatched a Macintosh apple to munch once he reached his destination . . . the pond . . . near the heavily wooded thicket.

His exhausted spirits seemed to improve as he tramped along the once familiar path of his youth. The fading sun spilled its rays upon his face while a light breeze whispered in the leaves on the trees. His eyes drank in the colors of buttercups, pansies, and other brightly colored wild flowers that filled his gaze as he slowly made his way along the over grown path . . . once well trodden and bare at the time of his youth . . . Thoughts of his father and mother filled his tortured mind. He wondered if they knew, in spirit, that he was on the threshold of changing the world and all mankind . . . now and forever more. The thought was more than his blood could endure. Nevertheless, Richard felt exalted to be returning to the somewhere and some when . . . of his younger days.

When he reached the pond, familiar sights greeted his senses. He laughed quietly, but aloud, as he thought about the times he and Stanley sat quietly by the pond as the gathering dusk surrounded them, and conjured up witches, evil sorceresses, and goblins flying swiftly to their nocturnal gatherings. Or, were they blindly seeking refuge from the Prince of Darkness as he sought unbridled orgies with them. He stifled a cackling laugh as he now recalled such thoughts that terrified them at the time. Now, he instantly felt young again. There, as if for the first time, were the sights of tall, stately reeds and tall grasses, all bunched together, each to their own kind, giving comfort to snakes, grasshoppers and crickets. Over there were the lily pads that provided a resting place for the frogs, who were just now beginning to announce their presence to each other by their croaking, chirping sounds. And there, over there in the opposite direction . . . were the bees and butterflies whizzing and buzzing in a symphonic dance. A funny thing though, he thought . . . Hawks and blackbirds courted in mid air: all of these seeming cacophonies of sights and sounds were well ordered and planned by Mother Nature. He had an instant, happy thought: The truly happy man is one who can enjoy nature in the raw.

Richard reached into his pocket and retrieved the apple he brought along for quick nourishment. As he munched on it, he thought about the ebb and flow of time. How the frogs, crickets, snakes, butterflies, all those creatures of God's creation had been doing the same things since time began. He wondered why it was that when he was alone at the pond, or when he and Stanley would sit near it, skipping rocks, talking about their personal goals and aspiration's for the future, deeper thoughts would seep into their idle conversations. He thought about how long ago that was. Time. What is it about time that haunts us all? "How time flies" was a phrase every school boy, every adult, sooner or later becomes consumed by it. Richard's knowledge of physics and Einstein's general theory of relativity seemed to answer that eternal question, for all of us. "Yes," he thought. It was that same venerable master of 20th century physics who said something like, "The distinction between past, present and future is only an illusion, however persistently," In other words, time is not what it seems. It does not flow in only one direction. The future exists simultaneously with the past.

"Ah," he thought . . . Perhaps Einstein was right, but what was there before time began? That is the ultimate question. It challenges our faith, even modem day scientists and philosophers. It is beyond current explanation. Can there be an answer to why such a state exists? Is this then, where scientific explanation breaks down and God takes over? Does it go beyond Stephen Hawking's singularity and Black Holes? Is it where the astronomer Robert Jastrow, in the book, "<u>God and the Astronomer</u>" addressed the issue saying, "He has scaled the mountains of ignorance . . . He is about to conquer the highest peak . . . And as he pulls himself over the final rock, he is greeted by a band of theologians who have been sitting there for a millennium." Or, what was it that the renown Princeton physicist Freeman Dyson said, "The more I examine the universe and the details of its architecture, the more evidence I find that the universe, in some sense, must have known we were coming." Richard continued to enjoy the serenity and quiet slumber of the pond. He found several rocks just right for skipping across the pond. He scaled a small, rocky mound, about three feet high, and began hurling them, childlike, upon the water. He succeeded in getting three, or four beautiful skips each, when he suddenly sensed that something was very wrong. Things were suddenly too quite, except for the occasional croaking of a frog. Things were not exactly this, nor that. On the surface there were the black birds making lazy circles in the sky above . . . and the pond creatures sang their songs. But, he knew another reality was just beyond his reason. His six senses told him something unusual was creeping up on him, like the early morning fog entering the Bay at San Francisco, where he would often go to for deep thought and reflection.

Suddenly, without a perceptible wind change, a hot, hellish blast of air brushed past his face. "What's that?" Richard said aloud, in a trembling voice, audible only to the frogs and crickets. For the first time he noticed, over by the wooded thicket, a huge, silvery, triangular shaped object barely visible in its shrouded mist. One thing was for sure; it was Leviathan in size . . . But, a thing of immense beauty and power. "No" . . . It can't be! . ..It was a craft of some significant design. It was hovering about thirty feet above the tree line . . . and vacillating back and forth like a falling leaf. It seemed to throw rays of shimmering light in all directions . . . like rays of the sun. The air around it crackled slightly producing an aura, a halo, resembling invisible butterflies in the air. One could easily recall shimmering heat waves on the road on hot dusky days in mid summer. Maybe that was the only way his brain could interpret whatever was happening. The awful majesty of the airship produced a sound too unearthly to be a sound at all. Time and Space around the pond seemed intertwined. He became lethargic and fatigued, as an eerie haze of unreality enveloped him. It nearly knocked him from his perch on the tiny mound. His head began to throb and his left eye developed a sudden tick of anxiety.

He could see, but he was unsure of what he was observing. He knew that the mind is very powerful and can play tricks on a person. The power of the unexplained was just that, unexplained. Richard started to see familiar scenes of human forms whizzing before his eyes, as if he were watching a movie. He had seen them before . . . in his recurring dreams. He felt as miserable as a prisoner of war. As Richard stumbled from his perch of safety, his blurred eyes remained fixed on the object that had now settled to the ground. It remained there. Its lights stained in unearthly shades of amber, purple, orange and blue-white. The craft became clearly visible to Richard as the pulsating lights stopped, transforming from color and mist to a defined triangular, physical object the color of Mother of Pearl. Richard nearly collapsed to his knees . . . like Paul on the road to Damascus. The sheep was now ready for shearing. The demons of air and darkness had appeared out of thin air; He didn't know where it came from. It had just, appeared! Then he heard a mechanical voice mention his name. It was not threatening . . . But it was a definite command . . . instructing him not to be afraid, and to approach the craft.

Richard straightened to his full height and began to walk like a robot toward the strange craft . . . now about one hundred yards away. He knew not why. He only knew that he was being drawn toward it by the mechanical voice. He had only gone a few steps when a thought came to him to run from it, but that was impossible. He was in fact somehow being drawn to it.

As he drew nearer, he noticed that the craft was now on the ground, supported by a triad of landing pads. He also noticed that upon his approach, a door began to open . . . from a seemingly seamless area at the bottom of the craft. A blue shaft of light shot out in all directions with a circumference of thirty feet. As it did so, three small human like forms floated to the ground. Once on the ground, all beckoned to him to continue his approach. He did not, or could not halt his advance. Some vice like force of attraction was tightening around him.

One of the beings was about a foot taller than the others and was, apparently their leader. He had an inordinately large head with dark slanting eyes, which seemed fathomless . . . and not surrounded by any whites. Either he and the others were stark naked, or they wore skintight suits that revealed no particular anatomical features. The skin, or suit, was either dull gray, or pale and wrinkled.

The larger entity made a few guttural, indistinguishable sounds, and the others stood motionless as the larger one advanced a few steps. Richard was not quite sure whether the next sounds came from the tiny, unmoving slit where its mouth should be, or the voice was some type of telepathic message. Nonetheless, he was dumbfounded to hear what followed.

"Welcome Dr. Stedman. We have waited a long time to meet with you again. Do not be afraid. We wish you no harm. We have been your constant companions since the days of your youth. We also knew your ancestors dating back to a quarter million of your years . . . A time when Saber-toothed tigers prowled the earth. We were there when your primitives made paintings on the cave walls of Lascaux, France. These paintings sent our calling card to the future."

213

"You know nothing of me," Richard said. "I have never seen the likes of you in life."

"Ah, dear Doctor, but you have," the voice said. "We have come to you in dreams. But, come aboard quickly. We do not have much time. There are things we wish to show you. Things I'm sure you will be of interest to you."

Once inside the machine, Richard became aware of a rectangular room with metal walls . . . bathed with a dull, green, florescent light coming from everywhere. He noticed a simply staggering bank of tiny, multicolored lights. They were burning with amber, greens, yellows and blues. He could not count the numbers of them. He was motioned to a solitary, toadstool like device, which he was sure was meant for him to sit upon.

He was left alone . . . for what appeared to be an endless time. He was not examined, pulled, or tugged upon. He just sat there, his eyes held transfixed on what lay before him. In another corner of the room he saw on the wall inscriptions that looked like scribbles of a kind of language, unrecognized by him. He tried to drink in the miraculous sights that surrounded him.

The two beings, whom he had seen earlier, entered the room and began making barking, or growling noises. He assumed they were holding a conversation. When they finished talking, they motioned Richard to follow them. He decided to obey them, primarily because he seemed to be compelled by some strange force to do so. One walked in front of him, the other brought up the rear. They left the small room and moved toward a door . . . where it was impossible to tell it had existed only seconds before. The room was larger than the previous one and almost square, but, not quite.

In one comer of the room was some type of reddish, phosphorescent device, four feet high. A panel, or screen, appeared that showed a panoramic view of the pond . . . and

214

even his home. The visual presentation was as clear as day. One of the entities gave a barking order and pointed to the other to activate a bank of crystal like devices that were in the bank of instruments. His hands literally flew across them. Another huge platform appeared out of the blank wall, revealing encased, horizontal rods, about six feet long. All were bathed in eerie, dull green light. The being touched a control ledger that made the rods began to pulsate in the fashion of a man breathing slowly in and out. The pulsating light that bathed the rods began to accelerate faster and faster, until they took on the essence of pure energy. It was a breathtaking sight to watch.

Richard hypothesized that the ship must have been powered by some type of gravidic power, or electro magnetic waves, or modification of both of them. He knew that gravidic waves are thought to travel tens of times faster than light. They would permit a craft to make quantum leaps like an electron in an atom that transfers from one orbit to another, perhaps above the speed of light where Einstein's mass, energy relationships no longer applied. Or, maybe negative gravidic waves, which would permit the occupants' biological clocks to continue to act as we know it to be.

The room vibrated ever so slightly . . . but that was the only motion Richard felt. The viewer screen closed, but one of the entities pointed to the ceiling of the room, which suddenly began to oscillate and move like ripples in a pond. The movement settled down and into focus Richard saw what looked like a giant spider web. He took this to be some kind of pathway, or star chart. The only one he could recognize was one that resembled the constellation ORION. He thought he could make out the three stars where the belt would be. In the upper left quadrant, Richard could make out the brilliant star Betelgeuse . . . And the anchor star on the lower quadrant of Orion . . . Regal. And could that be Cappella off to it right? He hoped it was, as his mind thought desperately for something familiar, any thing that would restore his sense of sanity.

The view now shifted, as if by a zoom lens, back to the middle star in the Orion belt . . . Where a tiny green light, blinked on and off in rapid succession. The operator of the device looked at Richard, pointed the green light and seemed to bow. "This must be their homeland," thought Richard. Far off in the distance was another quadrant of the heavens where a tiny & light, like a firefly was blinking. The entity pointed to it, then to Richard, and bowed again. The obvious guess was that it was our own Sun. One of the spider-like lines connected the two and displayed a third yellow light that was leaving a moving trail. The only conclusion to be drawn was that it was plotting the craft's current position. But what was most astounding of all were the other lights of different colors. They were tracking in different directions along the spidery type web. The web also displayed what could only be vortexes, or the singularity of "Black Holes."

It was unthinkable, beyond belief, pure magic. They were crossing light years, in seconds! One entity tugged at Richard's arm to follow him. The other being stayed behind, undoubtedly to operate the devices that were piloting the ship.

They walked back along other corridors, Richard had not seen before. They visited other rooms where he was shown other wondrous charts, formulas, and writings. All were unfamiliar to him except several mathematical equations that he knew were scientific proofs dealing with the quantum theory. Before Richard could grasp the full meaning of the magic he had just seen, the entity led him back through narrow pathways to the room where the toadstool seat remained. Richard, weak and dizzy from all he had just seen, could barely find the strength to slump upon it.

The alien leader appeared out of nowhere, absolute thin air, it seemed. The alien's sudden appearance was an incredible feat and startled him immensely. The leader had a small, round object in his hand, about the size of a large grapefruit. It was like a crystal ball . . . transparent. Inside it could clearly be seen an

216

object that resembled `jacks" that he played with as a child. It floated as if in a liquid, but it was clearly not liquid. On each spoke of the "jack, " . . . were nodules with tiny inscriptions and formulas on them. He recognized one of them as, E=mc2. The others were a complete mystery to him. He extended his hand holding the device and gave it to Richard. The leader spoke again and as before, Richard could only hear his voice in his head. As he did so, a golden beam of light, coming from a location the ceiling, suddenly struck and held him transfixed and unable to move. It bathed him in magnificent colors. The tall entity spoke again.

"Dr. Stedman. It is not necessary that you know my name . . . At least for the time being. We come from another time and place, unknown to your great scientists. It is not the dark star, or the 12th planet some of your great scientist talk about. Although both, do exist. We are from another dimension and the way has been opened to us since before the great flood. Your Dr. Einstein and others have been privy to our instruction. Some have even been bilocated to our domain, although they were not made manifest to our location . . . And their memories of their visits were erased . . . as will much of what you have just witnessed. We gave to Dr. Einstein and others a glimpse of our power . . . We have assisted them in their work . . . but not to their knowledge.

"They too had choices to make at that time in your history. Your Dr. Einstein, with his unheralded Philadelphia experiment where ships were made to dislocate, was just one example of our intervention. Our teachings were given to him too, as an instrument for upgrading the general knowledge of your kind. He refused our gift saying mankind was not ready to accept the knowledge for earth people.

"He kept it secret, even unto death . . . Trusting that mankind would one day develop a higher level of awareness to comprehend its full meaning and potential for the benefit of all

217

earth inhabitants. He was correct in his saying, "God does not play dice" when he did not agree with the theoretical assumptions of certain aspects of the Quantum Theory. Free choice is free to all. We do not force our knowledge upon your kind. However, many of his predecessors have been given what you call "God like powers" and certain other knowledge. We know that millions of earth people have suffered as a result of implementation of certain knowledge. Most because of their greed and brute like desires to conquer, enslave and subjugate all before them, proved their undoing. Certain of your priests, and popular religious leaders . . . from the Knights of the Templers to Popes, know many such things that we have imparted to them . . . Yet are undreamed of by the masses. They have been held by them, in secret, down through the corridors of time, sworn to secrecy by the guardians and their faithful followers. There are still alien strangers in your mist. I now offer you the same secrets of the universe, many undreamed of by your greatest scientists. You know one of those secrets. You call it "The Grand Unified Theory.

"The knowledge that you now possess, has the potential for advanced technologies that will appear as magic to your best thinkers of the day. Even so, they are but toys for play with us. We are prepared to permit you to expose that theory to all of the earth's peoples. It will require justice and courage for you to make the following choices. You will be permitted to announce the success of your scientific discovery. It will give modern earthmen a chance to dream, to move closer to those things that your people treasure most, unlimited energy . . . and power beyond imagining. We will allow you to become a celebrated figure, not only to your fellow scientists, but to all mankind. However, with our assistance, you may choose to keep it a secret until your kind develops a higher level of consciousness to comprehend its full meaning and potential. Should you choose this option we have the power to erase the essential mathematical proofs from the minds of your research associates at Berkeley. But, it is you, Dr. Stedman, who must make a decision. What knowledge will you take into the 21st Century? The Grand Unified Theory?

"Young Dr. Jessica Harrington whom we have given a glimpse of how to cure the AIDS virus with a vaccine, but she is unaware of our intervention and assistance. It is but child's play for us to speed up her work. Or, we can ensure that Dr. Stanley Davis, who is working on a manuscript that offers solutions to many of your society's greatest problems of poverty, poorly educated young, religious paralysis, and misanthropy. We have the power to make his manuscript a national best seller and translated into many world languages. But, it is you . . . and you alone . . . who must make the choice. We prepared you for this moment by bringing together some of the people we have worked in the past to Dr. Harrington's dialogue session two of your days ago. It was our experiment to prepare you for this moment in time. Now you have had time to rethink such issues. But, we will grant you an additional 24 hours of your earth time . . . to return to this location to give us your answer. You will bring with you at that time, Dr. Jessica Harrington, Dr. Stanley Davis, the man you call Clay, and Rev. Donovan. Let me forewarn you Dr. Stedman, we will be back! And you will be here, at this same appointed hour. Is this clear to you?"

All Richard could do was fondle the object the leader had given him, as a child would cuddle a doll. Then he was instantly transported outside the craft.

Richard emerged from a foggy dream and found himself once again sitting by the pond. The only problem was, he couldn't believe that nightfall was coming on fast. "How long have I been sitting here?" he thought. "When I arrived at the pond, it was approximately five forty five." He looked at his watch. It was now nearly seven thirty. "I must have fallen asleep." He murmured. For a few moments he stared at the lily pads and listened to the familiar sounds of frogs and crickets. But, for some subterranean reason, it was the wooded thicket where his eyes became transfixed. The more he stared at it, the more he began to vaguely remember . . . things! He recalled lights and indistinguishable figures . . . with strange forms. They were the same figures that tormented him in his dreams. Only this time, they seemed more real to him. It was now all so clear to him. Since childhood he had been visited by the aliens, perhaps even abducted and taken aboard the alien craft for examination. It also meant that Clay, Jessica, and perhaps even Stanley had been exposed to alien visitations, as well. He was relieved that he didn't have the headaches and sweats as in the past. Perhaps they would now disappear, forever. It also meant he was not going mad. He even felt refreshed of mind . . . But, tired of spirit.

He clamored to his feet, nearly falling backwards into the pond from the laborious effort. It was at that moment he noticed a strange object lying on the ground - next to where he had been sitting. "It couldn't have been there before." He thought. "I surely would have seen it . . . And remembered it." Richard wiped rivulets of perspiration from the corners of his misty eyes.

With trembling hands he reached with both hands to retrieve it. The object had the appearance of a large crystal ball . . . But it seemed to vibrate slightly to the touch. Upon closer examination . . . he noticed it contained within, another strange object. It had spindle like arms with smooth, round nodules on each spoke that reminded him of the game of "Jacks" he played as a child. It had strange writings on the nodules . . . And what was obviously minute formula on them. The "Jacks" were floating in the seemingly clear liquid. But he could detect no liquid. The warm, tingling sphere made him feel instantly powerful of mind. He knew he had seen it before. . . but he couldn't remember where . . . or when. He was too confused to give the matter additional thought. He clutched it tightly and staggered toward home . . . like a puppet whose strings were all mixed up.

When Richard arrived back at the estate, he was greeted by Jeremy. He had been anxiously awaiting his arrival hours ago, when he had seen Richard's distraught figure heading for the pond and the wooded area that gave the estate its name . . . Stedman Woods. Dinner had been waiting for him and was now very cold.

As Richard entered the front door, it was evident to Jeremy that he was in no condition to eat or hold a conversation. Richard waved a ghostly greeting to Jeremy and asked him if he would bring a strong drink, of his finest Kentucky Bourbon whiskey, to his library upstairs.

When he reached the upstairs he went immediately to retrieve his briefcase, to hold and fondle it, as one would cuddle a security blanket. Then, in like manner, he began to clutch the mysterious "Crystal Ball." He noticed it began to throb more vigorously than before. Again he felt very powerful, intellectually. He was convinced the object was living matter and not inert. He had the feeling it was an object of immense importance . . . whether now . . . or at some future time. Perhaps, it was as important as his Grand Unified Theory paper nestled securely in his brief case. Despite his inability to recall for sure just how the object came to be in his possession, he knew it was not at the pond when he arrived there . . . and it was going to play a significant role in his life.

Richard went to his armchair and quickly poured two strong bourbon drinks, and immediately fell into an abyss of tortured sleep.

After sleeping some three hours he walked down the stairs, being careful not to awaken Jeremy. When he finished eating a ham and cheese sandwich and drinking another generous helping of bourbon, then returned to his study. He felt a deep compulsion to call Jessica. He knew the hour was late, but he had to call her. He had to tell her something. Something relating to the bits and pieces of thought patterns that were just now coming . . . unsolicited to his consciousness. It was the thought of talking to her that calmed his spirit.

Jessica did not have a good day. There had been problems at the Center For Disease Control in Atlanta. A leak in one of the maximum containment alert areas housing live HIV virus caused a yellow alert in the alarm system. Fortunately, the backup contingency plans worked perfectly. She was able to handle the situation by conference phone calls with her distant associate.

She had also spent a great deal of time worrying about the potential her nearly completed vaccine could inadvertently create. She knew there was always the possibility that mutant strains of the virus, resistant to all available drugs, could develop. She was proceeding very cautiously, meticulously adhering to accepted experimental procedures. She constantly reminded her staff of the admonishment of Julius Caesar. "The biggest plan is built on the smallest detail."

The most critical result could be the creation of a type of super HIV that would lead to another, and more devastating AIDS pandemic. But, hope was still on her side. The pediatrics trials at Sloan Medical Hospital, using her "stealth" methodology, were going fine. Six month's trails of 3000 high risk volunteers across the country at risk for contracting HIV and 1,500 Ethiopian high-risk people were well underway. Sample tests showed that 95.8 percent of vaccinated volunteers produced ample levels of anti bodies that target and kill AIDS infections. The only problem to date was that most protease inhibitors are available only as capsules, not liquid form, and difficult for young children to take. But if a child is dying, crushing the capsules, and putting them into a palatable formula, is not a bad trade off.

After a late dinner, Jessica had relaxed in her study by reading the latest issue of The New England Journal of Medicine. She then watched the nightly television news, becoming only slightly annoyed, but curious, by one of the stories that chronicled multiple sightings of a huge, triangular shaped UFO, seen in the skies, in early evening, near the estate of Stedman Woods. "Good Heavens," she thought. "That's where Richard lives. This bit of news will make for a great conversation piece at our lunch date tomorrow." The hour was very late, nearly twelve thirty in the evening. Jessica, having decided to enjoy a relaxing bubble bath, her eyes and mind were nearly closed, when the phone rang. As she clumsily reached for the phone hanging on the wall above the tub, she uttered, "Now who in the world would be calling me at this hour. Whoever it is, it better be important." She could only utter a resentful, "Hello! This is Jessica." It was Richard, and he sounded strange, but she was pleased that he called. To Richard, her voice was like that of a hundred mandolins.

For the next thirty minutes she listened quietly, but in earnest, as Richard talked about the visit to the pond, near the thicket at Stedman Woods. He spoke of the "missing time." He told her of the strange object he had seen, and the even more curious object that he now had in his possession.

Jessica felt a deep compassion for him, ignoring a brief mental flash of a quotation from a forgotten source. "Never let trouble in the door if you can help it." He mentioned that he would have to alter their lunch plans. " Jessica, I have a great deal of thinking to do," he had told her. He went on to implore her to meet at his place at Stedman Woods at five o'clock tomorrow. Richard advised her that he would be asking Stanley, Rev. Donovan, and Clay to meet with him as well. His exact words that followed, were, "It will be a meeting of the gravest importance." For some unknown reason, Jessica had the feeling that what Richard really meant to say was that, "The meeting would be of epic proportions."

223

CHAPTER 14

Day Seven
The Covenant at
Stedman Woods

Richard stood zombie-like at the front door of his estate. He had been waiting for his friends for sometime. Suddenly they appeared as one. Stanley, Clay, Rev. Donovan, and Jessica, just stood there as one before Richard, feeling sheepish, restless and afraid of what might happen next. It was strange, but no one seemed surprised that all of them would gather together again. Each had a premonition that it was destined to happen, but they didn't plan it to happen. It was as if they had received some form of telepathic message which guided them to this moment. Only Richard knew they were not wrong.

But, they also felt foolish when Richard, speaking in a voice that sounded far away, asked them to accompany him to the area of the pond. Before leaving, Richard told them about the episode the previous evening. It was all coming back to him now. The group stood transfixed as he told them of the missing time, the strange craft, the crystal, and the Faustian dilemma given him by the alien leader. Since he wasn't sure they actually happened. He drew no conclusions, nor did he attach any special meaning to the events, except for the "Crystal Ball" which he cradled in his trembling hands.

As they begin their silent trek, each recognized the awkward position Richard was in. Walking before them was a world-renowned physicist, whose actions now bordered on the bizarre, if not worse. As they made their way to the pond they could not help questioning whether Richard's breakthrough scientific work was finally taking its toll on his senses. These negative thoughts dissipated when they analyzed their own behavior. Over the years, the dreams, the shapeless apparitions, the headaches, were their constant companions as well. They continued down the well-trodden pathway like a prison labor gang en route to perform hard labor. Only Richard seemed calm for the situation, as he took long, purposeful strides, five paces ahead of the group. They soon arrived at the pond and stood in childlike obedience, gazing at the pond, and the wooded thicket beyond. Hardly a word was spoken. Then, suddenly, without warning, the air became deathly still. Absolutely nothing moved, for minutes! No sound came from the creatures of the pond. No flying creatures took to the air. Then it happened! Now another small group of earthlings was about to be given a ringside seat to the future.

It was Clay, who first called their attention to a curious, boiling mist, high over the nearby thicket. It had suddenly materialized into view from a cloudless sky, like a light being turned on in a darkened room. It hovered some 1,500 feet above the ground. The misty cloud began to roll toward them, revealing golden light waves that shimmered in the fading sunlight. It stopped 150 yards from them, in the open pasture near the woods. A whirling sound animated from within it. When the whirling stopped, the rolling cloud slowly disappeared, revealing an immense, triangular object, gleaming in an aurora of colors, red, green, orange, and blue. The lights danced in a circle around the object at blinding speed. Then slowed to one pulsating mass. "It's a giant UFO," Clay screamed! The group turned as one, following the arch of Clays trembling, outstretched arm. When they saw the alien craft, all sank to their knees, groaning pitifully. Rev. Donovan made the sign of the cross and prayed to an unknown god. Clay clutched at himself and began to rant and rave in an unintelligible tongue.

The sight before them abolished everything they revere as true knowledge. Everything their brightest minds had conceived and touched, acorns, corn, berries, trees, rolling plains, television, airplanes, computers, paled by the magical sight before them. No! It abolished magic and mysticism as swiftly as modern medicine abolished witch doctors. It abolished all science fiction. Stanley could only blubber, "Our best scientist said UFO's were an impossibility." He fell into uncontrollable sobbing.

For a brief, dispassionate moment, Richard observed his friends. They were dumbstruck. Their minds taunted by the possibilities of what they were witnessing. Rev. Donovan formed more signs of the cross and blessed his fellow observers. Stanley tried to scream, but remained frozen to the spot, as he watched Clay walking toward the craft like a person in a hypnotic trance. Jessica, could only hold tightly to Richard, her mouth agape . . . eyes searching his, as if imploring him to make the nightmarish apparition go away.

As a scientist, Richard understood their plight. He knew that human beings relapse into a state of complete collapse and confusion, when they realized their world . . . their lives, suddenly transformed from innocence, in an amazing burst of realism. They were like primitives, who for the first time, saw an airplane in flight. His friends, not unlike his first encounter, were in a state of complete future shock, the kind that shuts down thought processes . . . as they realize that their own world, the reality they were comfortable with, and felt safe within its embrace . . . has been forever removed. UFO's were now a matter of history. But, there was more wonder about to consume them. As the group watched the brilliant object, now hovering twenty feet above the ground, a bluish light descended in all directions. Three figures emerged from the light and floated to the ground. Jessica, Clay, and Stanley, began to realize they had seen such phantom chalets in their dreams. At least now, they knew they were not mad. Somehow, they knew that, after today, those haunting dreams, and resulting headaches, would be no more.

As the alien figures drew near, icy breezes, and undreamed forces clutched at them, making voluntary movement impossible. The leader of the trio of entities spoke, somehow, to

227

their minds, counseling them that no harm would come to them. They were directed to approach the underside of the vast, hovering craft. As blue light bathed them, they were somehow made to float into the craft.

Two smaller creatures shuttled all but Richard down a small corridor. Intuitively, Richard knew his friends were about to be given a grand tour of the ship . . . and ultimately the heavens, similar to his own experience the day before. Jessica and the others looked back at Richard, much as small children would look back to their parents, just prior to boarding a bus for their first encounter with summer camp.

The giant ship gave a slight lurch. The leader again appeared from nowhere and motioned to Richard to be seated on the familiar, toadstool object. Then Richard could hear in his mind, the leader speaking in a gentle, but intense voice.

"Dr. Stedman, you have been witness to many things over the past hours, including visiting the farthest reaches of your galaxy. You also have been given formulas and visions, of which your best scientists have no knowledge. We have traveled outside your known dimensions, outside time, to places where your known science does not obey your known laws of physics. We have prepared you for this moment by permitting you to be a part of the dialogue session with your friends. You have debated current scientific, philosophical, religious and social issues. But, you are also aware that your philosophers and theologians have for centuries debated what it means to be human. And the answer is quite simple. It is the freedom to choose. We now offer you that same freedom of choice. This is not a Faustian bargain we are offering. Your choice will be our promise, our covenant, to you and your world. We have intervened in this fashion before. Human kind has never understood such promised fulfillment as "Eureka" moments. It will be no different in this instance. Only you will know.

"We have asked you to consider what major knowledge you would like to carry across the bridge into the 21st century. You were given 24 hours for your decision. Now it is time. Are you now prepared to offer your world such knowledge? What is your decision for the new vision of mankind for the start of the 21st Century? But, before you answer, you should know the object, the "Crystal Ball," as you now call it, contains awesome, but wonderfully, coded knowledge of the future. It will be yours to decipher in future years. It too carries its choices. Its truth, in due time, will become manifest you and your fellow scientists in future years. Although we have the power to destroy it and all of your kind, we urge that you take great care to guard it well. And, above all, take great care Dr. Stedman in arriving at the decision you are about to make. Your decision will be irreversible. What is it you wish us to bestow upon mankind for the new millennium? Your decision will be irreversible."

The awesomeness of the alien's propositions caused Richard to feel giddy, dizzy and faint. His body was shaking as a small child shakes a rag doll. But, he had already made up his mind. Through a maniacal grin, his simple reply was, " I am prepared to give you my answer. Let us now seal the covenant so that, Tomorrow, the world will be a better place . . . for all mankind. I accept your covenant by humbly proposing that . . . !

Outside the craft, on the highway bordering Stedman Woods, a local TV camera crew captured on video tape a huge, triangular object, slowly rising above the tree line, enveloping the area in a brilliant light, Then it streaked out of sight in the blink of an eye. The future had just happened. A new mythology was born in that moment. Mankind was now truly children of the universe . . . just in time for their journey into the 21st Century.

SELECTED READINGS

Eisley, Loren, The Unexpected Universe. A Harvest Book.

Gribbin, John, In Search of Schrodinger's Cat: Quantum Physics and Reality, Bantam Books, 1984, New York, NY 10103.

Gribbin, John, The Omega Point: The Search for the Missing Mass and the Ultimate Fate of The Universe.

Halpern, Paul, Cosmic Wormholes: The Search for Interstellar Shortcuts, A Plume Book, 1993.

Heilbroner, Robert L., The Worldly Philosophers, Revised, Fifth Edition.

Lederman, Leon, The God Particle.

Rucker, Rudy, Infinity and The Mind: The Science and Philosophy of the Infinite.

Russell, Edward W., Design for Destiny.

Searle, John, Minds, Brains and Science.

Sitchen, Zecharia, Divine Encounters, Avon Books, New York, 1995.

U.S. News & World Report, Schools That Work, Culture & Ideas, October 7, 1996.

Valle, Jacques, Dimensions: A Casebook of Alien Contact, Contemporary Books, 1988.

Von Baeyer, Hans Christian, The Fermi Solution: Essays on Science, Random House, New York, NY 1993.

Weber, Renee, Dialogues With Scientists and Sages: The Search for Unity.

Wright, Robert, Three Scientists and Their Gods: Looking for Meaning in an Age of Information, Times Books, New York, NY 10022.

ABOUT THE AUTHOR

Steve Scott, Sr., A native of Lebanon, Indiana, is the fifth of twelve children born to Lawrence D. and Violet E. Scott. He is a graduate of Lebanon High School and Indiana University, obtaining a bachelor's degree in radio and television. He was the first Black to graduate from that department and garnered three awards of merit for radio and television announcing.

After graduation from Lebanon High School in 1952, Scott served as a communications specialist with the Air Force and was the first Black accepted by the American Forces Korean Network during the war.

He began his business career in Indianapolis, Indiana as a supervisor for the Marion County Welfare Department and then became the first Black executive with a major television station in the state of Indiana for the NBC affiliate, the former WFBM radio-television station, as Director of Station License Renewal and Public Affairs. He retained that position when the stations were sold by Time-Life, Inc. to McGraw Publishing Company. He was the first Black in broadcasting to receive a "Casper" award for his work in hosting the TV program Job Line. He also received the honor of being named a Kentucky Colonel by the Honorable Louie B. Nunn, governor of the state of Kentucky. Scott held the position of vice president and general manager of radio station WTLC-FM. While with WTLC, Scott was the first Black elected to the board of directors of the Indiana Broadcasters Association. He later became the first Black executive appointed to a position with a major utility company in the state of Indiana: Director of Public Affairs at Citizen's Gas & Coke Utility.

Scott has served on numerous boards in the Indianapolis community, including Boy's Clubs of America, Girl's Clubs of America, Welfare Service League, Children's Bureau and the

United Way. He has also been active in the Urban League, NAACP, and Black Expo and headed the Mayor's Task Force to review the performance of the Federal CETA program. He currently serves on the Methodist Hospital Medical Group Board of Directors.

Married to the former Marilyn Gayle, Scott is the father of a son, Steve Scott Jr., and a daughter, Wendy. He is a member of the Witherspoon Presbyterian Church.